MYSTIC INVESTIGATORS

A MYSTIC INVESTIGATORS Book

PATRICK THOMAS

PADWOLF PUBLISHING INC.
WWW.PADWOLF.COM
www.facebook.com/Padwolf

WWW.PATTHOMAS.NET
www.facebook.com/PatrickThomasAuthor

MYSTIC INVESTIGATORS
© 2009, 2018 Patrick Thomas

COVER ART BY PATRICK THOMAS

BOOK EDITED BY ALYCIA J. MELLGREN

NIGHT CRIES originally appeared in CRYPTO-CRITTERS VOL. 1 ed. by Bruce Gehweiler
BARBARIAN SUMMER originally appeared in WARFEAR ed. by Leslie Ellis
WORKING GIRL originally appeared in the magazine BLOOD MOON RISING

ISBN: 13 digit 978-1-890096-88-5   10 digit 1-890096-88-1
Printed in the USA
Second Edition

"Took his heart out and hid it," said Mandi Cobb, my partner. There's nobody else I'd trust as much to watch my back. To be honest, there's almost no one else I trust period.

"Then why isn't he dead?" asked Pine.

"Old time mage trick. Mystically remove the heart and as long as it remains hidden, you can't be killed," I said.

"Karver, tell me you're joking," he said.

I shook my head. "Wish I was."

"How does he survive without something to pump his blood?"

"Magic," said Mandi.

"If it's such an old trick, how did this guy learn it? Everything we've found out about him points to the fact that he's a geek with no real skills."

"Internet," I said.

"The internet?" he said.

"Yep. There are plenty of idiots who post old grimoires online. With all the translation sites available, it doesn't take a genius to make the text readable. We've had a rash of these lately," said Mandi.

"So to stop this guy, we have to find his heart?" he said. I nodded. "How the hell do we do that?"

"And here's the rub," I answered. "The only thing in our favor is these people weren't bright enough to learn this on their own, so they don't always think through the hiding of the heart part. We found one in a shoebox under the guy's bed."

"So does this heart thing mean you couldn't catch this guy if we knew where he was?" he asked.

"We didn't say that," said Mandi, raising an eyebrow.

Pine wasn't one to ask questions out of idle curiosity and Mandi was obviously picking up some empathically. "Where is he?" I said.

"Bar outside of town. We have him under surveillance, but after seeing the type of punishment he can take, we didn't want to engage him near civilians," he said.

"Smart move," I said.

"Can we gas him or poison him?"

"Nope. Got to catch him like a rat in a trap," I said. "And since it's a guy, guess who gets to be bait?"

Mandi rolled her eyes. Pine chuckled a little too loudly for my tastes.

"Actually the gentleman lives an alternate lifestyle, so he wouldn't be interested in the lovely Agent Cobb," he said. "He might, however, find the dark and brooding Agent Karver strangely titillating."

"You're kidding," I said.

"Nope," said Pine.

"Oh joy."

"I'm sure we can dig up a nice leather outfit for you," he said.

***MYSTIC INVESTIGATORS*™ SERIES**
MYSTIC INVESTIGATORS   -   MEAN STREETS
ONCE MORE IN CRIME omnibus *by Patrick Thomas & Diane Raetz*
SHADOWS & BRIMSTONES omnibus *by Patrick Thomas & John L. French*

***THE MURPHY'S LORE*™ SERIES**
TALES FROM BULFINCHE'S PUB   -   FOOLS' DAY
THROUGH THE DRINKING GLASS   -   SHADOW OF THE WOLF
REDEMPTION ROAD   -   BARTENDER OF THE GODS

***THE MURPHY'S LORE AFTER HOURS*™ UNIVERSE**
NIGHTCAPS   -   EMPTY GRAVES   -   THE MUG LIFE
FAIRY WITH A GUN   -   FAIRY RIDES THE LIGHTNING
DEAD TO RITES   -   LORE & DYSORDER
BY DARKNESS CURSED   -   BY INVOCATION ONLY
SOUL FOR HIRE: GREATEST HITS

***MURPHY'S LORE STARTENDERS*™**
STARTENDERS   -   CONSTELLATION PRIZE

***DEAR CTHULHU*™ Series**
HAVE A DARK DAY   -   GOOD ADVICE FOR BAD PEOPLE
CTHULHU KNOWS BEST   -   WHAT WOULD CTHULHU DO?
CTHULHU HAPPENS   -   CTHULHU EXPLAINS IT ALL

Padwolf books by John L. French & Patrick Thomas
RITES OF PASSAGE: *A DMA Casefile of Agent Karver and Detective Bianca Jones*
CAMELOT 13 *(editors)*

Other books by John L. French & Patrick Thomas
THE JACK GARDNER MYSTERIES
THE ASSASSAINS' BALL

Other Padwolf books by Patrick Thomas
AS THE GEARS TURN: *Tales of Steamworld*   -   EXILE & ENTRANCE
NEW BLOOD (co-editor)

THE WILDSIDHE CHRONICLES OMNIBUS (contributing author)

Writing as Patrick T. Fibbs
UNDEAD KID DIARIES: OVER MY DEAD BODY
BABE B. BEAR MYSTERIES: BAD HAIR DAY
5 SILLY MONSTERS JUMPING ON THE ZED: *an Ughaboos picture book*

CONTENTS

FOR COLIN

BRAGGING RITES
A Hunt Adventure

It's never a good thing to see a student hurled by a window, but it's not exactly unprecedented at Franklin High School, the largest high school in Arcane County, Mississippi. Trolls, fey, weres and the occasional dragon numbered among the students and kids get into fights. It happens. It even happened to me back when I was a student here.

This time was different because it wasn't a student doing the throwing. I glanced out and saw an adult brag. I knew the school staff by sight and he didn't belong, but security was on it. My job was to try to get my class back into their seats.

"Let's get back to work people," I said, but I might as well have been herding cats.

"Ouch. That had to hurt," said Trina. Her mom's the Purlieu city witch, a position more powerful that the mayor and city council combined. Elected officials can be voted out, but the city chooses its own witch protector. A lot of the students here try to use their parents' positions and powers to circumvent school authority. Trina doesn't. Considering how much people fear and respect her mother, it just shows what kind of kid Trina is. "That one too."

A second look outside revealed two security guards collapsed against the school's brick walls and they weren't the only ones down. In addition to the one student that went by my classroom window, there was another kid on the ground. None of the four were moving and there were a few dozen kids still outside in the courtyard.

"Mr. Hunt, he's moving toward the rest of the kids," said Trina. "I could…"

"No," I said. Trina's a decent witch, but she's still a kid. I wasn't about to let one of my students engage a hostile psycho. It's not like I wanted to either, but someone had to stop him from hurting more people. "I'll take care of it."

"Listen to the big, bad bounty hunter," whispered Lonnie. The dwarf worked hard to convince everyone he was the born rebel.

I opened the second floor window. "I want all of you to go next door to Mrs. Applestone's class. And Lonnie," He looked up, his face fallen at the realization that I had heard him. "I want a fifteen hundred word essay on a famous bounty hunter in history by our next class." I taught social studies, but still liked to hand out the occasional report and had learned early on to give an amount of words rather than pages. Otherwise I got huge fonts and two-inch margins.

"But tomorrow's spring break."

"And a big, bad bounty hunter would care why?"

"Well, I don't know about the big part," he said.

I smiled. At four foot five, I'm well above average height for a boggart, but I still towered under most of my students. "Make it twenty five hundred words."

His face dropped even more, then lit up. "Any famous bounty hunter?"

"That's not related to me," I said. I'm hardly famous, but my grandfather Sift is a bit of a legend. Back in the day he brought in rouge fey, stagecoach robbers – even a killer dragon. Transylvania has engaged his services to capture vampires, which is infinitely harder than killing them. In more recent decades, Israel hired him to bring in Nazis. Especially impressive considering that since the ousting, most magic races can't survive a week outside one of the nine focal cities. Purlieu and the surrounding Arcane County is the focal for North America where the unofficial motto once was "Come here or die", at least as far as any race that depended on magic for survival. That's because the mystic races were forcibly relocated into the focals after the more powerful governments had the Earth mystaformed to limit where magic was located. The Allies felt they had no choice after Hitler's reign of terror and the damage he did both to and with mystic folk.

Which brings us back to my grandfather—Sift brought in der Führer himself. Everyone thought Hitler was dead, but he had only faked his demise by dragon fire and hid out in Argentina. It's Sift's most sensational capture, which means Lonnie wouldn't have to do much research to do his report and that would ruin the point.

I stepped up on the windowsill.

"You're not going to jump?" asked Trina.

"We're only on the second floor." My grandfather used to throw me from this height when I was a toddler. Boggarts aren't terribly powerful, but we know how to take a fall. "Now go next door," I said and hopped out.

One of my students gave a little scream as I fell. I'm not overly graceful, but I landed on the strip of grass below with only a minor stumble. Students who were taking their free period in the commons were rushing away from the brag, books and papers falling as they ran. A member of the goblin family, a brag has brown skin instead of the typical gray or green. This one was taller than me, but that's hardly a major accomplishment.

He lunged toward a pixie named Miranda who had broken one of her wings playing volleyball in gym class. Logic dictated that students shouldn't be allowed to play sports where the ball is bigger than they are, but school rules do. The Board of Education got sick of discrimination lawsuits and allows anyone who wants to participate in a sport to do so as long as their parent or guardian signs a waiver.

Pixies aren't used to walking and with such little legs are terribly slow. One of the other students could have picked her up and carried her, but having her small stature pointed out that way ticked Miranda off. The other students were so used to having her refuse, they probably didn't think about it until it was too late.

The brag looked like he was going to do a lot more than break her wing. Reaching down, I picked up the thickest textbook I could reach and chucked it at the brag's face. It got his attention, so I hit him with another two. It didn't hurt him, just pissed him off, which is what I was trying for.

I dumped the food off one of the nearby plastic cafeteria trays and flung it along the cement sidewalk, right at my pixie student. "Miranda, jump," I shouted. She realized what I was doing and listened, coming down on the tray as it passed beneath her. It stopped when it hit grass, but that was more than twenty-five feet from the psycho.

"Thanks Mr. Hunt," she said.

"My pleasure, Miranda. Now get inside," I said. There was no arguing as one of her larger girlfriends lifted her up and ran into the building.

"You want a piece of me, too?" said the brag.

"Sure, but what piece? I suppose I could mount your head on the wall of my den, but why would I bring something that ugly in my house?" I said.

"You think you're funny, boggart?" he said as his body began to change and I realized the student that had flown by my window had not been thrown. He'd been kicked. The brag transformed into a horse, although not entirely. His head changed proportions, but stayed humanoid. His already long, brown hair became a mane. "What are you going to do? Hit me with another book?"

I enjoy a challenge, so I hit him with three books. "Do I get a prize?"

"My hoof in your chest," he said, spinning and kicking out with both rear legs. He was strong and fast, but angry enough to both tell and telegraph exactly where he was aiming. Boggarts aren't strong, but we're quick, so he missed me. If I had been a little slower it would have been me flying past a window.

I clapped. "Impressive. Maybe if you shaved those legs and put on some fishnets, you could get a job in the chorus line on Narrow Street." (Purlieu's answer to Broadway.)

The brag spun and kicked again, but this time it was even wider so I had to dive underneath. One hoof caught my shoulder and I fought to not let the pain show on my face.

"Stand still, you shuck," he said. Now he was trying to piss me off.

"Ugly and a racist to boot," I said.

"Hitler should have killed all you shucks off," he shouted. It's not like he didn't try. Boggarts tend to be solitary and there have never been a lot of us, but over ten thousand Boggarts died in the camps. I doubt there are two hundred Boggarts in the two hundred miles that make up Arcane County, Mississippi. Beyond Arcane, the magic stopped, making leaving problematic for most of Purlieu's residents, so I doubted there were any more in all of the rest North America.

I've heard about the camps from my grandmother who was there. She survived, but none of my grandfather's blood family did. It was one of the reasons Sift went after so many Nazis. Sadly, I have students every year who don't believe the holocaust happened.

"So that's why you're attacking a high school? To pick up where the Nazis left off?" I said. All the students who could move under their own power had left, but that still left the two injured students and the security guards. I could run, but I doubt he'd be kind to the unconscious. I had to get him away from the school.

The man horse laughed. "It might be fun, but I'm here for personal reasons. I'm looking for Chlamydia."

"Maybe a brothel might be a better place," I said.

"I don't like funny, boggart."

"Must be rough living with that face then. Anyone ever put a saddle on the wrong end because they couldn't tell the difference?" I said.

"I'm looking for the succubus Clamydia."

"She prefers Mydia," I said.

"I don't give a damn. Her uncle did me wrong and I aim to take it out of her hide," he said.

Great, so this was partially my fault. Mydia was barely speaking to me as it was, which was rough considering we'd been friends since kindergarten.

This wasn't going to help.

"Her uncle's edict still stands," I said, although Mydia considered it a curse. Demons got caught in the ousting same as the other mystic races. Most can't get back to Hell, so the ones on this continent had to play house somewhere in Arcane. A succubus induces lust. Her mother claims the edict was to protect her, but her sisters didn't get one. Basically, Idmin has swore to kill anyone who has sex with his niece, which has made her the only succubus virgin, apparently ever.

"Idmin's in prison," he said.

"I know. I put him there," I said and paused for dramatic effect. I never wanted to follow in my grandfather's footsteps, but I kind of got rooked in. I was stupid enough to post bail for my good-for-nothing father, who repaid this kindness by skipping out on me. I owed the bondsman more money than I'll earn as a teacher in thirty years. Turns out, he figured my father would run. Since he couldn't get my grandfather to work for him anymore, he pegged me as the next best thing. Boy, was he wrong, but I got lucky and sneaky and managed to nail the former demon crime boss. He's doing a hundred and fifty, but will be eligible for parole in eighty. Gramps is over two hundred, so I'll probably still be around. Sometimes I have nightmares about what will happen that day.

"You're the Sift's kid," he said, sizing me up in a new way.

"Grandkid," I corrected. His kid would be my mother, the woman who abandoned me as a child to the Purlieu Orphanage. I have lots of parental issues.

"Then why am I still breathing?" he asked. Gramps has a rep, most of it deserved.

"Trying to set an example for the kids," I lied. Still I knew full well every window behind me had faces pressed up against the panes, watching. "Leave now and maybe you'll be breathing tomorrow."

"You expect me to be scared of a school teacher?"

"You've obviously never been in my class," I said.

"You there, get off of school property this instant!" I cringed when I heard the voice. "I've called the police."

"Who's that?" the brag asked.

"Principal Hannoy," I answered. He wanted nothing more than to have me fired, but with tenure and a friend or two in high places, it's proven difficult for him.

The brag laughed. "He's hiding behind an overturned desk."

"That's Hannoy." Unfortunately, that's when I heard another familiar voice. Mydia went against form and became a nurse – not many demons in the healing arts. She took a job here at the school not long after I did. The nurse's office always has a line of lovesick teenage boys faking illnesses just for the chance to have her feel their heads or look down their throats. I wasn't about to take my eyes off the brag, but from the sounds, she was outside, tending to the wounded.

"And there's what I'm looking for. Hey sweetie, you and me are going to go for the ride of your life," said the brag.

"In your dreams," Mydia said, putting the first boy on a stretcher, which two other teachers carried in.

The man horse growled and moved toward the succubus as she was tending to the second student. His eyes popped open at her touch and he smiled.

"Randell, how dare you pretend to be hurt!" she screamed. Explained why I hadn't seen him fly through the air. He used quick thinking and bad judgment for a chance to get close to Mydia. "You get inside the school this instant."

"Yes, ma'am," he replied, but didn't move.

"And you're banned from the nurse's office for a month," she said.

"But what if I'm really hurt?" Randell whined.

"You'll have to go to the ER," she replied. "And if you're not inside in two seconds, it'll be two months." The kid stood and ran for all he was worth. Mydia went to the nearest security guard.

Four girls had been practicing for a double-dutch tournament and luckily left their equipment behind. Distracted by the drama, the brag never noticed me tie a jump rope around his forward legs. Boggarts can manage to convince minds that they can't see, hear or smell us unless we want them to. In the old days, it was the same as being invisible. These days, we can be picked up by security systems, cameras and the like, not to mention the mind muddling field we generate works only a limited distance so it's not a free pass. It's how the Nazis caught so many boggarts. My people were used to hiding in plain sight for so long that the Nazis combined cameras, long-range binoculars and radios to lead their foot soldiers in a game of blind boggarts' bluff. It caught them off guard, before they could even think about evading capture. Still, one on one I was undetectable by most people, so the man horse didn't realize what I did until he hit the sidewalk.

"Stupid shuck. I ran Little Prussia for Idmin," he said.

"Do I look impressed?" I said, hoping I didn't, because I was. Idmin wasn't noted for his gentle ways and he didn't employ nice people. "Of course, that's twice you've said his name. If you're so tough, why not say it a third and see if the prison's wards really will hold him." Hell born demons can be called by repeating their names three times. "I'm sure he'd be happy to see you. Might even reward you, up until the point that he realizes your intentions toward his niece."

The brag shifted to goblin form and slid out of the rope. "I ain't leaving without her and if I have to hurt a shuck teacher and a few kids to do it, so be it."

"Hunt, they're safe," Mydia said, from inside the school. The brag stood and shifted back to man horse. Mydia stood with her hand alongside the doorframe where I knew there was a button, her eyes pleading. "C'mon."

"Nice to know you still care," I said. I stood between him and the door. If I ran, he might overtake me or trample me. Or he might overtake me, then trample me. If he made it through the glass doors, he could do some serious damage in those close quarters to the kids and Mydia, even Hannoy. "Lock it down." Mydia's brows went up and I saw worry in her eyes. "I'll be fine." I didn't know if I was lying, but if he got inside he'd hurt Mydia and anyone who got in his way, which if she got scared enough that her control slipped and her power flared, could end up being the entire male student body and faculty.

"You better be. I'm not done being mad at you yet," she said.

"You demons and your grudges," I said and she hit the switch. The protective wards Trina's mother installed lit up a shield around the school and everyone inside was safe.

"What the hell is that?" yelled the brag.

"Wards courtesy of the city witch." Now the brag was paying attention. "I imagine setting it off got her attention and she's on the way here right now, with a contingency of Purlieu's finest from the 13th Precinct." May be already moving if Hannoy was serious about the call.

The brag cursed.

"And of course there's me," I said with far more bravado than I felt.

"So you ain't going to let me leave?" he said. The truth be told, in goblin form he out-muscled me, forget about as a man horse, and I doubted throwing more books at his head would make him surrender. Still my grandfather taught me never to show weakness and that there was always a way to win. Of course, he also ended that statement with the phrase "proper planning". Still, all I had to do is keep him occupied until the cops arrived. One thing my grandfather and prodigal father had in common, besides my alleged mother, was a love of gambling and I learned the right way to do it from one and the wrong way from the other.

"Depends. Are you a betting man?" I asked. Profiling in the rest of the country is looked down on as a bad thing, but in Purlieu it's a fact of life. Doesn't mean it's right, but doesn't mean it's wrong either. Brag used to entice travelers and strangers to climb on their backs, then run so fast that the traveler fell off and died from the impact or ran them into the water until they drowned. That last one a lot of races did, but it's mostly the stuff of legend as these days most people know better than to get on something's back. We even have a safety video about it for the elementary schools. I've seen the video, but I'm not most people.

"What do you have in mind, shuck?"

"You take me for a ride. I stay on, you turn yourself in." Like either of us believed that would happen.

"And if you don't?"

"The usual I suppose. After all, I'm not exactly wearing a helmet," I said.

"How long?" he asked.

"Longer than yours. I mean, don't the other horses make fun of you? Or are you a gelding?" I said. He growled at the insult to his manhood. If I played it right, his ego wouldn't let him refuse at this point. Even if I played it wrong, I still delayed him a few seconds longer. "How long do you think it will take?"

"You wouldn't last five minutes," he said.

"Then why don't we say ten?" I said.

"You're on," he said. Before he could change his mind, I leapt on his back.

"I am now," I said. The brag froze, shocked that I had mounted him so quickly. "Clock's ticking."

The brag snorted and took off at a gallop out of the courtyard and onto the street beyond. At least we were away from the school. As we went down the block, I heard sirens in the distance. Great, now the cops show up.

My legs squeezed his flank and I dug my hands into his hair. The brag tried to pull his locks away, but it didn't do any good. As we turned a corner, he did a maneuver a horse would never do on purpose—he rolled in an attempt to smash me underneath him. It didn't work, so he did it again. I had to let go with one hand to protect my face and head. As soon as he regained his hooves, he ran me into the corner of a brick building. I leaned away as far as I could, but couldn't let go with my legs without falling off, so my right knee got smashed.

I managed to hold back a scream of pain, but if he did that again I was going to have trouble walking. Time to change the game. I let go with my legs and yanked myself further forward by pulling on his hair. Once my legs readjusted themselves, I reached one of my arms around his head, blocking his eyes. My other arm snaked around his neck. Neither was long enough to go all the way around, but for the moment, the man horse couldn't see and was fighting for air. I leaned my body to one side in an attempt to steer him. His ego wouldn't allow him to be lead, so he reared in the opposite direction, which was where I really wanted him to go.

The lack of air was slowing him down, causing the occasional misstep. In man horse form, he couldn't reach me, but if he shifted back to goblin my grip on his throat would be stronger and he'd pass out.

What happened next was equal parts luck and planning. A work crew had the street dug up to fix a gas line and there was a ditch. When the brag tried to roll me off again, he ended up in the ditch. That was the plan part. The luck part was that he was flank down. If he was head down, I would have been in some serious trouble. Instead, I pushed his face in the freshly dug earth on the side of the pipe and held him there until he passed out, then kept him there a little longer. He could have been faking unconsciousness like Randell and I wasn't about to do this again.

Once the brag was limp, I climbed out of the ditch as a police car, sirens flashing, pulled up.

"It's about time you got here," I said.

"We didn't want to spoil your fun," said Officer John Ludley. Ludley and I had a history. He used to bully me in middle school through sophomore year of high school. I spent the summer between my sophomore and junior years with my grandfather. When I got back, I made sure I was never bullied again. Ludley got the bulk of my revenge, but we became friends of a sort after that. He shaped up and went into the police academy and eventually was lucky enough to earn a spot at the 13th Precinct. They were considered PPD's elite. And the city witch was the de facto commander, although she left the day-to-day admin to others.

"Well, he's all yours now. He's unconscious. Think you can handle him?" I said.

"We'll try," he replied, walking over to the ditch. "Crap, he's still a horse? How are we supposed to get him out and into the car?"

A broomstick silently touched down next to Ludley. The blond woman who stepped off it pointed her finger at the brag and said, "As a matter of course, be a man, not a horse." There was a small light show as his flesh twisted, returning him to goblin form.

Ludley jumped at the words of the spell, realizing who was standing next to him.

"Think you can manage the brag now, John?" asked Karen, the Purlieu city witch.

"Yes, ma'am. Thank you ma'am," barked Ludley, who was obviously forcing himself not to salute.

Karen looked at me and rolled her eyes. She wasn't always thrilled with the deference others treated her with. I chuckled. "Your rhymes are getting kind of choppy."

Ludley shot me a horrified glance.

Karen shrugged. "Let's see you rhyme on the fly."

"I don't want to be a debater, so I'll have to prove it to you later."

"You call that a good rhyme? Is debater even a word?" she asked.

"Of course. I'm a teacher, I know these things," I replied.

"Well that certainly explains the plight of our education system," Karen said. "It looks like I have to baby-sit you again." Karen and I first met in the orphanage. I was younger and smaller and she looked after me. I tried to return the favor. She was adopted by a rich family and I was left to fend on my own for a while. Then my grandfather showed up to claim me. Turns out he didn't know dear old mom had dumped me on the orphanage doorstep and as soon as he found out, he came for me. My time there had been the worst two and a half years of my life, but it would have been far worse if it weren't for Karen.

I lived with my grandmother at her junkyard after that. Gramps would show up every few months. Karen and I wrote for a while, then lost touch until the business with Mydia's uncle. Imagine my surprise when the city witch turned out to be an old friend. Karen even ended up taking Trina out of private school and enrolling her in public so I could be her teacher. It was part of why I still had a job.

"We going to hide in the basement?" I said. It worked sometimes in the orphanage, until something big and bad moved in.

"Maybe not this time. Can I offer you a ride?" she asked.

"After this last one, I suppose even your driving will seem safe by comparison," I said. Ludley's gasp quickly turned into a cover-up cough and showed his horror at my tone with the city witch.

She put the broomstick between her legs and I stepped up behind her.

"So I hear you abandoned my daughter's class to play giddy up with this brag," said Karen, slipping into protective parent mode as we lifted off.

I wrapped my arms around her waist.

"I always wanted to be a cowboy and I did send them to another teacher," I replied.

"And my daughter tells me she offered to take down the brag, but you wouldn't let her?"

"True," I said.

"I appreciate that. My daughter thinks she's going to be the next city witch. And she may be, but she has a long way to go first. I appreciate you keeping her out of harm's way," said Karen.

"Just doing my job," I said.

"Right," she replied with a wry smile. "Which is why so many other staff were there helping you." I wasn't holding on for dear life, but I wasn't letting go of her waist, so she could tell when I shrugged. "How's your grandmother?"

"Doing well," I replied, not looking down. I've hated heights ever since I was a kid and Karen knew it. Today she wasn't pulling any fancy maneuvers, which I was grateful for.

"And Sift?"

"Last I heard, in Avalon." The city where all of Europe's mystic folk were ousted to. Each continent had one spot chosen, plus one in the Pacific and Atlantic.

"And just so you know, Hannoy is clamoring for your head. Claims you endangered students."

"Great," I said.

"Of course, every other report makes you out to be a hero," she said. "Including Trina, who I'm more inclined to believe than Hannoy."

"I appreciate that," I said. She asked for my version of events and I gave it to her. I finished just before we landed in the commons courtyard. The ward was down and it looked like most of the students were back in class, except for a few still being interviewed by cops.

As we stepped off, Hannoy rushed toward us, wagging his finger like it was a dog's tail. "It's unbelievable, Mr. Hunt, that you would do such a thing, especially on school grounds, near so many students."

"I quite agree, Dr. Hannoy," said Karen.

Hannoy was so taken aback he stopped mid-rant. "You do?"

"Absolutely," said Karen. "That Hunt would take on a known member of organized crime..."

"With total disregard for the safety..." said Hannoy.

"Of himself," said Karen.

"Needs to be addressed immediately," said Hannoy.

"I agree completely," said Karen.

Hannoy's pupils got as big as dimes. "You do?"

"Absolutely. Would you like it to happen here or at the 13th?" she asked.

"So I'll fire him and you'll arrest him?" said Hannoy, in a tone that sounded oddly turned on.

"What are you talking about? I'm talking about giving him the witch's ward," Karen said. Both Hannoy's and my jaw dropped at that. The witch's ward was a medal given out for heroism above and beyond. It was given to people who pulled children out of burning buildings, yanked grannies out of the paths of buses, threw themselves on grenades.

"Karen, I really don't deserve that," I protested.

"Nonsense," said Karen. "It shouldn't be up to a teacher to deal with dangerous intruders at a school."

"Exactly. That is security's job," said Hannoy.

"So when the security the school hires isn't up to the task, it's comforting as both a mother and city witch to know there is someone like Mr. Hunt here to protect the children when the regular measures, that the administration put in place, fail them. Wouldn't you agree, Dr. Hannoy?" asked Karen.

It was obvious he didn't, but he wasn't foolhardy enough to publicly disagree with the city witch. "I suppose."

"And we will talk about the school's failure," Karen said. Hannoy went pale. "And I will assign one of the 13th's officers to coordinate with your security guards. I think some mandated training and drills for the students and faculty is in order, don't you?"

"Anything to make Franklin High School a safer place," he said.

"Very good. So do you want the ceremony here or the 13th?" Karen asked.

"I'm not so sure it would be appropriate to have that kind of thing at the school," said Hannoy.

"True, with all the press taking pictures for the papers and sound bites for the evening news," said Karen. Hannoy's face lit up. "And you'd have to write a speech to give in front of the press and the assembled dignitaries."

"I would?" he said.

"Of course. You'd introduce me," she said.

I could imagine the wheels turning in his little head as he pictured himself in the limelight. "Of course."

"And say a few kind words about Mr. Hunt," she said. He waved that part aside. "It's no problem. We'll have it at the 13th. You'll be invited of course, but you'll be somewhere in the audience, not on the podium like you would be here."

"Wait, I may have been a bit hasty. The whole thing might be a good civics lesson for the student body. Wouldn't you agree, Mr. Hunt?" Hannoy asked.

"I'm getting a civics lesson just standing here," I said. Hannoy glared at me and Karen raised an eyebrow and tried not to smile.

"We can review what happened today, but I think we could let Mr. Hunt go back to his class," said Karen.

Hannoy grimaced. "Go," he barked in my general direction.

"Stop by the 13th later and I'll have a statement ready for you to sign," said Karen. I said I would. As I started back to class, I passed by the nurse's office and there was a line of boys alleging trauma from the events. Mydia stepped out in front of me and met my eyes for the first time in weeks. I had to look up to meet hers, although the view straight ahead wasn't too shabby, but staring there wasn't going to help matters.

"You did good," she said.

"Thanks," I replied. "Although I have to say that since you stopped hanging out with me, the quality of the guys seeking your company has really gone downhill. Although after me, almost anyone would be a downgrade."

"That almost would be a long list," she said.

"I doubt it," I said. I figured she was teasing, but my curiosity got the better of me. "Like who?"

"You don't have that kind of time," she said.

"Then how about you come over tonight and we rent a movie?" I said. "I've got cheese powder for the popcorn."

"No," she said. "Like I said, I'm not done being mad at you."

"Right," I said, turning and walking away without a word.

"Hunt." I turned and Mydia's face had softened. "But I'll be done soon."

I nodded and returned to my class. I got a standing ovation and took a small bow.

"Finally, some recognition for my fine teaching techniques," I said.

"That ain't the reason, Mr. Hunt," said Lonnie.

"All excited about learning more about the War of 1812, then?" I said.

"Nope. It's cause you're a 'B3H'," said Lonnie.

Now, I'm not yet thirty and I pride myself on not being too far behind on slang. "BFF" was "best friends forever", but I had no idea what a "B3H" was.

"Which is?" I asked.

"Big, bad, bounty hunter," said Lonnie.

I had to laugh. "Lonnie, about that report…"

"Yes?" he said hopefully.

"Make it a thousand words," I said.

Even with having to stay late to do the incident report paperwork Hannoy insisted I fill out, I have to admit I was feeling pretty good when I got to the 13th. I stopped by the desk sergeant and let him know I was here to see Karen. He had made it clear in the past what he thought of bounty hunters, so I kept it civil. Karen had told him to send me up, but he did so reluctantly.

Her office was on the top floor. When I got to the waiting area I got treated to an earful of a dressing down of epic proportions. The 13th Commander Maurice Mills was giving someone the what for, and I could hear Karen injecting her much calmer comments. I took a seat and picked up a magazine. There was a stack of the new issue of "Purlieu Beat" with a picture of Karen on the cover. I picked it up and flipped through it. Typical inspirational story of woman done good, the struggle as both city witch and a single mom. Not quite fluff, but not far removed.

When the door opened I was surprised to see Ludley and his partner come out, their tails between their legs. Neither had a badge on their uniform. I gave Ludley a look, but before he could answer, Mills stepped out and Ludley kept walking.

"Commander," I said.

"Hunt," said Mills with a curt but friendly nod. He was a bit of a hard-ass, but he treated me with respect, so he was okay in my book. "She'll see you now."

"Thanks," I said, bringing the magazine with me.

"Hi Hunt. Close the door behind you," she said.

I did as she asked. "I'm not so sure that's a good idea." Karen shot me a questioning look. I held up her magazine mug shot. "I might be overcome being so close to such a famous celebrity."

Karen dismissed the issue with a wave of her hand. "PR. They sent me a box. Take it with you."

"Only if you autograph it," I said.

"You want a witch to give you her written name. Are you insane?" she said.

"Depends who you ask. What's up?" I asked, pointing my thumb toward the hall.

"Quentin Johnson escaped from prisoner transport about an hour ago," she said.

"Who's Quentin Johnson?" I asked.

"The brag you took down," she said.

"You're kidding me," I said.

"I wish. It happened on your friend Ludley's watch. He and his partner were driving them to Stonefist for lockup. A car hit their squad car. Johnson crawled out the window and got onto a motorcycle and disappeared into traffic. Both officers are suspended with pay pending an investigation."

"Ouch." She handed me my statement. I read it and signed it.

"By the way, this is for you. I had Swimmer drop it off."

Swimmer owed the biggest bail bonds agency in the city. "Why?"

"Johnson had missed his court date last week. I figured you earned the bounty."

I opened the envelope and looked at the check. Ten grand. "But I didn't…"

Karen dismissed my protestations with a wave before they could begin. "I know money was the furthest thing from you mind. I know what Dumbley did to rope you. My offer to help get you out of that raw deal still stands."

"No thanks. I appreciate the offer, but I got myself in, I'll get myself out," I said.

"On the plus side, it wasn't Dumbley's client so you actually can keep the cash," she said.

"That'll really burn him. And I could use the money."

"And here I thought teachers made the big bucks," she teased.

Her assistant knocked on the door. "You've got a meeting with the mayor."

"I'll vamoose then," I said.

Karen pulled her broom out from behind the door. "Can I offer you a lift?"

"Your grin looks a little too evil. I'll walk," I said. Karen waved her hand shutting down the protective ward on her window and opening it. She sat on her broom and flew out, presumably toward City Hall. The window closed and the ward promptly turned back on.

I walked outside thinking of what I could do with my new found money, when I saw Ludley approach from behind and my left. I ignored him until he tried to put an arm on my shoulder. I ducked and ended up behind him.

I took him by surprise.

"Haven't seen you do that since high school," he said.

I shrugged. "I heard what happened. Tough break."

"I have to bring Johnson in," he said.

"I thought you were suspended," I said.

"I am, which is where you come in," he said.

"Excuse me?" I said.

"You have your bounty hunter license. I can be your assistant. No badge needed," Ludley said.

"I already took him in once. And he's not out on bail. Johnson escaped. And I'm not looking for a sidekick," I said.

"Assistant," Ludley corrected.

"Regardless, I'm not interested," I said. "I have to teach."

"Isn't it spring break?" he said.

Before I could answer, my cell rang. "Hey Mydia, change your mind about movie night?"

"I'm in an alley over on Wayland Avenue, behind the old theater. The brag from this morning is following me," she whispered. "I don't want him to catch me."

Mydia was scared of Johnson, but she also feared her demon nature. By living a mostly good life, she's kept her demon side stunted. If attacked, she might resort to violence. That would feed her demon side, maybe beyond the point where she'd want to reign it in. Unlike her sisters, Mydia's a full blood demon. The damage she could do if she let loose… I'd be willing to ride on Karen's broom if she hadn't left, just to get there quicker.

"I'm on my way," I said, but there was no answer. "Mydia?"

I looked at Ludley. "You still want to be my sidekick?"

"Assistant."

"Get me to Wayland now," I said. "Johnson's going after Mydia."

"My bike's around the corner."

We ran and he climbed on the motorcycle. "Get on."

"I'll drive," I said.

"Your feet don't even reach the ground," he said.

I pushed him back and assumed the driver's position. "It has hand controls so my leg length only matters if we stop."

"We're not going to stop?" he asked nervously.

"Not until we're there."

My reflexes are pretty good and I maxed out Ludley's speedometer. I could feel him stiffen when I took a corner so low we were almost even to the ground.

Only a few minutes had passed since the call, but the alley was empty and there was no sign of either of them.

"Damn," I said.

"You're the bounty hunter. How do we find them?" Ludley said.

"I don't know," I said.

"I thought boggarts had some magic ability to find people. That's what everybody says about Sift," said Ludley. My grandfather liked to cultivate the idea that the reason he was so good was supernaturally based, but I'd spent more than a few summers doing trace work with him. He had a couple of gimmicks and tricks, but what it boiled down to was a combination of being able to figure out how his quarry thought and pure bull-headed stubbornness.

What did I know about Johnson? He was mid-level mob management and had a love of violence. He had a sense of entitlement and felt Idmin owed him for some slight. Johnson took the demon's protection of his niece as a challenge. He could change mostly into a horse and could have carried Mydia off any direction, avoiding roads and streets in favor of back alleys and yards.

I hit myself in the forehead. As a man horse he had no arms. He had to have her in a vehicle. Some people would speed away from the scene of a kidnapping, but the brag knows enough not to. He'll be obeying every last traffic law so as not to be pulled over for a moving violation and be caught.

I switched positions on the bike. "You drive."

"Why?"

"Because I might be needing to get off in a hurry. Head toward Little Prussia and don't spare the speed. We're looking for a truck, van, or car with shaded windows doing the speed limit." Ludley nodded and the motorcycle took off. "And if you find yourself getting excited, let me know."

"Why?"

"Because we're looking for a succubus who's upset," I said and he nodded. Just being in the same vicinity as Mydia gets guys going and if she's upset the radius would only increase. Her power worked on adults even as a child – older children too – Me not so much. Her mother gave her an amulet to dampen her power when she went to school and it worked until she hit puberty. At some point in kindergarten, her mother asked her who her best friend was and she said me. Her mother did something to me that makes me mostly immune to her charms, but I fell in love with her anyway. Not that it made much of a difference because of her uncle's edict. She was one of the people I missed the most in the orphanage and one of my dearest friends. There was no way Johnson was going to touch her if I could help it.

We were almost to Little Prussia when Ludley slowed and mentioned, "I think we're close." He nodded toward his groin. "My early warning system went off."

I searched traffic. "There," I said, pointing to a stretch limo driving very cautiously. It's been my experience that limo drivers tend to take on the attitude of their passengers and this one was letting people in front of it instead of speeding to cut them off.

"I'll be pulling my disappearing act. You pull up alongside the back to get me a chance to get on, then call in back up," I said.

"Are you absolutely sure she's in there?" he asked.

"No, but it's the best guess I've got," I said.

"I can't call in backup on a guess or my suspension might become permanent," he said.

"Fine. I'll tap your shoulder before I jump, then fall back and follow."

Ludley nodded and I disappeared. As soon as I was close enough, I leapt to the back end of the limo. Ludley dropped back into traffic and I pressed my face up against the tinted glass of the back window to get a look inside – jackpot. Johnson had a gun trained on Mydia. Now I needed to figure a way in that wouldn't end with her getting shot.

The pigeons had left some droppings on the roof and disgusting as it was, I thought about scooping it up and throwing it on the windshield. Problem is, it wasn't enough.

We stopped at a light so I got off and ran to the front. Carefully I messed with his windshield wipers, then ran to a bus stop where two guys in suits were drinking coffee. I took the cups from their hands.

"Sorry, but it's an emergency," I said, letting them hear me. The garbage can next to them had a half eaten powdered jelly doughnut and I grabbed that too.

The cross street light was turning yellow so I ran and dumped the first cup of coffee on the limo's windshield. Luckily there was some creme in it. Next, I smeared the doughnut all over the driver's side.

He hit the wipers and squirted some washer fluid, but the damaged wipers only spread the mess around. I wiped the rest of the doughnut around in it. The powdered sugar and jelly mixed together nicely to make sure nobody could see out the glass. The driver opened his door cursing and had some tissues in his hand to clean the mess. I went right past him. Fortunately, the partition was only half way up. If I had been any bigger, I never would have squeezed through.

The light was green and horns were honking because of the snarl in traffic.

"What's the problem?" yelled Johnson.

"Someone threw some crap on the windshield. I've got to clean it…"

I wasn't about to wait for them to finish their conversation. Johnson had turned so the gun was pointed around from Mydia. I put one hand on the barrel and used the other to throw the second coffee in the brag's face. Like the Styrofoam cup says, contents may be hot, in this case, hot enough to burn his face.

I got the gun and opened the back door. "Mydia, run," I said, pushing her out. I hit the child safety lock on the side of the door and slammed it, then went out the other side and did the same. I jumped onto the roof, ran and kicked the driver right in the jaw. He fell like a brick. I went back inside the driver's seat and closed the partition the rest of the way, then took the keys out, making sure Johnson couldn't open it from the inside.

I stepped outside, put the keys in my pocket and pulled the unconscious driver out of traffic.

With any luck, the windows were bulletproof and he'd be trapped until police arrived. The smashing of glass shattered that hope. Johnson had gone man horse and kicked out the driver's side rear window.

I moved to the broken window and became visible. "I'd stay in if I were you," I said, pointing the gun at him.

"Then how will I kill you?" Johnson had shifted to goblin and was climbing out feet first.

I shot him. Just in the foot, but you would have thought I got him in the heart from all the screaming and whining.

"Any part of you that comes out, gets a bullet in it. You do a third time and I blow the gas tank.

"You're bluffing," he said and made a grab for me.

I shot his hand. One thing I learned from Sift was don't be afraid to hurt someone if your life was on the line. He also taught me how to do it with both minimal and maximum damage. "You have any marshmallows in there? Or any weenies to roast? Or do you still think I'm bluffing?"

"Okay, I'm not moving. Don't blow me up," he pleaded.

I just smiled and stood there until the cops arrived. They took him and the driver in custody, making sure Johnson was shackled before they let the EMT's near him.

I was taken back to the 13th and gave another statement. The cops questioned him, Mydia and I separately. They must have liked what they heard because they let me go.

Ludley came up to me, his badge back on his uniform. I had given some of the credit to Ludley and it looked like he got reinstated. He shook my hand. "Thanks. I owe you."

"Yes, you do, sidekick," I said.

"Assistant."

"Where's Mydia?" I asked. We hadn't had a chance to talk yet. Ludley pointed behind me. I turned to see the succubus charging at me. "Are you okay? Is…"

Mydia grabbed my face and gave me a kiss that would have brought me to my knees if she hadn't been holding me up. Like I said, I'm only mostly immune to her charms.

"I take it you're not mad at me anymore?"

"Nope. You still have a movie for tonight?" she asked.

"I can get one," I said.

"Do it. I'll be at your place in an hour."

Every man in the place hated for her to go, but loved to watch her leave. I wonder how many would go home to their partners and ask them to put on a nurse's outfit tonight.

"Hey, Hunt, one question," asked Ludley. "Were you bluffing about the gas tank?"

I gave Ludley a smile and left the 13th without saying a word.

ATTACK OF THE TROUSER SNAKE

A Terrorbelle Tale

I enjoy my job, which sets me apart from a lot of people—as if razor sharp pixie wings and naturally pink hair weren't enough to do that already. Not to mention a chest that's actually made a stripper complain to her plastic surgeon that he shortchanged her. Add to that mix shoulders wide enough for linebackers to look at me with envy and you only start to scratch the surface of understanding the joys of being equal parts ogre and pixie. I stand out even in New York City, despite the fact that I usually cover up my wings with a brightly colored trench coat.

My job is part semi-secret agent, with parts enforcer and investigator, plus anything else my boss decides she needs. On busier days this can include getting shot at, attacked by monsters or facing down more types of evil than I can shake a stick at. Not that stick shaking typically helps, unless it's the size of a small tree trunk and applied to vital organs. Basically, I'm hired muscle for a woman who fights back the darkness in a world that doesn't even believe in magic. Fortunately, it works for me. Fighting is all I've known since I was eleven. I need to make a living and I can't see myself at a typical nine to five. Although with the speed my wings can move at, I bet I'd made a great chef at a Japanese steakhouse.

Being one of Nemesis' three female agents keeps life from getting dull, but there are gaps between our assignments. During a job, things can get so busy that sometimes sleep isn't even an option. Makes how we spend our down time that much more important, even if we go about it differently.

Gani likes to experiment and study. You'd think the twin sister of Merlin would have learned enough about magic since the fall of Camelot, but she says there's always more to find out. And since her knowledge has saved my bacon more than once, I don't discourage her.

Rudy is a club kid, partying all night and sleeping away the day. Not exactly unexpected behavior from the daughter of Thor. I pity the idiots who get into a drinking contest with the valkyrie, thinking there's no way a woman could drink them under the table. Especially since the loser pays the winner's bar tab for the night. Rudy's not much into beer or mead, preferring mixed drinks and jello shooters, which can run upwards of fifteen dollars apiece in some clubs. It's not unheard of for her to run up a four-figure tab, but in her defense, she does tend to offer to out drink entire groups. She's even done it for charity a time or two. Things aren't pretty for the fools who try to welsh on their bet—Rudy can bench press a compact car fifty times. I consider that impressive—I have trouble after ten reps.

Neither research nor club hopping thrills me, unless you count spending time at Bulfinche's Pub to hang out with my favorite bartender Murphy. I like a little quiet time to myself. Nemesis' office is in a midtown skyscraper where she pays for about two thousand square feet, but Gani has folded over the space inside so it's got as much room as a mansion. She supplies her agents with apartments, but I only use my work residence when I can't be away from the office or I'm too exhausted to go home. Otherwise, I'm at my own place down in Hell's Kitchen. It's a third of the size of my work apartment, but it's all I can afford. And it has the added bonus of getting me away from work, which can be a godsend.

One of the benefits is I have neighbors. I've gotten to know most of them, like Mrs. Washington who treats me like one of her granddaughters. Or Mr. Rodriguez who runs the corner bodega. Ever since I stopped an armed robbery there, I can't pay for my fresh fruit if I wanted to. And they know things about me that I tend to keep secret, particularly my wings. Normally I cover up when I'm outside, but sometimes if I'm just going to the corner, I don't bother. My block is a home.

My neighbors have some vague idea what I do and tend to ask me for help when the police can't or won't help. Ever since I saved a couple of cops from zombie rats, I've had lots of friends with badges, particularly the pair I rescued, so I know it's not that the cops don't care. The truth is there are only so many officers and they can be limited by what the higherups tell them. My neighbors aren't a particularly wealthy or influential lot, so things shy of murder can sometimes get put on the back burner. And sometimes crimes not so shy of murder.

It started with a timid knock on my door by Horace Milford who lives two floors above me. He was in the grocery when I stopped the robbery and I wasn't exactly easy on the gunman in question. After disarming him, I threw him twenty feet. He would have gone further if there hadn't been a wall in the way. With my heritage, throwing a 160-pound man that far isn't too difficult. Reigning myself in so he wasn't seriously hurt was more of a challenge.

I have a peephole and a camera with infrared capabilities. I checked both. Never hurts to be careful—Nemesis has a lot of enemies and I've made a few of my own, so I never know who or what may be coming to pay me a visit. Getting into our office is akin to breaking into Fort Knox. Gani could easily make a billion in the home security industry. By way of contrast my home security system consists of a recently reinforced steel door. I've done the same to my bedroom. If someone breaks in, they have to deal with me. I'm a bit more dangerous than any alarm.

There was no one hiding behind him so I opened up.

"Ms. Belle…" My driver's license reads Terror Belle, even though it's really one word. My neighborhood is still very old world. I address all my neighbors who are significantly older than me with an honorific. Most of the older men refer to me as Ms. Belle. Despite eight years as a soldier and one of the all-female elite warrior Daemor, I'm barely legal to drink in New York, so I like it. "I need your help."

"Come in, Mr. Milford," I said.

The man actually blushed. "Would you mind coming out? My being alone in an apartment with a beautiful young woman might give people the wrong idea." It said something about the man, considering there was nobody in the hall. I had already suspected that his wife wore the pants in their family, but his next statement made it clear. "And I wouldn't want to upset Mrs. Milford."

I smiled. I'd lived in parts of Faerie where sex was how some people said hello to strangers. Those places tend to get lots of visitors, however casual intimacy has never been my style. I'd both offended and intrigued people when I turned them down. I found those offended preferable to those intrigued. Too many saw it as a challenge. I find decorum truly refreshing. "Sure. What can I do for you?"

"You know I manage the Jasper Hotel?"

I nodded. It was four blocks away. It wasn't exactly a no-tell hotel, but some people used it for that. No rooms by the hour, but it wasn't uncommon for people making a romantic rendezvous to rent a room for the night and check out after a few hours. It was half the price of the midtown hotels and didn't have the sleaze factor involved with the no-tells.

"You've heard about the deaths?"

"Yes." Gossip travels fast. Five people had died there in the last few weeks.

"What else have you heard?" he asked.

"Just that the police had ruled one a suicide and the other four as natural causes." Then I stated the obvious. "You think it was something else?"

"I do. All the deaths happened in the same room, which I thought was odd, but the detectives wrote it off to coincidence. Each victim was alone for the entire night, but on nights where more than one person stayed in the room, nothing happened. On the days of the deaths, the door's cardkey reader shows that nobody went in or out and the windows were locked when they found the bodies. And the room is on the ninth floor. Not that that is necessarily a deterrent for everybody." He looked at my wings when he said it. I didn't bother to explain that there wasn't enough magic energy in New York City for me to fly properly. I can hover and go up a bit if I have a running start and even slow a fall, but flying up to a ninth floor window is too high for me to manage. Not that he was accusing me and he rightly suspected that there were things that could fly that high. "My wife keeps going on about it being a locked door mystery—she's a big reader, but I'm more concerned that more people will die. I want to close down that room, but the owners won't let me. They don't want to lose the business and they accept the cops saying it's a coincidence. I don't know what to do, but I thought you might."

"Nothing rings a bell, but a friend of mine is more of an expert in these kinds of things. Let me give her a call. My cell is inside." I don't bother with the expense of a landline. "You okay waiting out here?"

"Of course," he said with a small bow.

My cell was on the kitchen counter. I hit "3" on my speed dial. One was my boss, two was Murphy. Three was… "Hey, Gani. It's Terrorbelle."

"Hi, T-Belle. What's up?" I was on speaker. I could hear something like rain and thunder in the background. I looked out the window. The sky was blue and cloudless.

"Is it raining by you?" I asked. Manhattan wasn't big enough for us to be having such drastically different weather patterns. Gani was supposed to be in her lab all day and Nemesis would have called if there were a mission.

"You called for a weather report?" Gani asked. I could hear the grin in her voice.

"Actually, I need a favor, but it sounds like there's a monsoon in the background. You go out for the day?"

"Nope, working on my weather control. I have a storm brewing right here in my lab. The entire area is barely a foot cubed."

"Sounds impressive," I said.

"I've done thunderstorms in miniature, but today I'm working on controlling the change between rain, snow, and sleet. I've been able to switch between them, but I want to have all three going at once without changing the overall room temperature," said Gani.

"Is it working?" I asked.

"So far," she said. "What do you need?"

I filled her in. "Any ideas on what it might be?"

I could hear Gani start to hum. It's the sound she makes when she's deep in thought. "Nothing springs to mind. Want me to meet you there to give it a once over?"

"That would be great." I gave her the hotel name and address and the background noise suddenly increased in volume and I heard things breaking. "Everything okay?"

"Not really. Thinking about your problem distracted me. It seems I forgot to figure in what the localized difference in temperatures would do to each other if I lost focus. I have a mini-tornado spinning amok. I've got to go. I'll meet you there in two hours."

"Great, but if you're going to play twister you really should do it with a cute guy," I said.

I heard her snort as she hung up.

I returned to the hall and told Mr. Milford I had called in a specialist and he thanked me profusely, kissing my hand three or four times.

I got to the Jasper a few minutes early. Gani can be very punctual, but not on days when she's playing in her lab. It wasn't so bad—she was only twenty minutes late.

Mr. Milford's pupils got a little wider when he saw Gani. Mrs. Milford probably would have slapped him for it. Gani is striking with a very regal air about her, especially when in her professional mode. She wore designer clothes I couldn't even name. Forget about her shoes—the closet devoted to her footwear was almost as big as my apartment. Of course, she has shoes that are older than some countries. Gani also sports waist length white hair that makes fresh snow look dingy. It was up in a bun today and she wore a pair of glasses. Gani looked like she was in her forties, pretty good considering she was pushing sixteen hundred or so. She's kind of vague on how old she really is, like it really mattered at her age.

Mr. Milford shook her hand and thanked her for coming, then took us up to room 914. We all went in. Gani took a quick walk around the room. No fancy gestures or funny noises—the good ones don't need to bother with hooey.

"Other than the residuals left by the deaths, there's nothing overtly mystic that was left behind. However, I'm sensing some things that seem to back up your theory. It feels more like they were killed, but so many deaths in the same place in such a short time make things run together."

"So you can't do an exorcism?" asked Mr. Milford.

Gani smiled. "I could, but there's nothing here to perform one on. Best guess is something from outside is coming inside."

"But how is it getting in?" he asked.

"There are plenty of things out there that a locked room wouldn't even slow down. Fortunately, most of them are fairly rare. We'll have to do this the old fashioned way," she said.

"Which is?" he asked.

I sighed. I hated the old fashioned way. "We set a trap with living bait." Which of course was going to be me.

"You want me to do it?" she asked.

"Not really," I said, but it'd be a nice change. Despite my heritage, I'm no mage. I can use magic to fly, but it's akin to a bird using updrafts. I don't store any magic in my body and the only two magic based objects I use— my gun and Daemor badge—have excellent built-in cloaks. Any creature than manages to survive in this day and age has better than even odds of sensing Gani's power levels. A magí could cloak easily, but Gani's no magí. Her brother is. She just taps into Merlin's power while he's otherwise indisposed waiting for the return of Arthur. It takes a lot of power for her to cloak the link, which can sometimes be more of a warning than the link itself.

So Gani's no good for bait. As far as the rest of the team goes, Rudy's a goddess and Nemesis is the daughter of night. Both can show up on well-honed mystic radars. I, on the other hand, have the same ambient signature as a human. It'd take a very skilled mage to sense I was anything else as long as my wings were hidden, so I almost always get to be the bait. It's gotten to the point where I had a t-shirt made up with a worm on a hook for these occasions. Gani and Rudy laughed, but Nemesis wasn't amused. We got a dress code memo after that. That from a woman who prefers black leather pants.

Worse, at least in terms of backup, Gani couldn't even stay in the building without possibly tipping off the killer. She did the next best thing and made an invisible rune on one of the walls. It allowed her to use her magic elevator to enter or leave the room, which wouldn't show up on the door log either.

"So technically, you could be our killer," I teased.

"True. Think you can take me?" she said, putting up her dukes like a boxer. As a fighter, she made a great mage.

"Without breaking a sweat," I lied. One on one, if I had the element of surprise, I'd bet on me. If she had time to plan, I might survive, but I'd have to probably kill her to do it. Thankfully she's one of the good guys.

Before we left, I asked Mr. Milford to get me a list of all the employees and to cross-reference who was working the days of the deaths. Not that a killer couldn't come in on a day off, but it was a start. I also asked for copies of the bills of all the people who had stayed in the room, whether they died or not.

Gani left via her elevator. I walked home, packed a bag and returned to the Jasper, this time to check in. Mr. Milford made sure he met me at the desk, whispering he had left copies of everything I had asked for under my pillow.

I went up to 914 and everything was where he said it would be so I checked in with Gani on my cell.

"What are you wearing?" she asked.

"Gani, I didn't know you thought of me that way," I joked.

"Sorry to disappoint, but I'm just interested in your choice of attire since this is an after hours gig," she said.

I smiled. "Yes, I have my bait t-shirt on."

"Just make sure the killer ends up on the hook, not you," Gani said.

"I'll do my best," I replied, said goodbye and hung up. Pulling out folders, I tried to find a pattern in the paper trail. There was no smoking gun on the bills—some ordered room service, some didn't. There wasn't a movie that they all ordered on pay per view. Some used the hotel phone, some didn't.

Normally I'd prefer to interview the staff myself, but this wasn't an assignment for Nemesis. She's not well known in most circles, but those in power, be it mystic or political, tend to at least be aware of her reputation. This gives her some pull with the powers that be, which gives her agents some leeway when we bend the occasional rule. Since I was doing this on my private time, I knew enough not to count on that. That meant if I screwed up, it would reflect poorly on Mr. Milford and I'd hate to get him fired for trying to help.

A scan of the employee files revealed only three who were on the clock the nights of all of the deaths—a night clerk, a maintenance worker and an IT guy.

I used my cell to call Mr. Milford. I had a few questions. I wasn't sure why an IT guy worked at night, but Mr. Milford told me he went to school during the day and apparently guests got cranky if they couldn't access their e-mail and surf the web. The IT guy was typically tied to the computer system just as the night clerk had to stay in the general vicinity of the desk. The maintenance worker, however, could go anywhere, maybe even figure a way around the card locks. The IT guy might be able to erase the logs. The night clerk had control of the security monitors and could edit security footage. Maybe they were working together, maybe it was someone else entirely—after all it didn't have to be an employee.

"Were there any guests who were here all the nights in question?" I asked.

"Give me a moment," Mr. Milford said. I could hear the click of a keyboard. "No, not all five. Any ideas yet?"

"Lots," I said. "But nothing more solid than that."

"I normally leave in about a half hour. I could stay if you need me," said Mr. Milford. It was sweet that he was acting protective, but I could handle myself better than he could. Still, the male ego is a fragile thing.

"Better to keep things normal. We don't want to alert anyone to why I'm here, but thank you," I said.

Next, I checked the room over. Normally that would have been the first thing on my list, but as Gani and I had already done a check earlier I was just looking for anything non-mystical we might have missed. Despite a thorough search, I didn't find a single trap door or secret passage. The only way in, besides the door and windows, was the pipes in the bathroom. Not that those couldn't be used. To be safe, I put the toilet seat down and the stoppers in the sink and shower. It wouldn't stop anything, but the noise removing them would let me know something was coming.

The next few hours were pure boredom. I didn't talk on the phone because that might be enough to scare whatever was doing the killing off. I didn't turn the TV on because it was too much of a distraction, especially for me. We didn't have television in Faerie and I can very easily get sucked into a program. Not a good idea when I'm supposed to be keeping watch for a killer. It would make me a real target instead of just bait, so I just held a book in front of me. I can read three languages, so I made sure the book I chose wasn't written in one of them to avoid another distraction. I periodically turned a page of a French edition of the collected Three Musketeers to make it look like I was actually reading it.

I ordered room service. It came and nothing happened. It smelled good, but some poison can actually enhance the smell and taste of food. Besides my days as a Daemor made me too paranoid to eat any of it. I even examined under the cart to make sure no nasties were hiding.

Next, I ripped apart my intended meal looking for anything hiding in the food. It might sound crazy but there were living creatures small enough to hide in food that could kill you. My phone rang. It was Syndey. I rolled my eyes. I liked her, but she came on about as subtle as a subway train. We had met while I was filling in as a bouncer in a vamp club, a task that fell in the "anything else my boss came up with me to do" category of my job. There was a problem and a bloodsucker got the drop on me. Sydney stepped up and hit him with a chair from behind, giving me enough time to take him down. She saved my life. The only thing she asked in return was for me to go clubbing with her–often. Other than a quick trip to Bulfinche's Pub, I'd been too busy, but Sydney called me every other day to see if I was free.

If I didn't answer, she'd just keep calling. I opened the flip top. "Hi, Sydney."

"Hey, Terrorbelle. Darcy got invited to a party on Park Avenue. Going to be some rich guys there. You want in?" she asked.

"Can't," I said.

"You working?" she asked.

"Not exactly," I said.

"We got a limo. We can swing buy your apartment to pick you up."

"I'm not home."

"Where are you?" she asked.

"At a hotel," I answered.

"Belle, you having a nooner?"

"It's nighttime and no, I'm not," I said.

"Is he married?"

"Who?"

"The guy you're having the affair with. I mean why else use a hotel?" she said.

"I'm not meeting a guy," I said.

"Come on, you can tell me," she said.

There was a knock at the door. I looked through the peephole. It was Glen Baxter, the IT guy. He looked a little different from the photo on his ID badge having grown what he probably thought passed for a goatee. Maybe with a little eyeliner and some age it one day may be a real one. Not that I should talk. According to his file, he was a year older than me.

"Sydney, I have to go. There's a man at the door," I said.

"I knew it. Call later and tell me all about it. Toddles," she said.

It was easier not to argue. "Bye."

Baxter knocked again. I opened the door cautiously. "Yes?"

"Sorry to disturb you, ma'am. I work for the hotel and we've been having some problems on this floor with the wireless network. Have you noticed anything?" he asked.

"No, but I don't have my computer with me," I said.

"Do you mind if I come in and check your wireless router?" he asked.

"I don't usually let a guy do that until the second date," I said. He laughed, a little harder than the joke was worth. Normally, a woman alone in a hotel room should close the door and call the front desk to check his story, which of course would scare Baxter away if he was the killer. Still, I shouldn't appear too accepting. "Can I see some ID?"

He handed over the plastic badge on his collar and smiled, probably thinking he was being charming. Maybe he was, but since he was one of my only three suspects I had trouble seeing him as anything other than a possible serial killer.

I looked it over and smiled back, returning it to him. "I guess it'd be okay for you to come in."

"Thanks," he said, moving toward the corner by the TV. The router was a small plastic circle on the ceiling with a blinking red light. It had been green when I checked in. "Ah, here's the problem. The router is stuck in a loop. I just need to reset it."

Baxter stood on a chair then took a pen, stuck it into a pinhole, and held it for several seconds. When he took it out, the LED went off, then the green light blinked a few times before staying on.

"That should fix it. Management bought the cheapest routers they could find and sometimes this happens," he said, making no move to go.

"Well, I'm sure you have other rooms to check," I said, knowing that my router shouldn't be affecting the ones in the other rooms.

"Actually, my dinner hour just started. I have some free time," Baxter said, looking deep into my eyes, trying for seductive. He got somewhere between puppy eyes and a dog in heat.

"I'm good," I said walking to the door. "Got to wash my hair, do my nails, that sort of thing."

When I pulled on the knob, it didn't turn. I could tear it off the hinges, but I was still playing a helpless female. He might just be on the prowl for a consensual quickie, but I doubted it.

"The door's stuck," I said.

"No, it's locked. Computer thing."

I gave him one last chance. "Well, open it then."

The smile that took up residence on his face looked nothing like seductive, closer to seduced. "I think not. Your phone service is down and the button I pressed up there jams cell phones. It's just you and me."

"I can see you're very excited by the prospect." It looked like something massive had pinched a tent in Baxter's extremely baggy pants. And the tent poled was writhing. "But I'm not interested."

"Pity," he said, unzipping his fly with one hand, pulling out a washcloth soaked in some chemical I could smell five feet away with the other. "How'd you like to meet my trouser snake?"

"I doubt you'll like how the introductions will turn out," I said, pointing my gun at Baxter's groin. Something snake-like popped out and it wasn't little Baxter. It wasn't little either, easily as thick around as a litter soda bottle and about six feet long. I popped a shot off, but the thing moved too fast and the bullet ended up grazing Baxter's inner thigh. The creature's accomplice fell to the ground, screeching in a high-pitched voice, while the creature itself disappeared from view. It moved too fast for me to be sure, but I think I knew what it was and it wasn't good. Not willing to take him at his word about the cell jammer I hit send on my phone and no service flashed on the screen

"You shot me," Baxter cried.

Moving to the bathroom, I pulled two towels down and threw them at the wounded man, then closed the door. I didn't want the creature getting away through a pipe. More people would die if it did.

"You helped that thing kill five people and planned to make me number six. Look somewhere else for sympathy."

"The first guy killed himself," Baxter whined. "The bullar was trapped in stone and convinced him to sacrifice himself. It broke the curse holding him."

Damn, I was right about what it was. I made wary circles with my gun, but the creature stayed hidden. "It was no curse, just a larval state. They need a human sacrifice to awaken and twelve more to transform." Probably used some sort of telepathic mind games to drive him to take his own life. This was only the second I'd seen, but Bullar become Kulshedra, which is a bigger, flying snake that breathes fire. Another hundred sacrifices turns them humanoid, looking like a hairy giant woman. It takes ten times those numbers if they kill the people themselves. Magic makes the rules, I just try to learn enough of them to keep me alive. Someone offering up a person makes it a sacrifice, which is why it was keeping Baxter here. Bullar eyes hypnotize their victims so they can put their mouths over the person's and literally suck the life out of them. It didn't matter if the intended sacrifice had a knife wound or was knocked out with chemicals on a washcloth for it to count.

"My leg hurts," Baxter complained.

He was annoying me and playing up his irritation factor, maybe figuring his snake-like partner would pop up and help by hypnotizing me. "A flesh wound is less than you deserve. Push the towels against it. It doesn't look like it got your femoral."

"How do you know that?" he whined but did as instructed.

"You'd have lost more blood and be unconscious or dead by now," I said, taking off my coat. I may not have eyes in the back of my head, but razor sharp wings are the next best thing. I'd shred the bullar if it came at me from behind. It might not kill it, but it'd damn well hurt it.

Baxter's eyes got a little wide at the sight of my deadly appendages, but it still wasn't enough to shut him up. "I'm hurt bad. You need to get me to a doctor."

"Or put another bullet in you to put you out of my misery," I said. I'm not above killing, but I did a lot of it in my time as a soldier in Faerie. I needed a damn good reason to end a life these days and annoying me didn't quite cut it. "Now be quiet."

I thought I heard something rustle. It sounded like the monster was under the bed. Now I could bend down and peak, but that would leave me vulnerable. I could use an explosive round to blow the bed up, but the blast would blind me for half a second. That's too long a window to be vulnerable when facing a fast adversary. Also, while the construction in the Jasper wasn't shoddy, it wasn't thick enough to make me confident that it could stop shrapnel from going through any walls, ceiling, or the floor. I didn't want someone from another room hurt or killed so I went with option three.

I kicked the bed across the room with one foot, flipping backwards in the process. I'm not a superior gymnast by any means, but with my muscle power, I don't have to be to accomplish basic maneuvers. I get it done and don't worry about making it pretty. And I cheated by using my wings to help me hover during the spin, which also would shred the creature if it tried to attack me from behind.

Startled by the loss of its cover, the bullar leapt at me, especially impressive considering it had no legs. It sort of sprung like a coil. Magic changes the rules that way sometimes. It was too damn fast and somehow managed to change direction in mid-air toward my head. I watched its open jaws land on my face, its mouth covering mine. Years of training helped me not panic, take a deep breath and shut my mouth the moment before contact. If it managed to suck out my breath, it'd start to drain my life force. Bullar allow their victims to keep breathing in a creepy symbiotic mouth to mouth. It lengthened the death, which was more pleasurable. In a twisted way, the bullar combined feeding and sex into this one deadly act. The stolen life force allowed them to move onto the next stage in their evolution.

The serpent bit down hard to get my attention. I was angry enough I almost made the mistake of looking in its eyes. My Daemor badge, which I wore these days as a belt buckle, combined with my training gave me some resistance to mind control, but it wasn't a free pass. If it got control of me, it'd force me to breath and I'd die.

Of course, if I didn't get it off me soon, nature will make me do the same thing and I'll die anyway.

It was too close for a safe shot, so I grabbed its tail and pulled. Its teeth sank even deeper into my face, like dozens of sharp, pointy anchors. I was pretty sure yanking it was hurting me more than it. Worse, it was trying to widen its jaws even further, opening my mouth. Once that happened, I couldn't stop it from sucking the fight right out of me.

My love life has never been much to brag about, but I have standards. Even on my worst day, I'd never let a creature like this French kiss me. It had to qualify as the second most disgusting kiss I'd ever had. Its nine sharp tongues raked against my lips, cutting as they licked. It had enough control over the little things that it was using some of the tongues to try to pry my lips apart. To add to the fun, it began to suck so the tiniest opening would let my breath escape. Its serpentine body swelled out with the effort.

The edges of my vision started to have tiny lights swirl around as the bullar's belly ballooned up even more, but it gave me an idea.

I couldn't pull it off me without tearing parts of my face, so I needed another way. Being a firm believer in the turnabout is fair play philosophy, I wrapped one massive fist around its neck and squeezed, cutting off the serpent's air supply. For good measure, I twisted its body around like a balloon animal with my gun hand to make sure the bullar couldn't breathe either. I didn't want to let go of the gun, so my grip was weaker than I would have liked, especially since it used its tail to try and pull my arms away.

Talking would literally be the death of me, but there were other ways of getting my point across. The bullar's scales were dense enough to deflect most small arms fire and its eyes were too small a target, hence my hesitation to risk a shot. I didn't want to take a ricochet or have one hit someone in another room. Instead, I arched one of my upper wings until its razor edge was at the bullar's neck, just below where I squeezed. My skin was already past pink and on my way to becoming blue, but I learned long ago never to show weakness. Instead of struggling, I raised an eyebrow and held it, pointing with my eyes at my wing tip, then I nicked the serpent's skin between and under its scales. I felt flesh part and blood ooze.

I considered decapitating it without a warning, but I might not cut through on the first try and, even wounded, the bullar could still do me some damage. My face may not be the prettiest on the block, but it's the only one I've got. I had enough scars without any on my face.

The serpent made a noise that was more growl than hiss. I pushed the wing in until it cut down to muscle. If it didn't let go in the next few seconds, I'd have to try to take its head off regardless or pass out.

I won the game of chicken and the bullar let go of my face only to snap around and sink its fangs into my gun hand. I managed to hold onto my automatic, but my grip loosened enough for the bullar's tail to snake around my throat.

I had managed to take in a deep breath. The wing tip that I had threatened it with sliced out, managing to catch it partially between scales. A normal snake, even a boa constrictor, would have been sliced in half. If I had a better angle or leverage to get between its armor, the wound would have been more than an inch deep.

At the same time, I smashed the fist it had wrapped its jaws around into my forehead. Hitting myself might seem like a bad idea, but I have a very hard forehead.

One night when I was dragged out clubbing by Rudy, some guy was trying to impress women by smashing walnuts into his head to open them. When I expressed that I was less than impressed, he challenged me to do better. The bar had a couple of real coconuts to make drinks from and I spilt one open on my forehead.

The impact with my head hurt the bugger enough for it to open its jaws. I got my hand free for an instant before its maw opened even wider and it made a second try. Instead of pulling away, I pushed my hand down its throat, gun and all. It clamped down hard enough that my fingers started to go numb.

It hurt, but I'd learned to work through pain years ago. Physical pain was the easiest. I sprinted across the room and used my wings to hover near the ceiling. Baxter had hit a button in the router to jam my cell phone. I'm not a high tech gal, but there were simple ways of dealing with complicated gadgets. I reached up with my free hand and ripped the plastic device off the ceiling and crushed it between my fingers.

I had to let go of the bullar to wreck the tech, which it took as an invitation to wrap its tail back around my windpipe. I had managed several deep breaths and tensed my neck muscles, which where strong enough to halt the tail squeeze, at least for a bit. The longer this went on, the more the advantage would go to the serpent.

It knew this, but wasn't patient enough to wait, deciding instead to cut off my windpipe by putting the tip of its tale in my foolishly open mouth. I was distracted by my multi-tasking—I was trying to fight the creature and dial my cell phone at the same time. I bit down on the appendage as I hit "3" on my speed dial.

I obviously couldn't respond, so a few seconds later the wall morphed into elevator doors and opened. Gani looked out, ready to sling a spell. Dropping the phone, I ran toward the elevator and motioned Gani out, all the while forcibly unwinding the tail from around my throat. Maybe it was in pain from me biting its tail, maybe I had better leverage, but this time I won the tug of war and got it off, if you could call the resultant circles of bruises around my neck winning.

I mentally clicked the gun's clip to armor piercing shells and snapped my swallowed hand like it was holding a whip. Once the serpent was in the lift, I fired. There were a series of tiny bulges as the bullet ricocheted along the creature's digestive tract. I fired a second shot and this time some of the bulges were trickling blood between the scales, which fortunately didn't extend inside of the creature. Switching the clip to explosive rounds, I fired again, squeezing the serpent's neck tight behind the bullet. The blast blew half its guts out a new hole. The bullar wasn't dead, but its jaw's grip on my hand weakened.

Gani made a complicated hand motion and purple lightning jumped from her fingers to the bullar. It convulsed and fell off my hand onto the floor.

"You need to finish it?" asked Gani, stepping inside her elevator.

I looked down at my bloody hand and walked out. There were times I needed to finish a fight. Sometimes honor or revenge demanded it. This was neither. "Nah. All yours."

The bullar spoke for the first time. "Oh mighty mage, I can offer you great power for serving me."

Gani laughed. "The only way I'm going to serve you is over rice with a garlic sauce."

"Glen Baxter, attend your master or all you are entitled to shall be lost," said the bullar as purple lightning filled the elevator, making a strobe effect in the hotel room as it filled with the aroma of cooking meat.

I'm not sure what the snake promised the geek, but it was enough to make him drag himself to his feet in an attempt to help the monster.

I was tired and hurting so I just pointed my gun and cocked it. "Take another step and you lose a kneecap."

"I don't believe you," Baxter said, pulling a switchblade from his pocket and charging me. I caught his hand and twisted it back, dropping him halfway to the floor, followed by a swift kick to the front of his leg. Baxter screamed in agony and fell the rest of the way to the floor. "You broke my knee."

"I warned you'd lose a kneecap. And it's only dislocated, not broken," I said, pulling the cheaply made knife out of his hand and snapping it in half in front of him, then putting the pieces in my pocket. Shoving him facedown on the carpet, I literally sat on Baxter to pin him as I ripped his belt off and made a tourniquet below the hip but above the gunshot wound. It wasn't too deep and had already started to clot, but was still bleeding.

"So can I assume you'll be confessing to the cops to the murders?" I said.

"Are you crazy? You can't prove a thing and I didn't kill them," Baxter said.

"You offered them up to your trouser snake and made sure they couldn't call for help. That's the same as killing them in my book," I said.

"I'd have to be an idiot to confess," he said.

"You'd have to be an idiot not to," I said. Gani exited her elevator carrying a charred serpentine carcass and plopped it on the floor in front of Baxter's face. He whimpered as smoke rose up and the smell of charred flesh entered his nostrils. Baxter tried to roll away, but couldn't move me off his back. "Especially once his family comes looking for him."

"Family?" he said.

"He didn't tell you? Each Bullar is part of a family of twelve. Very close. They have to team up to overpower and devour the mother, after which they go into the stony larval stage the suicide victim found him in. Once all twelve get the necessary human sacrifices, they join together to evolve to the next stage. A hydra. Now that their brother is dead, they can never move on. Your bullar at least explained to you how important evolution was to him, I assume?" Baxter nodded, his chin digging into the carpet. "That was why he did all this after all. Can you imagine how angry the other eleven are going to be that you cheated them of their chance? Can you imagine what they are going to do to you for killing their brother?"

"Me? You two killed him," he said.

"Well, that's your story. Mine is you called us and asked us to set him up. Isn't that how you remember it?" I asked Gani.

"Not so much asked as begged is how I recall it," said Gani.

"But I was loyal to him. I tried to kill you." His tone had gone up an octave. I hate to hear a grown man whine. It gives me a headache.

"Prove it," I said, taking a picture of him and the corpse with my phone. "Smile."

"Wait, don't I have to be offered as a sacrifice for them to kill me?" Baxter said.

"For the power, sure, but they'll be going after your for revenge. Besides, you're kind of puny to be split eleven ways," I said.

"I don't want to die." Baxter had tears streaming down his face.

"I imagine your victims felt the same way," I said.

"You have to protect me," he said.

"Not my job," I replied. "You'd need to be someplace safe 24/7. Bullar don't want people to know they exist. It makes their killing run smoother. If you were in jail, they probably wouldn't go after you, at least until you got out."

"And the guards would have to protect you if they did come for you," added Gani, tsking me so Baxter couldn't see.

"But that'd hardly be fair to them," I said.

"Forget about them. Someone's got to protect me," said Baxter.

"The only way they'd protect you is if you confessed to having a hand in these murders," I said.

"I'll confess," said Baxter.

And confess he did to the cop that met us in the lobby. As soon as he was taken away, Gani turned to me with a grin.

"You naughty girl, you."

"Me?" I said, with mock innocence.

"You made all of that up. Bullar and hydra have nothing to do with each other and if a bullar had family, they wouldn't care less about each other," said Gani.

"It worked, didn't it?" I said.

And it did to a point. After explaining how he doctored the computer logs, Baxter put the mention of giant magic snakes in his statement and the DA's office almost took him for a nut and let him go until my boss made a call.

The night before sentencing, Baxter called the ADA to try to withdraw his plea. After all, no snakes had shown up at Riker's to get him, so he figured he might be safe. Gani whipped up an illusion of a flock of floating snakes outside his cell and all talk of withdrawing his plea on account of insanity was forgotten.

I got invited to dinner at the Milford's by way of a thank you and had a week's worth of leftovers forced on me. And Sydney still didn't believe that I wasn't having an affair at the Jasper, especially when I explained that I had been attacked by a trouser snake.

A STITCH IN TIME

A Case of the Soul Collector

A stitch in time saves nine. The sad part is I wanted Judy Nein dead and it seemed like everyone kept stitching her back up. Turns out she wanted to be dead too, but our ideas of what that entailed differed. In mine, the dead stop all bodily functions and get buried or their ashes scattered to the wind. In Nein's, you kept moving and talking and when a part fell off, you simply found someone who was good with a needle to sew it back on for you. It helped if they had a strong stomach and deft hands. Not to mention industrial grade thread.

The dead started coming back a few years back in serious numbers. It should have changed the world, but day-to-day life is pretty much the same for most people. Sure, plenty of religions had a field day. There were those who claimed it was the end of days or the resurrection, but not everyone who died came back. Some ministers started preaching that only the truly righteous were chosen to come back, but they shut up damn quick when their holy ones got into unholy slaughter. Not all of the nearly dead turned into psychopathic killers, but it wasn't rare either. It got soul collectors federal marshal status. The upper tier, of which I'm one, are sanctioned by the UN with authority to operate in any member nation. There's a lot of money to be made contracting out, but often the living conditions are lacking. And the conditions of the dead are even worse. And despite the blessing of the UN, there are countries that don't want me back. Hell, my own mother cringes when I show up on her doorstep.

The Nearly departed don't all come back the same way. There are hundreds of different dead. Judy Nein was a basic zombie, but with enough mind to hold onto who she was. She was low on grunting, moaning, and lumbering behavior, but she still rots. The people in her Chicago neighborhood seem intent on telling me her good points, pushing that she's an excellent dancer. I'm not sure why. If Fred Astaire came back to tap dance on the throats and spleens of the living, I'd have to take him down too, although I might dress up in a top hat and tails for the occasion.

In the plus column for Nein, there's no evidence that she gets the munchies for human bits, brains or otherwise. On the minus side, Nein ain't above the occasional bovine gray and white matter snack. That snack habit came straight from a butcher's daughter. Most of the neighborhood treated me like a leper, but this young lady got it in her head that soul collectors are hot. Some people would look down their noses at me for taking advantage of that infatuation. Those people have never had groupies. Women throwing themselves at me, wanting nothing more than hot, meaningless sex are hard to say no to. Well, the ones that use pale makeup and wear dark, depressing clothes are easier to turn down, but some of them have bodies that could model lingerie if they'd change the makeup scheme from midnight to spring.

And this butcher's daughter was gorgeous, legal, and insisted on sex before she'd tell me anything. It would take a stronger man than me to turn down that offer. I didn't even try.

After she told me that tidbit, she hinted she knew more, but wouldn't share unless I paid her bribe again. This time we broke a piece of furniture, but it turns out she was bluffing. I had figured she was, but I just couldn't take that chance. It was well worth being sure. And I got some nice pork chops.

Only someone who'd been dead themselves wouldn't know that the Nearly departed number in the tens of thousands while the licensed soul collectors in North America barely top a hundred. Could get some more, but the old timers like my mother aren't interested.

Soul collectors can't and don't go after all the dead. Time and manpower won't allow it. A collector gets called in only when one of the Nearly crosses the line. It's the law, not that I haven't been known to bend or break a few in my time. It's all thanks to one of the first of the mass Nearly departed. The gent was a big shot lawyer and when he showed up at his law firm three days after his funeral, the senior partners refused to reinstate him, so he did what lawyers do—he sued them. Case went to the Supreme Court and ended with the Nearly dead getting some civil rights protection. Of course, the fact that the son of one of the justices had also recently returned to the land of the living didn't hurt matters. A two-month moratorium was put on declaring someone legally dead.

Nein was do-gooder neighborhood hero before she bought it, a crusading grandmother type, working to clear the drug dealers and pimps out of her neighborhood. Judy Nein got nailed in a driveby, presumably in retaliation. Nein rose up at the morgue and walked out, straight back to her streets. It might have been better for her if she had waited until after the undertaker had worked on her. Embalming fluid makes the walking dead toxic, but they don't lose so many pieces. At least Chicago is cold most of the year, but she's too involved in her neighborhood to head off somewhere smarter like Nome.

Nein didn't fit the rogue profile, but someone called in a complaint, which led to me being called to look into things. It wasn't the way a case usually went down. Normally, I only go in after there are multiple complaints from credible sources, an independent investigation, or a pile of bodies. Three federal investigators couldn't find skin or shroud of Judy Nein, so some muckety muck asked me to look into things. That's the beauty of doing what I do. Nobody can order me to do anything. I can be asked, pleaded with, begged, coerced and threatened. Ordered, no. When I turn the feds down, they can dock my pay. They've done it too. It's when I hire out of the country. I usually fill up my Cayman account and in a few weeks, they send some CIA spook to find me. I insist on back pay and a bonus for wasting my time, plus anything else that'll turn the screws a little bit.

Other than the one anonymous complaint, there wasn't any evidence that Judy Nein had done anything wrong, so I hadn't gone in orbs and guns blazing. If I found out she was hurting the living, she was going down. If she wasn't, I'd find out who made the complaint and take out my displeasure at having my time wasted on them. I'm not paid by the hour.

I canvassed the neighborhood twice, talked to the woman's family and friends. They were protecting her down to the last person, with every bit of the intensity of witnesses to a mob hit denying they saw anything. Only these folks weren't doing it out of fear. They were doing it for a few of the more noble emotions. Despite myself, I was admiring and envying the dead Nein woman. There probably weren't enough people to make up a handful who'd be willing to lie for me out of the goodness of their hearts.

I was tired. Except for the butcher's daughter, the locals had made it clear I wasn't welcome, but my job wasn't done. Being too stupid and stubborn to give up wasn't a requirement for being a soul collector, but it made me more effective. I wasn't going anywhere yet. I stopped to lean against a lamppost and took a nip out of my flask and opened a candy bar—white chocolate. I gave up smoking as I didn't want to overly hasten my own death. There are too many on the other side waiting for me and most of them aren't waiting with open arms. Booze helped take the bite out of the cold Chicago wind and I figured it was a slower death than cigarettes. Also helped me relax enough to do my job. As for the white chocolate, I liked it. It was one of the few tastes that helped deaden my extra senses.

Not all soul collectors can sense the nearby dead–lucky bastards. There were two Nearly and a dead body nearby. The corpse wasn't coming back. I'd have to let the locals know where to find it. Odds are somebody cared about the person he was and was worried. There was also a dead left arm, but I already knew that. It was mine. Although technically it wasn't mine, it was just attached to me.

The stark weather only served to remind me how stupid I'd been to a woman I cared about. I had been a real ass and too stupid and stubborn to ask for her forgiveness yet. I took a second sip, mulling over my next move and debating a second trip to the butcher shop to check to see if my lady friend had figured out a break in the case. Short-term sex helps keep deep thoughts on the state of my love life at bay. There's a difference between making love and having sex, but enough of the latter helps block thinking about the former. I looked over and there was a beat cop in uniform heading my way. I was planning to tell him about the corpse when the baby-faced officer of the peace took out his nightstick. Cops never used that move as the start of a friendly conversation. I learned that as a kid when I used to get rousted just for standing on the corner. I hated it then and wasn't thrilled by it now. The difference is I hadn't been a kid in a long time.

I pegged Babyface as the same kind of prick who made my life miserable as a kid, but I might have been wrong. It doesn't happen often, but I did it enough to keep me honest. Partially anyway.

"Can I help you, Mr..." Babyface asked, obviously fishing for my name. I wasn't about to give him mine. I had almost managed to forget it after all these years. I wasn't even going to volunteer the one I had it changed to ten years ago. Not to this prick. Babyface was actually smacking the stick into his open palm as he spoke. I suppose it probably intimidated kids and the simple minded. As a kid, I had bones broken by one of those. Today, I was angry enough that I wasn't scared, which was stupid and dangerous. A guy with a stick could hurt or kill me. I've had Nearly swing trees at my head, so one guy with a stick seemed way down on the threat scale. Besides the day a punk like Babyface here manages to nail me while I'm watching is the day I hang up my orbs for good and head off to the rest home.

"Nope. I'm good," I said, taking another slug from the flask followed by a square of white chocolate. I could almost hear my mother's voice in my ear telling me I should eat better. And sometimes she does just that. As far as the feds are concerned, I'm one of the most badass collectors they've got, but they've never had to deal with dear old Mom.

"What exactly are you doing here?" he demanded, acting like I should be paying him a toll for standing on the sidewalk.

"They let you on the job with eyes that bad?" I said. Yeah, I was being an ass, but Babyface was probably harassing kids like I once was when he's not messing with visitors to the neighborhood.

"Excuse me?" the cop said, his face turning beat red. I probably wasn't cowering properly. I'd been meaning to take lessons, but never had the time.

"I'm drinking and eating," I said. "I'd offer to share, but I don't like you."

"Put it away."

"Candy illegal in Chicago, is it?" I said. "Al Capone's great-grandson running chocolate now?"

"The booze wise guy. We have open container laws here," he said, pointing to my flask with his stick.

"Not done yet. I am done with the candy though," I said, crinkling and dropping the candy wrapper at his feet.

"Oh, you're done. And that's littering with your loitering."

"Oddly enough, I usually prefer loitering with my littering, but I hear it's good to spice things up," I said.

"I'm going to teach you respect," spat Babyface.

"No need, I already know it. Do it at karaoke all the time. Want to hear my Aretha? Not as good as my Elvis, but after a couple drinks, nobody cares," I said.

"You dumb punk," said Babyface, poking his nightstick into my Adam's apple. I smiled. The next second and a half was probably a blur for him, but I was actually a little slow for my tastes. Probably the liquor or maybe I'm just getting old, although I'm a little young for that. My reflexes and strength are better than average for a human, but not necessarily as fast as some of the dead. Except for my left arm. Not surprising considering its condition.

I twisted his arm around his back, forcing him to his knees. By the time he realized what was happening, I used his own handcuffs to restrain his hands behind his butt, pushed him on his stomach, and was sitting on his back.

Babyface was furious. "That's assault on a police officer! You're going to jail for a long time."

"Wrong, Sparky. You just assaulted a federal agent and not only are you going to jail, but you pissed me off. Cops don't go assaulting citizens without cause. I'm going to make sure you get kicked off the force," I said.

"Bullshit," spat Babyface.

I took the leather glove off my left hand. Babyface looked at the mummified flesh and cringed. "You're a god-damned Nearly!"

"Nope," I replied, suspending my badge in front of his now bulging eyes. When he read what I was, I felt all the anger and tension fade from his body.

"Crap."

"That about covers it," I said, wiping some white chocolate goo off my fingertips on to his uniform shirt. I belched, starling myself. Odd, I couldn't remember having hot dogs. "Nothing left but to call and turn you in. You know the penalty for assaulting a federal collector in the course of his duties. There's no way around that. Unless..." I let the last word dangle like a gutted night crawler in front of a prize bass.

"Unless what?" asked Babyface. I knew his type. He became a cop because he was a bully at heart and the badge let him get away with things that most other people would be put away for. Made me sick to my stomach and that's saying something.

"I'm working a case, but haven't been having much luck. I'm looking for one of the Nearly."

"Judy Nein," he whispered.

"You got it in one," I said. "Where is she?"

"How should I know?"

"Beats me," I said and took out my cell phone, making sure Babyface could see me in his peripheral vision.

"Wait!"

I raised my eyebrows and lowered the phone.

"I heard there is a party for the Untouchables tonight," he said.

"I thought Eliot Ness and the rest were long dead. You trying to tell me that they've become Nearly?" Nearly from that long ago are rare, but hardly unheard of. Ness was supposed to be one tough S.O.B. in his day. It could get ugly.

"Who?" asked Babyface, obviously a product of our fine education system. "The leader of the Untouchables gang is Howell, not this Ness guy."

"So how does that help me find Nein?"

"Duh. Howell and the Untouchables killed her," said Babyface.

"So why are they still walking around?" I asked.

"Probably because she hasn't gotten a hold of them yet," said Babyface.

I shook my head. I expected this level of density from one of the Nearly with a half rotten brain, not one of the living. "I meant why haven't you arrested them?"

"Are you crazy? No one will testify and anyone going in to get them would end up dead," said Babyface, addressing me as if I were the idiot.

"You realize Chicago's finest outnumber these Untouchables, both in numbers and firepower?" I asked. "You can call for backup."

Babyface had a blank look on his face.

"You didn't even try to get them arrested, did you?" I said.

Babyface shrugged. "No one asked me. It's not my job."

"Never read your job description, have you? Where and when are they meeting?" I asked. Babyface told me. I had time on my hands, so I made the call to have him picked up. I told them about the corpse.

"Hey! You said if I helped you out with finding Judy Nein, you'd forget about this," barked Babyface like an annoying, yappy dog.

"When did I say that?" I asked, not even pretending innocence. I'm not that good an actor. Or that innocent.

"Before when..." A light went on inside the inky workings of Babyface's brain. "You tricked me!"

"You should see me with a deck of cards," I said. My left hand could literally move faster than the living eye could follow. It wasn't like I was going to let a bad cop stay on the streets. I may have come to this law enforcement thing later in life, but I wasn't going to let one bad apple drag the rest of us down. I was still sitting on Babyface's back, so I shifted back and forth on purpose. I'm sure my moving squished some tender organs, or at least I hope it did. "Now shut up and stay still."

They say it's not a party until somebody breaks something. I did my part for the Untouchables shindig by smashing a window in the back of the bar they were tearing up and letting myself in. There was enough noise up front that nobody realized they had a gatecrasher.

I sat in a storage room where I had an obscured view of the festivities. The ghost of a cat was trying to chase a mouse, but the little squeaker wasn't having any of it. From the looks, they'd danced this tango before. At some point the ghost cat had caught the mouse, but couldn't hurt him, so now the mouse ignores the kitty's tenth life. If the mouse is lucky, the spectral feline will never figure out how to affect the physical world or how to possess something or things will turn out quite differently.

I appropriated some salty snacks that were probably meant for bowls on the bar. I tossed a couple of cheese twists to the mouse. The cat tried unsuccessfully to swat the snack away. I ate some more, which made me thirsty, so I helped myself to beer. I was technically on the job and there were several armed men in the next room, so I wasn't supposed to be drinking. In deference to this, I stopped at two. Or maybe four. Depended if the other two empties were there when I came in.

Other than playing some really bad music and not being able to dance well, the Untouchables hadn't been guilty of anything while I was watching. I picked out Howell early on. He was the one the men were kowtowing and brown nosing and the one the ho'ed out women were flirting and cozying up to.

I had started in on some cheese and crackers that were on a top shelf when something finally happened. The front door flung open and smacked the wall like a drunk trucker's hand on the gentle curves of a rest stop waitress's buttocks. Two Untouchables came in with a girl in tow. Judging by her struggles, I'd surmised she wasn't there for the party or even willingly for that matter. Her dark hair was pulled back in a shoulder length ponytail that the punk on the left was yanking her around by. Kid couldn't have been more than sixteen.

Howell let out a yell. "All right. The festivities can get started now that the favors are here."

The scumbag tore the girl's t-shirt down the middle and put his hand in a place where it would never belong. She tried to kick him in the groin, but he caught her knee and used the handhold to spread her legs as if her attack had been some sort of intimate invitation.

I gritted my teeth and narrowed my eyes. I hate when I have to choose between helping somebody and doing my job. It never turns out well, although maybe it would if I stopped choosing the person, but I have to look at myself in the mirror each morning. My mug ain't pretty, but I ain't too ashamed of what I see. In this business, that's a lot.

My gun had a full clip, but the chamber was empty. I tend to keep it that way, as I hate having my sidearm fire while it's in my holster. Bullets hurt. That gave me ten shots, plus another half dozen clips, but there were at least two dozen Untouchables. The extra clips weren't going to do me any good. Even with my speed, I wasn't going to get a chance to reload in these close quarters.

I put my gun in one hand and two orbs in the other. Orbs will collect the souls of the living as well as the dead, it just takes longer. It's also way illegal, but it's been done and not one licensed soul collector has ever been convicted for doing it in self-defense. We lost two who did it for revenge. One went to prison, the other went up against me. I'm still here, soul intact. She's… not. I still miss her.

I was willing to do whatever I had to in order to make sure I walked out with the girl. Anyone who got in my way was going to have to take their chances. I stepped out of the storage room wishing I wasn't too stubborn to have worn my vest today. It's good against bullets, claws, and fangs, but the weight slows me down and blocks my power flow.

Before I got out into the bar proper I knew we had company. The door flung open again. Instead of slapping the wall again, it flew off its hinges, snapping in half. A tiny woman in heels that barely got her to the upside of five feet, stepped in. Her floral housecoat was seamless, but her skin looked like a patchwork quilt. A pair of coke bottle glasses rested on her nose.

It was Judy Nein and she came ready to dance the demolition tango. The zombie woman got to Howell in short time. With one hand, she batted him further than the ghost cat in the back had ever dreamed of swatting that mouse. Nein got between the girl and those that meant her harm, which was a rather large task for such a small dead woman.

Nein quickly got her reward for saving the girl. It was engraved in her chest using hot lead, and it was sent special delivery by the Untouchable who had been next to Howell. A pale hand shot out and crushed the hand holding the gun. I could hear the snap, pop, and crackle of bones being pulverized from where I was. Many people cringe at the sound, but truth be told I find it comforting, so long as it's not coming from my skeleton.

A gun wasn't going to do anything but get me shot, so I holstered mine and took out an orb in each hand to make my entrance.

"Everyone stop and put down your weapons," I said, strolling into the nest of gun toting vipers as if I was the one who was untouchable.

"Who the hell are you?" Howell demanded.

"Federal soul collector," I said.

Howell smiled. "Come to take this bitch away? Good."

"Not exactly," I said. Howell's smile turned upside down. "Nein and I are going to have a long discussion, but right now the lot of you are under arrest."

"You are out of your jurisdiction with us, collector man. We ain't dead," Howell snarled like a spoiled child.

"Not yet." It was my turn to smile. "Kidnapping is a federal crime."

"We didn't kidnap nobody," said Howell, the picture of perfect innocence. Luckily, I could see through it even without the negatives.

"I've been here for two hours," I said.

"You got a warrant?" said Howell.

"Collectors don't need one. Living Protection Act," I said.

"You have to get out of here first and I don't think that's going to happen," said Howell, pointing an automatic weapon between my eyes. His cronies followed suit.

"Nein, get the girl out of here. We'll finish our business later," I said.

"Dead bitch ain't going..." Nein grabbed the girl and sprinted out of the bar before Howell finished his sentence. "...nowhere."

Howell blinked as if the fluttering of his eyelids was the rewind button on a remote control.

Much screaming and cursing ensued, but none of it very creative. "Collector, you going to pay for that."

"Sorry, left my wallet in my other pants. I'll get it when I go back to see your mother later." I got to enjoy him curse some more for that one. "This is your last chance to lay down your arms and surrender." There was laughter until I let some of my power flow into my hands and the orbs. It was an impressive light show. I know one soul collector who moonlights doing fx for movies and rock concerts. "Anybody screws with me and I'll be taking your souls into custody instead of your bodies."

"That's illegal," said Howell.

"No, it's not," I lied, upping the mystic wattage. I lit up the room, each of my hands holding ball lightning. Eight Untouchables turned tail and ran. Ten more put down their guns. That left four plus Howell.

"You only got two orbs. That ain't enough for all of us," said Howell.

"Each holds a dozen souls. I've got plenty," I said. In actuality, usually three is the upper limit, but it seemed foolhardy to share that information at that moment. And I had a trick up my sleeve. Actually, I had a .22 in one and a knife in the other. For a time I kept a grenade in my coat pocket until the pin got stuck in my keys one day and I accidentally pulled it loose. Fortunately, the car was a rental.

This trick was actually inside me and made me glad I had forgone the vest.

I kicked my light show into overdrive. Tendrils of blue crackling light jumped out from the orbs in my hands into the chests of anyone holding a gun, like five leashes forged from electricity. There was fear bulging behind the eyes of the gang bangers as they stopped trying to stare me down and started trying to figure out how to outrun lightning.

I muttered some nonsense that I thought sounded ancient and mystic and upped the power behind the tendrils so they tripled in width.

For the finale, I dimmed the tendrils and shouted, "Idyo!" It was a word that always made me cringe when a certain Creole lady yells it at me.

It meant idiot.

"I've already claimed your souls. The only thing stopping the orbs from exhuming them from your body is my will." That was all bluff. The body will fight to keep its soul. "Shoot me and I'll die, but it'll be worse for the lot of you. Put down your guns, get on the ground and put your hands behind your heads. Now."

Howell's quartet of compatriots complied. As each gun hit the ground, that tendril came off of them and moved to Howell's chest like five day-glow snakes.

"I ain't going to jail," said Howell. All other sounds in the room seemed dwarfed by the tiny click the hammer of his gun made as he pulled it back to the killing position.

I'd never pull my gun in time, but I really was only a heartbeat away from exhuming his soul. I didn't care what kind of scum Howell was, taking a living soul was not without consequences and I'm not just talking the legal kind. The screams and pain wouldn't leave me easily. At least they wouldn't be lonely.

"Your funeral," I said, meaning it. I just thought of what he had been about to do to the girl and the rest was easy.

My ability to sense the dead helped me notice something Howell didn't. Judy Nein had returned and had snuck up behind him. Her pale hand clamped over the gun, her pinky blocking the hammer from falling. Before Howell knew what was happening his gun was gone and he was suspended a foot off the ground with Nein's hand clasped around his throat. Especially impressive considering her height.

The dead woman seemed more annoyed than angry. Her patchwork face looked up one end of Howell and down the other.

"You're the punk who killed me? I'm disappointed," said Nein.

Howell glowered at the dead woman. "I'll kill you again and we'll see how disappointed you are then bitch..."

Nein cut his air supply by squeezing his windpipe. Howell kicked and clawed at her single hand with both of his for all the good it did. If Nein wanted him dead, he couldn't stop her. I might be able to but wasn't sure I wanted to. Nein would be doing the world a service by getting rid of this punk. Plus, I'd have the proof I needed to take Nein down.

Problem was, I was starting to like the woman and I don't easily like many people, especially dead ones. Worse from my point of view, I owed her for helping me out and I hated being in anyone's debt.

I stepped closer, but still out of her powerful reach. "So, Nein, how's this going to go down?"

Nein looked at me and smiled. Her teeth were the only parts of her that were perfect. Dentures.

"Please, call me Judy. Or Gramy. Everyone calls me Gramy. You the Collector that's been looking for me?"

I nodded.

"You come to take me?" she asked. The grandmotherly way she stared at me over the rims of her spectacles made some deep part of me want to feel guilty. I smiled. Doing what I do, I often worry that parts of what makes me human will wither and shrivel up then die. Nice to know it hadn't happened yet.

"Hasn't been decided. Way I see it, right now it could go either way. I'm just investigating an anonymous complaint," I said. I had turned off the light show, but my orbs were humming, although only Judy and I could hear them. One of the punks on the floor tried to crawl away backwards. He was one of the pair that had dragged the girl in. I kicked him twice in the kidneys to express my displeasure at his leaving early and uninvited. He got the message and stayed still.

"Who would have complained about me? I'm just doing my part," Nein said.

"I made the call, you dead piece of..." said Howell, before Nein cut him off again.

"Manners," said Nein. "There's a lady present."

"So, you going to even the score?" I asked.

"Kill him? Heavens no. What kind of example would that be for my grandkids? But I just can't allow him to run around here. He'll hurt too many people. Do you think it would help if I testified against him? I did see him pull the trigger."

"No, ma'am, I don't think it will. It's hard to get a conviction on the words of the dead alone without any other evidence," I said. Nearly tend to freak out juries and also often lie to serve their own ends more often than not. After all what difference does swearing to God to tell the truth make if, for all intents and purposes, it seems like God's already decided he doesn't want you?

"What if we had a jury with some Nearly on it?" she asked.

"Almost never happens." At least outside of California.

Nein sighed. "I'm going to have to at least break some bones to keep him from going after other people if he's not going to go to jail."

That was all I needed. Nein hadn't crossed a line that I would have if I were in her place.

"He will for assaulting a federal collector in the course of his duty. That's a minimum of ten years in a federal prison without parole. He also was part of a kidnapping conspiracy, which I witnessed, so the girl won't even have to testify. And his assault was more of an attempted murder. That will add some serious time and make two strikes. I'm guessing his legal record is less than spotless. If he's got at least one other conviction in his past, that would make three strikes which means he'll go away for life," I said.

Nein smiled and nodded, then brought Howell's face so it was level with her own. With her free hand, she slapped his face then made a finger gun and pointed it between his eyes.

"Who's the bitch, now?" Nein giggled and dropped Howell on his ass. She covered her mouth and looked at me as if ashamed. "I normally don't use such language. I hope you'll forgive me and not mention that to my little ones. I wouldn't want them to know that their Gramy cussed."

I cuffed Howell and started securing the rest of them, using duct tape.

"They won't hear it from me, ma'am," I said. I called the locals for a pick up. It didn't take long for them to take the Untouchables away.

"Such a nice boy for a collector. That pays well, does it?" Nein asked.

"I do okay," I admitted. It pays very well and I don't spend much. I charge most things to my government expense account. Financially I'm ahead of the game. Not that it was anyone's business, especially one of the dead.

"It's a secure business with a good future?" she asked.

"There's no sign of business slowing down," I admitted, although the sign might end up being fire in the sky or a horde of flesh eating locust.

"Are you single?" Nein asked, her dentures shining.

"Yes," I answered hesitantly. Nein was sounding like my mother.

"Seeing anyone?"

"I'm between girlfriends at the moment," I answered. I didn't get the impression that the butcher's daughter was interested in me long term. "But you're a little old for me. Not to mention a little too dead."

Nein laughed. "You have to come for dinner and meet my granddaughter. She's a lovely girl, with a great personality."

"That usually translates as ugly as sin," I said.

"Hardly. She's very pretty and graduated medical school in the top ten percent of her class. She just doesn't take the time for a social life."

"So she's hot?" I said, perhaps a little too lecherously.

"Maybe fixing you two up isn't such a good idea," Nein said.

"Nah, eating a dinner you cooked wouldn't be such a good idea," I said, as visions of a decaying zombie preparing food ran through my mind. Trust me, rotting flesh doesn't add anything to a meal. "Dating me would make her happy."

"Making her unhappy would make me break your legs," said Nein, showing me her white smile.

"I can respect that." And I did. This case was closed and it's not like I had anywhere I had to be. "Call for take out and I'll think about it."

SPAWN OF LIGHTNING

From the World of Agents of the Abyss

Amonster made from bits of dead men should have a difficult time passing himself off as a man, but Adam Frankenstein had long ago learned to copy the mannerisms of those around him so well that even his appearance didn't stop him from mixing with humanity. It should have been far more difficult for a creature such as himself to gain access to a security conscious Nazi concentration camp. Adam Frankenstein not only got into Maly Trascianiec but got a guided tour of the facilities. This was aided by his history. The patchwork man had lived relatively uneventfully among the German people since the end of WWI after serving Germany as a decorated fighter pilot. The unusual condition of his skin and his many scars were now passed off as war wounds. These days, Frankenstein's scars seemed far tamer than the ones the people of Germany were seeing firsthand.

Because of his triumphs as a pilot, Adam Frankenstein had been recruited to help train the new generation of German air wolves. Even from the early stages of the Nazi's rise to power, the patchwork man had been repulsed by them. Understandable since they had risen to power on a platform of blaming minorities of those different than themselves. Few were more different than the creature who now lived as a man. His earliest memories were of being chased by villagers with torches and pitchforks that wanted him dead because he was not like them. He spent years barely escaping death at the hands of others and the Nazi's rounding up of the Jews and Roma brought flashbacks of his past, and he was torn between standing up to help them and finding a cave to curl up in.

Knowing he could not stop the roundups alone and very unwilling to go back to an existence of running and hiding, he took the military commission pressed upon him, but worked with the German resistance to fight back. Frankenstein's latest assignment brought him to a pilot school outside Minsk, Belarus to train German pilots to fight the Russians. The airfield was less than an hour's drive from Maly Trascianiec and the officers there were only too happy to oblige a holder of the iron cross with a tour of their camp.

Frankenstein had no desire to see the horrors within. There were rumors and very loud whispering about what was happening in the many camps. Medical experiments that boggled the mind; torture, rape, and even worse atrocities. Those in the camps wearing their brightly colored single or paired triangles were being readied to being slaughtered en mass. Adam Frankenstein was only one man—he knew he could never single handedly free an entire camp. Even if he did get them out, where would he put hundreds or thousands of people? He didn't have the resources to transport, house, or feed them. However, he knew those who might. Earlier in the struggle, he had saved some individual families before they got to the camps and gotten them away from German controlled lands. Besides, it was too late for those brought to this camp. They had all been slaughtered earlier in the week. A new batch of prisoners was due in a few days. Once they arrived at the camp, it would be too late, but before… there was still hope.

What had made him force himself to view firsthand the latest horrors that men had wrought was the tale of a drunken scientist who swore they were piecing pieces of Jewish corpses together in an attempt to infuse them with life. It sounded all too much like the process that had long ago birthed him in his reluctant entrance into the world. Despite his recent acceptance among men, he was never truly one of them. Frankenstein sought to spare this new creation the same hard fate of his terrible beginnings. If he happened to find a friend or even a brother in the process, so much the better.

The tour was designed to take them only through the sterilized areas of the camp. Nothing too bloody, nothing too horrible, nothing that would churn the stomach of a seasoned veteran. From a distance he could see ash rising from the ovens and even had he not come here forewarned of the mass murders, he would still know. Frankenstein suppressed a shutter. The masses that once chased him would only have burned him. How much worse would it have been to have suffered these tortures first?

"So what do you think of our camp, Captain Frankenstein?" asked the lieutenant who had served as his tour guide.

"Very efficient," said Adam Frankenstein, keeping himself aloof as any good officer would to a lesser rank. He knew the reputation of the camp. No one had ever escaped Maly Trascianiec.

"Would you like to dine in the Officers' Mess?" asked the lieutenant.

"I'm actually far more interested in things I have heard. I am told that there is the most amazing medical work being done here. Things that will save soldiers lives. Or perhaps…." He let the word hang in the air. "Create them."

The soldier grinned knowingly. "Oh, you mean the jigsaw soldier."

"Stop speaking!" shouted a major who had been approaching, hoping to greet the holder of the iron cross personally. "That is classified, even to a war hero such as Captain Frankenstein." The major looked at the pilot, an apologetic look on his face. "I'm sure you understand that some things are too important to the fatherland to come out too early. I will have to insist that you stay away from building 22."

Adam Frankenstein bowed his head to the superior officer, to hide a smile at being so easily given the location of what he was looking for. "Entirely understandable. I hope you will forgive my curiosity as such a thing would certainly assure the fatherland victory against all enemies."

The major laughed and slapped the reanimated captain on his back. "Yes, I understand, but be patient. All of Germany and the world will see the fruits of our labors soon enough."

"Excellent. I am famished. How about we visit your Officers' Mess," said Adam Frankenstein.

When the meal was over Adam Frankenstein was shown out of the camp and drove a few miles away, hiding his Kübelwagen on the side of the road. Under cover of darkness, he made his way back to the camp. He had noticed a gap in the sentry's patrols that would not do anyone trying to get out of the camp any good but was enough for someone foolish enough to break in to use. He scaled the twenty-foot fence in a matter of seconds and was over and hidden behind an outbuilding before the sentry passed him again. He made his way as slowly and stealthily as he could, not an easy task for someone who stood well over six and a half feet tall. It was difficult to do without being seen and thus far he had been lucky, but he knew that luck was a fickle mistress, just as likely to offer her favors to his enemy as to him. One row over from his destination he felt the barrel of a rifle pressed against the back of his head and knew that Lady Luck had moved on to a new lover. The whore he thought, just like his former bride.

"You stand and keep your hands behind your head," said the soldier.

Adam Frankenstein stood slowly and the soldier watched as the creature rose to his full height, gripping his rifle tighter with every inch. "I am sorry."

The soldier mistook the apology as the start of an excuse as to why he was here and the beginning of a plea for mercy. It gave him a false sense of superiority, assuming the gun made him top dog, so he was quite shocked a moment later when the huge man's hand shot out to grab him around the neck and snap his spine like a twig.

The body of the dead German soldier would raise alarms. Adam Frankenstein stripped the soldier of his uniform and dragged the body to where a pile of rotting corpses lay outside the crematorium. The area had not been on the tour route. He threw it in the center of the pile then realized it stood out. It wasn't wasted away and malnourished, so it looked more like a man while the other corpses seemed to be bags of skin with some bones inside. The reanimated man threw a few more corpses on top to better hide it.

After disposing of the soldier's uniform, he made his way back without being noticed until he stood outside of building 22. A pair of armed soldiers stood sentry duty. Adam Frankenstein had learned much about human nature in his hundred plus years of life. He especially knew soldiers. As a captain, he outranked both of the sentry's and marched up to them like he belonged. They both moved to stop him but did so differentially.

"I'm sorry sir, it's by invitation only in there and everyone on the list is already inside."

"I understand." Adam Frankenstein pulled a sheet of paper out of his pocket. "I have a message from Himmler for Colonel Gustave." Invoking the head of the SS, as was assuming the colonel was inside this building, was a risk, but something this big would demand the involvement of the camp's commandant. "If you could deliver it to him, I'm sure it would be appreciated."

After he handed the paper to the soldier who had spoken, the man nodded and turned to go inside. In that instant Adam Frankenstein's hands wrapped around both men's skulls and squeezed. During the First World War, he had heard soldiers brag how they had crushed skulls and they made a sound like a melon popping. Adam Frankenstein knew them instantly to be liars because a shattered skull makes a unique sound that's as close to a melon popping as a bullet is to heavy artillery fire. At this point he assumed he would be discovered as soon as he walked through the door, so he didn't worry about body disposal.

Adam Frankenstein stepped inside and what greeted him stopped him in his tracks. Despite the many embellishments on the story of his creation over the years, the truth of the matter was he was brought to life in the equivalent of a college dorm room, with a wire that was attached to a lightning rod on the roof of the building. It was the one he asked to be created for him that was birthed in a castle.

The Nazis had their creature laid out on a concrete slab and dressed in a private's uniform, but the shirt was unbuttoned. Adam Frankenstein could see where the various parts had been sewn together. The stitching was much more delicate and neater than his own. The Nazi scientists weren't bothering with anything as risky as a thunderbolt. They had a very large generator, easily the largest he had ever seen with a turbine of some sort, its wires hooked up to their creature.

The assembled officers and scientists were so intense in their quest to create life in the ultimate soldier that none of them even noticed the prototype enter and move to stand in the shadows. Adam Frankenstein was faced with a dilemma —stop the Nazis from making another patchwork man or to allow another creature such as himself to be brought to life, to know the same pain and loneliness of forever being an outsider. In the end, he could no more stop the spark of life from entering this creature than he could end his own life. And even if he had tried, he would have been too late as the generators sent their man-made lightning to course through the patchwork of corpses they had assembled.

Adam Frankenstein had been present at the birth of one other like himself, his reluctant and runaway bride. This was different. For one, he was much older and not quite trying to make himself fall in love with this creature. And this one had not been built at his request.

The Nazi's creature was strapped down to the table with thick pieces of leather that would have easily held any man, no matter how strong. The scientists just did not realize how strong a thing made of corpses and born of lightning would be. They may as well have tied their jigsaw soldier's wrists, ankles and chest with twine for all of the good leather shackles did.

The creature broke one arm free, then the other. Both legs burst their bonds simultaneously. One scientist mistakenly moved forward with a full syringe in hopes of quieting their super soldier, but it was too little and too slow. Drugs did not work the same on patchwork men, so even if the scientist had managed to jab the needle in, it would have done him no good. He was flung across the room to smash into the wall. A second scientist, faster than the first, but still far slower than their monster, picked up the syringe and jabbed it in the back of the creature's neck. It was a mistake. That scientist had not yet been seen by the creature and could have probably escaped. Instead, the pain caused by the jab of the tiny piece of metal enraged the spawn of lightning. That scientist's neck was snapped with a backhanded slap.

The soldiers in the room lifted their rifles and pointed it at the creature, but the colonel shouted, "Nein! He is not to be harmed."

There was a mistake. Enough bullets might have destroyed him and saved them.

A half a dozen soldiers waded in trying to use their gun butts to beat him into submission. It was clear he felt the blows, but the battering seemed to anger more than hurt him, merely throwing him off balance.

Adam Frankenstein remembered the pain of his birth. The searing and burning of the untold volts of electricity that coursed through him stayed with him long after the lightning had stopped, torturing the very flesh it was animating. Because the brain was previously used, Frankenstein had inherited some basic motor control and language capacity but was without memory. He imagined it must be the same for the new patchwork man. The creature was not striking out in hate or violence. He was in searing agony, his main desire to be left alone.

The half dozen soldiers were tossed about the room like so many rag dolls. Adam Frankenstein was impressed. This new creature appeared to be even stronger than he was at his creation. Of course, the corpses that made up his jigsaw of parts were fresher than those Victor Frankenstein had dug up, so the serum may have worked quicker on fresher tissue after the man-made thunderbolt strike. The muscles actually grew before his eyes, increasing in both mass and size.

The original patchwork man still stood in the shadows, careful not to even breathe, not wanting to alert anyone in the room to his presence. Luckily, the soldiers and scientists were far more concerned with their own creation. Colonel Gustave decided to try and reason with the creature.

The commandant stepped forward, his arms outstretched to his side in a non-threatening posture.

"Please. We mean you no harm. We are very pleased that you have joined us, Private Blitzkrieg."

No one else in the room made a move, more than content to let the colonel have his try, not to mention be the focus for the next attack. The creature did stop, looking up at Colonel Gustave.

"What did you call me?" The creature's vocal cords had not spoken for some time and it was obvious that just speaking was an effort. The jigsaw soldier's voice was slow and gravely with a broken Yiddish accent. The memories of motor control were due to their choice of brain, taken from a very learned rabbi. It seemed an odd choice by men who were attempting to exterminate the Jewish race, but it was based on the assumption that a brighter man would help their Private Blitzkrieg serve them better. He was envisioned as the first leader of their jigsaw corpse troops. "Why do you call me that?"

"Because it is your name. I am your creator," lied the Colonel, but he knew full well that the scientists who had done the actual work were in no shape to dispute his claim.

"Why have you created me?" asked Blitzkrieg.

"Because you will save us from our enemies. Come let us retire to someplace more hospitable. We will go to the Officer's Mess. And although you are just a private, I think we will make an exception this time," said the Colonel with a chuckle, extending an arm towards the exit. Adam Frankenstein had already backed out the way he came and thrown the bodies of the slain sentries on a neighboring rooftop so they would not be found by the exiting men.

The colonel led the creature born of Nazi generated lightning across the camp, chatting with him about simple things, speaking of the greater glory of the fatherland. Blitzkrieg half listened, looking around him, not only at the men who followed but also at the camp itself. He had literally just been born and everything was new to him. Colonel Gustave tried to lead him down certain rows. The sewn together bits of corpses of the jigsaw soldier had made him slightly taller than the average man, but the reanimating process had increased his size to almost seven feet tall. They had planned well with his uniform for it was strained by the muscle beneath only slightly. His high vantage showed him the one building that stood higher than the others in the camp.

"What is that?" he said, pointing to the gas chambers.

"It is nothing. Come with us. We will feed you well, then we shall all drink and make merry," said Colonel Gustave.

Blitzkrieg was having none of it. Something about that building disturbed him, but what exactly escaped him. Without conscious thought, he turned and walked towards the gas house. A soldier made the mistake of getting in his way and was swatted aside for his trouble. The colonel looked nervous but waved at the other soldiers to stand down as they followed slowly in his wake.

Adam Frankenstein followed as close behind as he could manage without risking discovery.

When Blitzkrieg arrived, he stopped short and stared at the building.

Reaching to use the door, he found it locked, so he simply pushed until the door tore off its hinges. After stepping inside, he was greeted by mounds of sorted clothes and a large pile of shoes. The jigsaw man moved further in, opening the next door and setting foot inside the chamber of death. The colonel and his men went as far as the outer door and looked inside after their creation. When Blitzkrieg turned to face them, tears fell from his eyes. Memories were assaulting him with the force of bullets.

"I know this place. People died here. People were killed, their breaths choking them until they breathed no more." Blitzkrieg's posture changed. Where before he was hurt and confused, now he was filled with anger. His hands balled into fists and he turned to Colonel Gustave. "You must have done this."

"They were enemies of the fatherland. It was necessary," said Gustave. "For the greater good."

"There is nothing good in this. It must be avenged."

There were no more words; the creature's rage spoke volumes as he charged for the colonel who was smart enough to slam the heavy doors. The creature smashed into them, pounding them with his fists until even the heavy metal looked like it might buckle.

Colonel Gustave, his face blanched white with fear, knew it would not be long before his Private Blitzkrieg waged a war upon his own creators, so he gave the only order he could.

"Release the gas!"

"But sir, you said he was not to be harmed," said one soldier.

The colonel hit the private in the back of the head. "The gas will just kill him, but leave his body intact. There is more serum left. We can take him far from here into the Blagovshchina Forest and revive him again. We did not realize that the brain we gave him would have remnant memories that would be triggered by these sights." The gas poured in. Even the monster needed to breathe and he began to choke, but it did not stop him from trying to bust down the door. "We will do it again and we will do it better. We will learn from our mistake."

The pounding made Gustave more nervous than he wanted to show in front of subordinates.

"We will adjourn and meet again tomorrow morning to discuss how to better handle things the second time. You two will tend to Herr Private." Colonel Gustave singled out two privates for this possibly dangerous duty.

"Colonel, if he should escape from the chamber, can we shoot him?" asked one of the privates.

The colonel knew that the creature was valuable and should not be harmed, but the pounding at the door made him realize that if he escaped, the creature would be coming for him.

Gustave gave a curt nod. "Do what is necessary."

Adam Frankenstein had been a soldier, a wanderer, a farmer, a criminal, and even a killer, but still, he could not take life lightly. The men, he hesitated to call them soldiers, who worked in this camp turned the blind eye to the atrocities committed here, cloaking themselves in the protection that they were only following orders. It made them just as guilty as those who did the actual killing. It mattered not if they justified it by saying the majority were Jews and Russian prisoners. German, Jew, Roma, or patchwork creature, all deserved life and those that took it had no moral protection against losing their own. Frankenstein knew he was in their number, but at least he fought for life. He knew that would hardly matter when his time came. It didn't stop him from hoping.

Despite his great capacity for violence, Blitzkrieg was virtually a newborn and thus by Frankenstein's reasoning not yet fully responsible for his actions. So it was hardly a difficult choice when he stepped out of the shadows behind the two soldiers who were looking inside the gas chamber with a mix of apprehension and glee then smashed their skulls together.

Quickly Adam Frankenstein maneuvered the door open, but the gas had taken its toll. Even though Blitzkrieg was still banging on the doors he was doing it from his knees. The century plus old patchwork man took a deep breath and stepped inside to pull out his brother creature.

Adam Frankenstein remembered his own unusual birth and knew how strongly he reacted to small acts of kindness. It was plain in the eyes of his brother creature that he felt the same way.

"You saved me," said Blitzkrieg. "Why?"

"Because I am like you." Blitzkrieg looked at Frankenstein's German uniform. He rolled up his sleeves to show Blitzkrieg his own scars and mismatched skin and limbs. "I only wear these clothes to give me an advantage should we be discovered. I also use them to fight these monsters from within. They think they have created you, their monster soldier, but they are the true monsters. We will get you out of here."

Blitzkrieg had been gulping air greedily, pushing the effects of the gas from his system. Slowly he rose to his feet.

"This place shall not stand. It has caused too much death for my people."

Adam Frankenstein's brows rose up. "You can remember a time before the thunderbolt?"

Blitzkrieg shrugged. "Not quite remember. Not as if I was there. I see things as if I was watching from a distance. The horrors they did. Laughing, enjoying the savagery. We must free the prisoners."

Frankenstein frowned. "There are no more living prisoners inside the camp. Except you."

"I have to make sure they can't do this again," said Blitzkrieg.

"There is more to this than just those here. There are hundreds and thousands of them with weapons that can destroy either of us. The fight must be done in stealth," urged Adam Frankenstein.

"Perhaps, but first I will find and make the colonel pay," said Blitzkrieg.

"Its more important that we get you out of here," said Adam Frankenstein laying his hand on Blitzkrieg's shoulder, forgetting what it was like to be touched so soon after riding the lightning.

Blitzkrieg lashed out with his arm, smashing Frankenstein first into a wooden wall and then through it. Beams collapsed on top of the older patchwork man. Blitzkrieg made his way out into the camp. He had not gone far before more soldiers attacked him. They fired at him, trying to contain their bullets to his extremities. The lightning and the chemicals that brought the bits of corpses to life were still doing their work. The flesh mended itself back together, ejecting the spent bullets as it did so. Those that were daring or foolish enough to try for hand-to-hand combat were crushed, battered, or torn apart.

Blitzkrieg lifted up a young soldier who most likely lied about his age to get into the army. Holding him by the throat so that they were eye to eye, he demanded, "Where is the colonel?"

Being a gung-ho soldier while surrounded by fellow soldiers and carrying a loaded gun is hardly the most difficult thing in the world. Maintaining that bravado, that willingness to accept even a painful death for one's cause can be overwhelming for some when they find themselves facing their own death in the eyes, even if the orbs were mismatched and different colors. It is especially hard when death was squeezing one's windpipe closed.

The soldier had difficulty speaking with his semi-crushed larynx so he merely pointed with his left arm. Blitzkrieg turned in the direction he indicated and walked. He hadn't intentionally planned to use the young soldier as a human shield, but that is how it worked out. The other soldiers were hesitant to shoot one of their own, so followed at a distance.

Finally, Blitzkrieg arrived at the colonel's office and dropped the soldier who gave him directions, battered but alive. The two soldiers that were posted at the door only got one shot off each before their necks were snapped. Blitzkrieg didn't even bother to try to open the door, merely smashed it in. Colonel Gustave had climbed part way out his window but was half a second too slow. Even with mismatched legs that were slightly different lengths, Blitzkrieg still moved too fast. The colonel was caught by the ankle and dragged back inside.

"Let go of me, I order you," yelled Gustave, pointing his finger at the patchwork man. Blitzkrieg took the colonel's right hand in his left and crushed it until the bones became fragments. Gustave collapsed sobbing.

"Please, do not hurt me. I am your father. I gave you life."

"But what of all those lives you have took? What of their fathers? Or children? Did you think you would never answer for them?" said Blitzkrieg.

The colonel dismissed the murders of tens of thousands with a twitch of his face. "They were Jews, Russians, Gypsies, Jehovah Witnesses, homosexuals, and communists. They did not deserve life and from their ashes, a new German army will rise with you at its head." Colonel Gustave swelled up with pride as he spouted what was obviously beloved propaganda. "Not all the bodies were put in the crematorium. The strongest were put aside and hidden. Ready to be sawed apart and put back together, Herr Blitzkrieg. Together we will conquer the world for the Third Reich."

"There is no we. I will have nothing to do with such horror," said Blitzkrieg.

Colonel Gustave smiled. "Ah, but you will. That is the next part of the plan, one we should have had ready to go immediately. You will be indoctrinated to be the perfect Nazi soldier."

Before Blitzkrieg could respond, a potato masher grenade flew inside the office. Blitzkrieg could tell by the look of horror on Gustave's face that it was a deadly weapon of some sort. The jigsaw man threw the colonel atop it. Gustave's body blocked and absorbed much of the force of the explosion and the resulting shrapnel. Blitzkrieg bent over to examine the pieces of the colonel. He was quite thoroughly dead and dismembered. Part of him felt robbed of the killing, but the rest of him was satisfied that it was done.

Before the smoke cleared, a group of soldiers eased their way in the doorway still pointing their rifles ahead, each covering the one in front who held another grenade. The soldier armed the grenade and threw it. Again, the creature was too fast and plucked the explosive out of the air as if it were a falling handkerchief. Blitzkrieg stepped up to the first soldier and rammed it into his chest, tearing through bone and muscle. The jigsaw man lifted up the soldier and threw him out the door into a group of other soldiers who were waiting to come in. Before the explosion, Blitzkrieg managed to rip the throats out of the two men who hadn't had time yet to fire their rifles at him.

The blast wounded more soldiers, using the thrower's own bones as shrapnel. Watching one of their own turned into a bloody and deadly weapon was enough for the rest to retreat, dragging their wounded comrades behind them. Switching to a new tactic, a few ran to look for gasoline to burn the building down. The rest stayed, determined to keep the creature inside until they could incinerate it.

Rifle fire pummeled the wooden walls of the office slowly, turning the boards to kindling and Blitzkrieg realized he was trapped. There was a loud crash, barely heard above the incoming gunfire as Adam Frankenstein smashed through the wooden back wall of the office.

"Hurry! We have to get out of here," he said. "They are going to burn this place down."

Blitzkrieg nodded when his eyes caught sight of something on the colonel's desk. Instead of leaving through the gaping hole, Blitzkrieg walked to the desk.

"What are you doing?" questioned Adam Frankenstein.

"These papers here—I know they are important." Blitzkrieg was looking at Jewish holy books, scrolls of the Torah and kabala. "They should not stay here to burn. They should be saved."

Adam Frankenstein walked to the desk as Blitzkrieg gathered up the holy writings. He saw familiar notebooks and papers and recognized the handwriting as that of his creator Victor Frankenstein and Victor's maternal grandfather Johann Conrad Dippel. The original patchwork man rushed and picked those up and clutched them to his chest.

"Are those holy documents too?" asked Blitzkrieg.

Frankenstein tucked the papers in his jacket with great care. "For us they are. They contain the secrets of how we came to life." As the outside walls and roof began to smolder, the two patchwork men ran out the hole in the back wall, straight into a group of soldiers who had moved to cover the rear of the building. The battle was short and very one sided. When it was over the two men, who some would call monsters, escaped the camp by pulling down a guard tower and running over the rubble into the night.

They did not stop running until well past the first light of morning.

They found the Kubelwagen that Adam Frankenstein had hidden the night before and they rode together the rest of the way to a shack Frankenstein had set up in the Blagovshchina Forest. He had the foresight to have forged papers ready for Blitzkrieg that passed him off as another war veteran. It would help explain the scars.

"What am I to do now?" asked Blitzkrieg.

"We in the German resistance could use someone with your strength. It would help you to destroy that which you have come to hate."

"Is that what we do? Destroy what we hate?" asked Blitzkrieg.

"No, not always. Sometimes we destroy that which we love. There are even times when we don't have to destroy anything at all. But tonight won't be one of those nights," promised Adam Frankenstein.

Blitzkrieg was fed and given a change of clothes. They were too small even though they were tailor-made for the elder patchwork man. Next Adam Frankenstein took Blitzkrieg on a motorbike with a side-car through the forest until they came to a large clearing covered with camouflage netting.

"What is this?" asked Blitzkrieg as Adam Frankenstein cleared away the camouflage as the sun went down.

"A trophy from the last war. I defeated the French pilot known as the Phantom. Several times in fact, but the first time I managed to get his plane down intact. I decided not to give it to the military, but to keep it for my own. The newer planes are much faster, but they don't have the Nieuport's maneuverability. And I've made some additions of my own, including a newer engine and a second cockpit. Helpful when I need to smuggle someone out. The black paint helps hide me at night. It was a challenge to bring it to Belarus with me, I'll tell you." Adam Frankenstein got Blitzkrieg situated in the rear cockpit and then loaded him up with three bombs, each the size of a small child.

"What are these?"

Frankenstein smiled. "Remember the grenades from the camp?" Blitzkrieg nodded. "Each of these is a hundred times more powerful. We will use them to destroy the camp."

"We will drive this to the camp? Won't they see us coming long before we get there?" asked Blitzkrieg.

Frankenstein grinned widely as he climbed into the front cockpit, putting on his aviator cap and goggles. "No, my friend we will not drive. We will fly." He then hopped out and quickly spun the front propeller around until the engine coughed to life. Moments later they were careening down the dirt runway until they took off into the air.

"What should I do with these?" Blitzkrieg asked indicating the bombs.

Frankenstein laughed. "Be careful not to jostle or drop them. When we get over the camp you will let each one go as we go over a target and they will blow it to kingdom come."

It was much faster to fly than drive, even keeping to just above the treetops. Frankenstein kept his plane too low for anti-aircraft artillery to accurately get them unless he was foolish enough to fly directly over them. He wasn't that foolish. As a teacher of the flight school, he knew where the artillery was located so his pilots could avoid them during their training and so he could do the same on his dark night missions.

Their first target was the gas chambers. What Blitzkrieg could not do with his fists the night before, one bomb accomplished in an instant. Next was the crematorium where the Nazis were storing the stronger bodies they were saving to build their army of jigsaw soldiers. The third explosion took out the armory, which in turn caused a larger explosion, which damaged the road leading to and from the camp, making a rapid land pursuit of the aerial bombers difficult. As chaos rained beneath him, Frankenstein pulled up into the sky tipping his wings once in a salute, not to the butchers that called themselves soldiers, but to the dead he could not save. His respects paid, he took his fellow patchwork man up into the night sky. A lightning bolt flashed through the darkness and Frankenstein smiled at the good omen. Tomorrow he would tell Blitzkrieg of the train headed for the camp with new prisoners and his plans to make sure it never gets there.

NIGHT CRIES

A Story Of The Nightcriers

"**Y**ou're nuts," I said.

"That's why you love me," Jeanie said, a smile peaking out from her lips, cloaked in black by her favorite shade of lipstick. It was also her favorite shade of clothing, hats, shoes, boots, socks, and underwear-hair dye too. Jeanie's the type who is only wearing black until they come up with something darker.

"No, I love you because you're such an optimist," I said. Jeanie punched me in the arm.

"There's no need to get insulting, Kent Spenser. A girl can only take so much, even if that girl is me," she said.

"That's not what it says about you on the bathroom wall," I countered.

"Who'd write something like that about me?" Jeanie asked, flinging a perpetually hanging lock of hair off her eye and onto the top of her head. Unlike the rest of her do, it didn't stand straight up in defiance of gravity. Her drunken mother always complains it makes her look like a sheepdog. I think it makes her look hot. I think looking like a sheepdog would be a step up for her mother.

"Um, I might have done it," I said, a sly grin on my face as gravity again won the battle and the hair dropped back over her eye.

"Why would you trash my rep like that?"

"First, you couldn't care less about what anyone else thinks." Despite what Jeanie says, it wasn't her body or her ability to tie a cherry stem into a knot with her tongue that first attracted me. It was her the world better get out of my way attitude that did it. Although that cherry stem thing was a close second. "Besides, I wasn't trashing you. I was bragging."

"Well, in that case, I hope you made me a copy." Jeanie leaned in and kissed me, her tongue ring poking playfully around in my mouth.

"Keep this up and I'll have to expand on my commentary," I murmured as best I could with my tongue engaged in much more important activities than mere speaking.

A hand poked me in the back, more roughly than was necessary. "Mr.

Spenser, Ms. John, this is a high school hallway, not a make out hot spot."

Jeanie got that glint in her eye and turned her gaze on the man who had interrupted us. "Mr. Martin, I don't see why it can't be both."

"And Ms. John, therein lies your problem."

"And why don't we talk about your problem, Mr. Martin. Could your intensity in bothering us be because you haven't gotten to play kissy-face with anyone since bell bottoms were in?"

"Bell bottoms were in again a couple of months ago," I whispered. "And did you actually use the word kissy-face in a sentence?"

They both ignored me.

"My personal life is none of your concern, but for your information, I make out a lot," said Mr. Martin, protesting too much.

"It doesn't count if you had to blow her up," said Jeanie.

"I've had enough out of you, miss. How'd you like a trip to the principal's office?" asked Mr. Martin.

"Is it all inclusive? Do I get to fly first class and get some spending money?" asked Jeanie.

"March, Ms. John," said Mr. Martin, pointing down the hallway.

"Excellent. I'll be sure to tell Mrs. Washington that you are harassing me again," said Jeanie, taking a couple of goose steps.

"What are you talking about?" asked Mr. Martin.

"You are harassing us, while Dillon and Muffy swap spit a stone's throw from us."

Mr. Martin looked confused. When Jeanie started, I had decided to get comfortable and was leaning against some lockers. I nodded and pointed down the hall to where Jeanie's least favorite preppie scum —her term, not mine —were in passionate lip lockage. The pair was the ultimate high school couple cliché.

"So apparently the captain of the football team and the head cheerleader can treat this high school hallway as their personal make out palace, but not us?" asked Jeanie. "Is that fair? Is that just? Or is it just plain discrimination because you don't like the way we dress?"

"What's wrong with the way I dress?" I asked.

Jeanie turned and looked me up and down. "Not enough black. Too colorful."

"I'm wearing jeans and a navy t-shirt," I said.

"Exactly. Now, would you be quiet? Please just stand there and look pretty. I'm working here," said Jeanie with a wink.

I obliged, tossing my own hair back, and placed one hand on my hip and the other on my head, followed by a suggestive, and rather comical, wiggle. Jeanie had to stifle a giggle.

"Mr. Martin, you are aware that personal appearance is considered an extension of free speech, that is covered by the Bill of Rights? I know you teach math and not social studies, but the first amendment is pretty basic stuff. And as long as we conform to the school's dress code, you as a teacher are not permitted to treat us differently than other students. If you do, it is considered discrimination, in my case it is religious discrimination, again infringing on my first amendment rights," said Jeanie.

"I don't care about your little devil worshiping cult..."

"Now that is discriminatory and inflammatory. I am the High Priestess of the First Church of the Hidden Truth. Would you treat a rabbi like this? Or the pope or the Dalai Lama?"

"You're no pope."

"But like him, I am the head of a major religion," Jeanie said. A while back, she was getting hassled at her job for the way she dressed, so she started her own religion, with herself as the High Priestess. She put up a notice on her conspiracy web site and in less than a week she had five hundred members. Last time she mentioned it, she had almost seven thousand. "Like him and the Dalai Lama, I have my own robes of office." Jeanie had made it one of her duties to dress a certain way. When her boss finally fired her, she sued for religious discrimination. Acting as her own attorney she won four hundred thousand dollars. "Do we have a case of religious discrimination here, Mr. Martin? Because I can assure you, we do not worship devils or demons and I am insulted by the insinuation. I'd hate to have to file another lawsuit, but I have the forms on my hard drive. I'd just have to change the name."

Mr. Martin was gritting his teeth and his face was beet red. Veins were popping out all over his neck and forehead. "This has nothing to do with religion."

"Then why just stop us and not the preppie scum?"

"I didn't see them," he sputtered.

"A likely story," said Jeanie. Just then the morning bell rang, signaling the start of another school day. "A pity we'll have to stop this, as I'm sure you have a class to get to."

The teacher was none too happy at being dismissed. "As I'm sure you do."

"Nope. Independent study actually. I'm where I need to be," said Jeanie.

"What about you, Mr. Spenser?" asked Mr. Martin.

"English," I admitted reluctantly.

"You'd better get there before the late bell rings," said Mr. Martin.

"I guess I better go then," I said. I didn't have Jeanie's clout, so I wasn't about to go head to head with a teacher.

"I'll walk you," said Jeanie, grabbing my arm and leading me away. We left the math teacher fuming in our figurative dust.

"One day, you're going to push him too far," I said.

"Maybe."

"You know it wasn't religious discrimination."

"But it was still discrimination. He hasn't gotten over me showing him up," said Jeanie. The love of my life is a certified genius. She could have gone to college at twelve but wanted to stay in regular school. Jeanie refuses to graduate a day early. At eleven, she took the SAT's and missed a perfect score by one answer, which pissed her off. She protested the single question she got wrong and proved her answer was right, which meant she ended up with a perfect score. I took mine as a junior and did okay. As a freshman, Jeanie took Mr. Martin's AP Math, a college level course. She was constantly correcting him and was right every time. Finally one day he said no one could possibly compute the value of pi in her head to fifty digits. Jeanie proved him wrong, although she was glad he hadn't said sixty, because she realized from the 52nd place on, she had miscalculated.

"Go figure," I said.

"And what's with almost making me crack up back there? It would have totally screwed up what I was trying to do."

I repeated my wiggle. "Too sexy for you?"

"Too funny."

"What project are you spending your morning on?" I asked.

"Budget cuts are about to ax the art program. I'm going to try to get us a grant," said Jeanie. In her high school career, she had gotten our school grants to pay for a computer lab, high-speed internet access, to rebuild our stage and theater, and to save our music program. Jeanie has taken advantage of each—learning computer programming, starring in a school play, building sets for another and mastering how to play eight different instruments. In short, Mrs. Washington the principal thinks she walks on water, so the odds of her getting in trouble with the principal were fairly slim, even if she had refused to get a grant to help pay for a new football field and scoreboard on principle. It also explains her independent study freedom. She actually has enough credits completed online to get two masters once she can supply the college with a high school diploma.

"I figured it would be more research on conspiracy theories."

"A girl can't live on conspiracy alone. Besides, if it's out there in a book or on the net, I've seen it. Nothing new for me to learn there."

"Not unless you can capture a man in black and interrogate him."

"I'd rather find a mothman."

"You're not still on that kick."

"The mothmen are real."

I sighed. "A lot of people in this town certainly seem to think so."

"How can you not?"

"The last sightings were in 1967." Point Pleasant, West Virginia had a slew of sightings in the sixties. Ended with a bridge collapse that killed forty-six people or so some say. Others say it was just an accident. It doesn't take a genius to figure out which side of the fence Jeanie falls on.

"Not true. That was the last mass sighting. There have been regular sightings every few years; some have been of a mothwoman. As near as I can figure, the mothpeople have just gotten smarter, better at hiding. And they are not just around here. They've been seen in New Jersey."

"That's the Jersey Devil."

"But eyewitness accounts are amazingly similar. Glowing eyes, bat-like wings on humanoid figures that can fly. You up for heading out to the old TNT plant Friday night?"

"I know that's where most of the old sightings were, but we've been out there dozens of times and we've never seen anything," I said. "It gets old."

"Being alone in the dark with me is getting old? I must be slipping up somehow," said Jeanie.

"You say that all the time, but all we ever do is watch," I said as we reached the door of my English class.

Jeanie tilted her face down and gave me her big, doe-eyed stare up through her hair as she rocked her shoulders back and forth. "Maybe this time will be different."

"You always say that too."

"Maybe this time I mean it. Are you willing to take that chance? Plus I just got two pairs of infrared goggles I'm dying to try out."

I sighed and the late bell rang. I leaned far forward for a quick goodbye kiss. Jeanie is five eight, but I'm six four, so we have a bit of a height differential. "Gotta go."

"You coming?" she asked.

"Just breathing heavy," I said, which got me another punch in the arm.

In her little girl voice, she pleaded, "Please?"

"Fine," I said, running into class just in time to be marked late.

When Friday night came, we sat in the dark. Jeanie stared out, searching the night with her infrared goggles. I was searching a little closer to home.

"Stop staring at my chest," said Jeanie.

"I can't. These goggles are picking up on your heat signature, so I can see through your shirt. The view is incredible," I said.

Jeanie gave me a look like she didn't believe me, but took a look down at her cleavage. "You're right," she said, then slapped me across the face.

"What was that for?" I asked.

"For being a peeping Kent," she said.

"Hey, I'm not the one who brought the goggles. Although since I can see through your shirt, it really doesn't make sense to keep it on, now does it?"

Jeanie chuckled. "Original, but not happening, Spenser."

"Can't blame a guy for trying," I said.

Jeanie leaned over and kissed me. "No, I guess I can't. But I will blame you if we miss out on our chance to see a mothman."

I sighed, a little louder than was probably wise.

"What?" she asked, annoyed.

Foolishly, I answered. "I just don't understand how someone so smart can be taken in by all this conspiracy crap."

"Crap?" Jeanie's tone was unhappy.

"Mothmen, Area 51, Bigfoot, Men in Black, Elvis wandering the highways and byways."

"They are all real."

"Then how come we don't have pictures or video? Except for that Bigfoot film," I said.

"Which was a hoax. It was just some guy in a modified gorilla suit, but the government let it get out because it was a fake, so it would make the entire idea of a sasquatch seem silly."

"Which of course, it isn't," I said sarcastically.

"No, it isn't. Area 51 exists. It is a matter of record. The men in black use misdirection to keep the government's secrets. They did the same thing with the fake alien autopsy film. Any real proof gets stolen or destroyed before it can be shown to the public."

"Seems like an awful lot of work to keep the public in the dark. I just don't buy it," I said.

"That's what they are counting on. What would it take to convince you?" Jeanie asked.

"Show me a mothman and I'll think about it," I said. I was tired of the same old argument and I opened my arms. "Friends?"

Jeanie moved in and we hugged. "Always."

"You know, now would be a great time for make up sex," I said, ever optimistic.

Jeanie gently pushed me away. "We haven't had first time sex yet."

"I'm willing to combine the two," I said.

"I'm not," she said.

"Okay, I'm willing to wait," I said.

"But how long are you willing to wait?" she asked.

I answered truthfully. "To forever and back. I'll be here as long as it takes."

"Good answer." Jeanie leaned in, her mouth slightly open.

"Thanks." I met her halfway.

We made out for a while, still wearing the goggles. When we came up for air, I opened my eyes and saw something in a nearby tree. It looked like a pair of red eyes. I pushed myself back, pulling Jeanie with me, screaming the whole while.

"What!?" asked Jeanie.

I pointed. "Mothman!"

Something in the tree stood and bat-like wings unfurled. Then there was a screech and my goggles went dead. By the time I got them off, all I could see was a shape flying up into the night.

I looked at Jeanie. Her goggles must have died too because she was holding them in her hand and staring, her mouth agape.

"Now do you believe me?" she said.

I wanted to say it was a bat or a sandhill crane, the explanation the government experts gave everyone back in the sixties, but I saw what I saw. It was no bat or bird. It looked like a cross between a woman and a giant bat.

"Maybe," I said, searching all around us frantically. There could be more of them. They supposedly ate dogs. Maybe they had moved onto people. "We should get out of here."

I could see Jeanie was torn between searching the area or trying to somehow follow what we saw, but despite having one of her greatest fantasies realized, she was scared too. "Okay," she agreed without arguing.

We made our way quickly back to Jeanie's convertible. Without a word we climbed in and sped off. We didn't speak until we were miles from the old TNT factory.

"What the hell was that?" I said.

"Mothman," said Jeanie, a smug smile on her pretty lips.

"Looked more like a mothwoman to me," I said.

"You got that good a look at it?"

"Yes. What the heck happened to your new goggles? Why'd they cut out like that?" I asked.

"It happened right after the mothwoman screeched. Many of the reported sightings had some sort of electric failure–lights, radio, TV."

"How could that happen?"

"Off the top of my head, I'd say an EMP," said Jeanie.

"A what?" I said.

"Electro Magnetic Pulse. It knocks out all active electronics in an area."

"Could a creature make one?" I asked.

"Unlikely. Usually, it takes a nuke or some very expensive equipment. Back in the 1920's, a physicist named Arthur Compton came up with the idea that electromagnetic protons could knock loose electrons away from atoms that had low atomic numbers. In the fifties, they figured out that gamma radiation from a nuke does that to nitrogen and oxygen atoms in the atmosphere. The loose electrons interact with the Earth's magnetic field. A fluctuating electric current is produced..."

"And that makes the magnetic pulse," I said.

"I'm impressed," Jeanie said, smiling.

"I'm no genius, but I did take physics."

"Sorry. The magnetic field that is the pulse induces an intense electric current in any conductive materials in its range," Jeanie said.

"So someone holding onto a piece of metal would be electrocuted?" I asked.

"Interesting question. I don't think the EMP lasts long enough. They'd probably just get a bad shock."

"Wouldn't a surge protector stop it?" I asked.

"Not really. Normally a surge protector is dealing with current coming in one direction. This would induce the electricity from within. A small pulse would temporarily jam electronics. A medium one would wipe a computer and a big one would fry everything. So if we're dealing with an EMP, it's obviously a small one. "

"So why couldn't a creature do it?"

"I doubt anything organic could manage it."

"What if it could burp up a large number of protons? Like an electric eel or something."

"Gross. I don't see how. An electric eel's head and tail are opposite poles and the electricity comes out of one or the other. They have five or six thousand electroplaques which are little organic batteries," Jeanie said.

"I'm constantly amazed that you know this stuff," I said awed.

"I can read and retain five pages a minute. I read at least two or three hours a day. You do the math. But the idea of having something organic that could emit protons..." She started to get that far away, deep thought look in her eye, which normally I find adorable, but she was driving. We started to swerve into the other lane.

"Keep your eyes on the road, please," I said.

Jeanie laughed. "Your idea is out there, but... I wouldn't rule it out entirely. It would explain an awful lot. There's much speculation that the government has EMP weapons, but they are supposed to use microwaves to push the protons around. I'm fairly confident organic life can't produce microwaves, but could there be another way?"

"Pull over," I said. Jeanie looked at me and we would have gone up on a curb if I hadn't grabbed the wheel. "Your mind's got a new idea. You're lost to me for at least a few hours, so it's much safer if I drive."

"You're probably right," she said, stopping the car. We switched seats. I drove and she did whatever she does when that part of her brain switches on. I dropped her off at her house and walked myself home. It was only about a mile, but the entire way I kept looking back over my shoulder, paranoid that someone or something was following me, but I saw nothing.

When I reached my abode, I put my key in the front door, part of me wondering if they changed the locks again. It had been almost two months since my foster family had tried it. I don't know what goes through their heads. Do they think if I can't get in, I'll just go away without telling my caseworker so they can keep getting the checks?

The door opened without incident. The house was dark except for a flickering light from the TV blaring in the living room. I shouted, "I'm home." I didn't get a response, but then I didn't really expect one. I went to the fridge and saw they had padlocked it again. I opened one of the kitchen drawers and pulled out the hammer. It took me only two swings to bust the lock.

The first time I did that, Mr. Darrow told me never to do it again. Then he threatened and shoved me, which was stupid. He is a fat slob who smoked, not to mention he was drunk at the time. I slugged him once in the gut, which ended that conversation. This made the third time this year that he locked up the grub, which was pointless since he never bothered to hide the hammer. My personal theory was he got so drunk he couldn't remember what he had done before. He could probably hide his own Easter eggs.

I rummaged through the shelves. The contents really weren't worth locking up. There was a gallon of milk that had gone chunky, some cheese that had gone moldy, about a case worth of beer and some beef jerky. I grabbed an unopened package of jerky and a couple of beers. I wasn't a big drinker since I had gotten sick drunk when I was fourteen, but after the night I had I felt like I needed something stronger than chunky milk.

I headed upstairs to the large closet that was my bedroom and plopped down on the twin mattress on the floor. I was chewing some jerky and washing it down when Denise walked in.

"Hey," she said.

"Hey yourself," I said. Denise sat down next to me.

"You're getting in late. You and gothette finally do it?" she asked.

I had been in this sad excuse of a household for a little over two and a half years. Poor Denise had been here all her life. She was the closest thing to a sister I had ever had, although she'd made it clear making that an incestuous relationship would be fine with her. She used to get dressed and showered with the door open. A few times she came into my room dressed only in a towel and each time the towel somehow fell off. I was flattered, but —except with Jeanie —I'm very shy. Denise was cute, like a hot girl from a heavy metal video, but she was damaged goods. Then again, so was I. Regardless, I never made a move on her. It didn't feel right to take advantage of her that way and it would have done her more harm than good.

Not that I haven't thought about it. I still sometimes fall asleep with the vision of her towelless and dripping wet from the shower. I usually wake up the next morning needing a shower of my own, of the freezing cold variety.

Denise was looking for love and had confused it with sex. She spent most of the time I'd been here sleeping around with any guy at school who'd have her. There were plenty of takers, but not a one of them willing to give back anything but pain and contempt. She tried to turn over a new leaf and thought she'd try a geek, thinking he'd be more sensitive. Guy was in the computer and chess clubs. Denise actually really liked this guy, name of Troy. He seemed to reciprocate. Brought her flowers, took her out to dinner and the movies, said he loved her.

Denise brought him home. Her mother was out working and her Dad was passed out in his room, so the meeting the parents thing didn't exactly work out, but Troy didn't seem to care. She took him up to her room, with every intention of making him a very happy boy.

The problem was, as soon as she shut the door, Troy changed. The sweet guy veneer disappeared to be replaced by the horny guy out for everything he could get. Instead of taking things slow and easy, he pushed too far, too quick. Denise told him to stop. He didn't. Spouted the usual drivel about how he had spent lots of money on her and he knew she had put out for guys who gave her nothing. Wanted a return on his investment with interest. Denise told him to get out. Troy ignored her and tried to rip her blouse. Denise screamed for her daddy, who lay uncaring in a drunken dreamland. My room was only next-door, so I heard her.

I threw open the door. Denise was crying on the bed, holding a pillow to cover her torn blouse with one hand and punching Troy with the other. There was some kicking going on, but she was too upset to be aiming strategically.

"Get off of her," I ordered.

"You live with the slut. I'm sure you get some every night. Tonight, she's mine, so go the hell away, Spenser. If you're that bothered, you can wait around for sloppy seconds," said Troy.

Denise was the only one in the house who had shown me any kindness, and I'm not just talking about her letting me see her naked. Even if she hadn't been nice, I wouldn't have let the dirt bag hurt her.

I grabbed him by both of his shoulders and yanked him off of her. He punched me twice—once in the stomach and another in the face. I returned the favor, then managed to get his arm behind his back. I forcibly led him to the stairs, planning to get him out of the house. When we got to the top step, he flexed his knee back and brought his foot up into my crotch. The pain made my world go white and I pushed him forward without thinking. Troy tumbled down the stairs. At the bottom, there was a crack and he screamed. Troy jumped up cradling his shoulder.

"You broke my arm," he yelled, following it up with some truly impressive profanity. "I'm going to sue your ass."

"For what? My CD collection? I've got no money, no family to go after," I said.

"Then I'll have you arrested," said Troy.

Denise had come out of her room and stood next to me. "Call the cops. I'll tell them how you tried to rape me."

"You're a whore. Why would they believe you?" Troy asked, confident he had outsmarted us.

"Because I witnessed you do it," I said. "Call them. The number's 911. Hell, I'll dial it for you." I noticed his face was bleeding. "And the fact that Denise has your skin and blood under her fingernails won't hurt our case once they get done with the DNA testing."

Troy looked at us, cursed and ran out the front door.

"You want me to call the cops?" I asked.

Denise shook her head. "I just want to forget this ever happened." We later found out Troy didn't go home until the next day, convinced the cops would be waiting for him. He told everyone he fell and broke his arm, never once mentioning Denise or me.

"Okay. You going to be okay?" I asked.

"I guess, thanks to you." Denise kissed me on the cheek and I could feel myself blushing. "Thank you."

"You're welcome," I said.

" Kent, would you mind coming in to my room with me? I don't want to be alone right now."

"Sure," I said.

We went inside and she picked up a t-shirt from her laundry pile. "I'm going to change. Do you mind?"

I was surprised at the shyness considering the towel incidents, but she had been though a traumatic experience. I turned and closed my eyes.

"I'm done."

I turned around and saw a piece of lingerie on her desk. Denise followed my eyes and picked it up, embarrassed. "I was planning to be with him. I even got a special outfit." Denise held it up to her chest. "Then he had to be a jerk and ruin everything." She threw the satin top hard against the wall where it collapsed slowly and fell to the floor. "Kent, why did he act like that?"

"Guys can be jerks," I said.

"You're not," she said.

"True, but I'm rather exceptional," I said with a smile.

"I wish I was. There must be something wrong with me." Denise started crying.

I reached over to her desk and ripped a piece of toilet paper she kept in her room. I had one in my room too. We lifted them from school. The

Darrows usually forgot to take care of the little things like tissues, toilet paper, soap, so we learned to adapt. I handed her the squares.

"Denise, you are trying too hard," I said.

"More like I'm behaving too easy," she said.

"There is that," I said.

Denise stared at me. "Aren't you supposed to tell me I'm not to make me feel better?"

"You have enough people lying to you. One more isn't going to make you feel better. Those guys don't see you as a person, just a toy."

"Damn," she said and the waterworks increased.

I put my hands on her shoulders and made her look me in the eyes. "Troy was a waste of your time, but that doesn't mean every guy will be. Don't give up on yourself. In a couple of years, you can move far away from here and start over where nobody knows you. You can reinvent yourself to be anybody you want," I said. I tried every time I got moved to a new home.

"Reinvent myself. I like the sound of that." Denise leaned forward and hugged me. I hugged her back. Neither one of us let go for a long time. We were both desperate for human touch. "Kent, would you stay in here with me until I fall asleep? Please? I'll be good."

"Okay," I said. I went over to her bed, which was actually on a bed frame and lay down close to the wall. Denise pulled a blanket off the foot of her bed and snuggled up next to me with her head in the crook of my shoulder. She wrapped both of us in the blanket. We woke up the next morning still holding each other and Denise hugged me and kissed me on the cheek. The peep shows stopped after that, but Denise seemed less damaged. And to tell the truth, so did I.

I even told Jeanie about it and she believed me when I told her nothing happened. She even asked Denise if she was okay and if she wanted Jeanie to beat the crap out of Troy. Denise declined, but Jeanie did get him kicked out of computer club. And joined chess club to figuratively kick his butt there.

Ever since, Denise has taken a real interest in my life, which explains her question about Jeanie and my love life.

"No, we didn't," I admitted reluctantly.

"The girl's a fool. You want me to talk to her for you?" asked Denise.

I thought about it, but after deciding that it wouldn't help, I went with my first instinct. "Naw, but thanks. You want jerky or a beer?" I asked holding up both.

"Broke the lock again, huh?"

I nodded. Denise plopped down next to me and took a beer and a piece of jerky.

"My Dad catches us and we're going catch hell," she said, but she downed a good size gulp just the same.

"I'll take the heat," I said.

"So why you drinking? Not your usual scene," Denise asked.

"I had a rough night," I said, debating on whether to tell her what happened.

Before I could decide, in walked Mr. Darrow, stinking and staggering. "Which one of you wrecked my lock? Judas Priest, who the hell said you could drink my beer?!"

Denise cringed. I opened my big mouth, curious as to what might come out.

"You did," I said, a plan forming.

"Me?" He looked at Denise for confirmation and his daughter nodded. "Why would I give you snots my beer?"

"You lost the key for the fridge and you needed our help to get in. You said you'd give us a soda for helping, but once we got in you realized you didn't have any. So you said you didn't want us to go away empty handed after we helped you, so you gave us the beer instead. We told you we were underage, but you said there was no way you were going to let the government tell you what you can and can't do," I said. When drunk, Mr. Darrow would go off on tirades about the government being too involved with everyone's day-to-day business. Also, when smashed, his memory was notoriously unreliable.

"Damn straight, they can't. I'd like to see them try," he said. "You kids enjoy them beers and thanks for your help."

Mr. Darrow staggered back out and down the stairs.

As soon as we heard him back in the living room, Denise let out the breath she had been holding and started giggling. "I can't believe that worked."

"Neither can I," I said. We finished the beer and jerky.

"I'm going to bed," Denise said, leaning over to kiss me on the check and give me a hug. I did the same. We still both needed that human contact. She walked to the door and stopped, then looked back. "You know if she ever dumps you..."

"I know."

Denise nodded and went to her room.

I didn't sleep well. The entire night I felt like I was being watched. I even dreamed I could see red eyes looking in my window.

I hated Saturday mornings. I loved that I could sleep in and didn't have to go to school, but I always wake up hungry. On school days, I get free breakfast and lunch. One of the few benefits of being a poor foster kid. On weekends, I had to forage for myself and I already knew there was nothing good in the fridge. I finished the two pieces of beef jerky that were left in the bag I had taken before I hopped in the shower. Denise was already up and gone to visit friends. Both of us spent as little time at the house as we could.

I decided to head over to Jeanie's place. I'd see what she had come up with and maybe grab some breakfast. Her mom usually hit the bars and got hit on in return, which meant she was rarely home Saturday and Sunday mornings.

I knocked on the door but got no answer. I knocked again and heard voices.

Opening the door a crack, I said, "Jeanie? You home?"

A man's voice answered. "Mr. Spenser, please come in." Then I heard the voice yelp.

"Kent, run. It's the men in black," screamed Jeanie.

I hesitated, caught between belief and disbelief and saving my skin or that of the girl I loved. That second was too long. A man in a black suit and tie came up behind me, blocking me from running away. He was silent but motioned me into Jeanie's living room, so in I went.

"Mr. Spenser, it's fortunate that you came to us. We were going to have to collect you," said another similarly attired man.

"Collect?" I asked.

"They're going to make us disappear because we saw the mothman," said Jeanie. I assumed there was a reason she changed the gender back, so I didn't correct her.

"Nobody is going to disappear Ms. John. We are not 'men in black'. My name is Agent Smith and I work for the Department of Wildlife Conservation and Agent Jones there works for the Center for Disease Control."

"If you are federal agents, then why am I handcuffed to this chair and why were you covering my mouth?" asked Jeanie.

"Because when we entered your house, with your permission I might add, you attacked us with a lamp and wouldn't stay quiet. Attacking federal agents is a serious offense, I can assure you. We were merely assuring our safety and yours. As for the covering of your mouth, I suffer from migraines and your screaming was annoying me," said Agent Smith. "It is my understanding that you both came in contact with a sandhill crane last evening."

"We saw something," I admitted.

"But it wasn't a crane," finished Jeanie.

"It's very common for the sandhill crane to be mistaken for a monster, especially in the dark," said Agent Smith.

"We had infrared goggles," said Jeanie, her normal cool demeanor so far gone that we wouldn't be able to see it with the Hubble Telescope. Her conspiracy theories seemed to be fast becoming fact, facts Smith and Jones were trying to dismiss as a flight of fancy by a silly girl. For once, Jeanie didn't have the upper hand and it made her angry. She was volunteering too much information, stuff that she should be hiding. If the stories of men in black kidnapping witnesses were true, she should be agreeing with whatever they said in order to get them to leave without us.

"Well, the goggles they sell in sporting good stores are impressive toys, but not at the level of those the military uses," said Smith.

"I'll have you know..." started Jeanie.

"That we spent a lot of money on those hunting goggles," I said cutting her off. There was no reason to tell these two that what Jeanie had bought was US military surplus. She did have money and didn't mind spending it. "But it was dark. It didn't look like a crane, but I suppose you two are the experts."

"Precisely," said Smith. Jones, who still hadn't said a word simply nodded.

"Do you have a card so we can call you if we see the crane again? I assume it must be endangered for you to be tracking it," I said.

"Very close," said Smith, handing me a business card.

"I'm curious as to how you found out that we had encountered it because we didn't mention it to anyone," I said.

"They must have cameras that filmed my license plate and they came after us," Jeanie said.

"Actually, we noticed the special report on the First Church of the Hidden Truth's web site," said Smith.

I rolled my eyes back and looked at Jeanie.

"I knew they were afraid of me. You monitor my site!" said Jeanie.

"Actually, we have a search engine monitoring the web for reports that might be related to the crane and since it has been mistaken for a mothman before, that was one of our search parameters," said Smith.

"Well I apologize for this entire misunderstanding and I wish you the best of luck finding the crane," I said.

"I'm afraid we are going to have to take your friend into custody for her assault," said Smith. Jones nodded a bit too eagerly.

"Again, a misunderstanding, but from where I stand you seem to have unlawfully imprisoned her in her own home. Proper procedure would have been to take her to the nearest federal building or police station, not handcuff her to a chair and try to manually gag her. Both sides here made a mistake, but if we can all agree to disagree, we can call this whole thing a wash," I said.

Smith frowned. "I suppose as long as Ms. John is willing to correct her web report to state what she saw was, in fact, the sandhill crane and direct her viewers to report any more sightings to our hotline."

"I'm sure..." I started.

Jeanie cut me off. "That there is no way in hell I'm going to do that. The first amendment protects my freedom of speech. Let's not forget in my case we're also dealing with freedom of religion."

"That is unfortunate," said Smith. "I did mention that Agent Jones is from the CDC, yes?"

I nodded.

"Well, this particular sandhill crane is believed to be infected with East Nile virus."

"There is no such thing. You mean West Nile virus," corrected Jeanie.

"No, I don't. East Nile is a mutation of West Nile. Mosquitoes no longer need to act as a carrier between the two species. Infection can spread directly from bird to human and then from human to human as an airborne contagion. We are going to have to take you into custody to quarantine you."

"Wait, you were going to let us go a minute ago," said Jeanie.

"Are you going to correct the mistake in your story?" asked Smith.

"No," said Jeanie in grim determination. I wanted to smack her, but it wouldn't do any good. One, she'd clobber me. And two, I've always known Jeanie would die before she betrayed her convictions. I just never thought that I'd be dying alongside her.

"Very well. We will also have to take anyone you've had contact with," said Smith.

"I've been alone all night," Jeanie said honestly.

"I went straight home and went to bed. I didn't see anyone," I lied. As much fun as it might be to have these guys arrest Mr. Darrow, there was no way he wouldn't give up his daughter. I wanted to keep Denise safe.

"Wait, if we are so contagious, why don't you have infection prevention suits on?" asked Jeanie.

"We've been vaccinated," said Smith, who saw Jeanie was about to speak and cut her off. "If you've been infected, it's too late to get the inoculation. And as each batch of the vaccine costs almost a thousand dollars, it would be too costly to vaccinate the entire populous."

The conversation seemed to be over. The pair of men in black led us to a nondescript four-door sedan, which of course was black. The windows were all tinted dark enough so somebody on the outside couldn't see in. We were put in the back seat, which was set up like that of a police car —-mesh wire over all the glass and doors that could open from the inside. The window separating front and back was blackened to the point of opacity.

They got in the front and drove off.

I looked over at Jeanie. For the first time ever, I saw her frightened, which was comforting in an odd way, because I was terrified.

"I'm sorry I got you mixed up in this," she whispered.

"Me too," I said. Jeanie curled up against me and wrapped my arm around her shoulder.

"Can you ever forgive me?"

"We'll see," I said.

Jeanie actually leaned back and stared at me like she was surprised. "You would have preferred I gave in?"

"Honestly? Yes. So you don't get to prove your conspiracy theories, but we'd get to live," I said.

"We may still get to live. They may just bring us to Area 51," she said, getting the familiar look on her face when she's trying to pull a scam.

"Why?"

"Breeding stock for the gray aliens. I'll probably have to have a bunch of alien children," she said, her sense of humor creeping back in.

"Wait, if I have to die, so be it, but if anyone is having sex with you, it's going to be me," I said.

"Oh, you won't be left out. You'll probably have to stud for a harem of female aliens," she said.

"With the big heads, saucer eyes, pear shaped bodies and long fingers?" I asked.

"Yes."

"Do they have breasts?" I asked.

"Some reports say they do," she answered.

"An entire harem, you say? All of them willing to put out?" I said smiling.

"Wait a second. You sound like you're actually looking forward to it," Jeanie said indignantly.

"Except for the whole alien thing, it's every teenage male's fantasy," I said. "Since by this time tomorrow I may be real busy, I'll give you the chance to be the first one to use my stud service."

"Here? Now?" asked Jeanie.

"Why not?" I said.

"Because we've been kidnapped by two men in black who are in the front seat and would be able to watch the whole thing," said Jeanie.

"Through that glass? Come on. I'm sure they probably have the whole alien sex thing rigged up to their personal pay per view, so what's the difference?" I said. "Besides, if we're going to die, I don't want to go as a virgin. Worse, I don't want to go without having made love to the woman I adore."

Jeanie mulled it over, frowned and then smiled. "Well, I was considering saying yes for prom night."

"Seriously?" I asked.

Jeanie nodded. "I hadn't decided for sure. Part of me still wanted to wait for marriage, but other parts were having trouble holding out that long. I had thought about it back on my eighteenth birthday but chickened out. Prom night seemed perfect. I know it's cornball, but that way we could have the entire weekend together, not a quickie in the backseat of the car. Ironic how life turns out, huh?"

"We don't have to..."

Jeanie put her index finger over my lips and whispered "Shush." Then she kissed me like I had never been kissed before. Every other time we had made out, we both had held back, not wanting things to get out of control. That wasn't an issue now. Jeanie climbed on top of me, straddling my pelvis. She pulled my shirt over my head. I got my hands under her shirt. I had the twin mountains of the promised land in my hands when the right car door opened.

Jones grinned and waved at us.

"No!" I screamed.

Smith opened the left door. "I hope we're not interrupting anything."

"Actually, if you could come back in like ten minutes..." I started and

Jeanie grabbed my face, turned it away from Smith and gave me another amazing kiss. Then she took my right hand in her left, dismounted and got out of the car. I followed close behind, putting my shirt back on.

Neither of us said a word.

I looked around, expecting to be at some secret installation. I was surprised to see we were at a low rent hotel on the outskirts of town.

Jones motioned us to follow him toward one of the rooms. He opened the door and we went inside. Jones then left, but Smith followed us in.

There were two full sized beds, a bathroom, and a TV.

"This is your new home away from home. Make yourselves comfortable. We'll be here until later tonight," said Smith.

"That's great. If you wouldn't mind stepping outside, I think we'd like to take a nap," I said.

"Go ahead. Do whatever you like, but one of us is going to be in the room with you at all times," said Smith.

"Do you mind if we both use the bathroom?" I said. Jeanie was actually giggling.

"Glad to see you have your priorities straight or at least something straight, Mr. Spenser." He glanced at my bulging jeans. "You may use the bathroom together or separate, however, the door will remain at least one-third open at all times. There is a window in there and I would hate for either of you to be hurt trying to climb out of it," said Smith. Jones returned, snacks in hand. "Mr. Jones will be with you for the next few hours. I will be back."

Smith left.

I figured I'd try again. The escape option sounded even better than the sex one, I'm sorry to admit. "Mind if we use the bathroom together?"

Jones waved with a flourish toward the restroom, then used his hands to indicate the door had to stay open.

"How about giving us ten minutes alone?" I pleaded.

"Ten minutes? It better be a lot longer than ten minutes," said Jeanie.

Jones shook his head but pointed to the bed.

"It'd be better if we didn't have an audience," I said.

Jones shrugged, sat in a chair and opened a bag of popcorn he had probably gotten at the vending machine, like we were some movie he was about to watch.

Jeanie moved to one side of him, I went to the other. She got down on her knees on the floor and leaned forward. She hadn't bothered to re-fasten the buttons I had undone in the car and she was showing a lot of cleavage.

"Please, just give us a little bit of time alone," she purred.

Jones turned and stared right where he was supposed to. I picked up the lamp with every intention of hitting him on the head with it. Jones never even moved his eyes, but his hand reached inside his jacket, pulled out his gun and pointed it between my eyes, all before I got the lamp six inches off the table.

Slowly, I lowered it back down and stepped away. Jeanie did the same.

I shrugged, trying not to break down and cry. "We had to try."

Jones raised his eyebrows and nodded, seeming to agree. There appeared to be no hard feelings on his part. Nice to know we had been kidnapped by a professional.

We sat on the bed, waiting. Smith switched every two hours with Jones. Jeanie and I spoke in whispers until night fell. They didn't feed us, even though we asked for them to get us something from the vending machines. All we had was the cheap coffee the motel supplied with the room. We loaded it up with sugar, but it still wasn't the same as a meal. Despite being worried about what was happening, I was starving.

When the bedside clock read 11:00 PM, Smith spoke for the first time in hours. "It shouldn't be long now."

"What shouldn't?" asked Jeanie.

"You'll see," was his only answer.

There was a high-pitched screech and all the lights went dead. Smith stood and reached for his gun, but he never reached it. At first, all I saw was a pair of red eyes through the crack in the pulled curtains. Then there was shattering glass from the window being smashed inward. The curtains caught Smith like a fish in a net. The mothwoman from the night before was standing over him, pummeling him until he was unconscious.

Jeanie and I backed up against the back wall of the motel room. I stood in front of her and for once she didn't tell me I was being too macho.

The mothwoman stopped and stared, focusing on me. She tilted her head and smiled. The oddest thing was, it seemed familiar somehow.

Seeing we were scared, she didn't come any closer. All we did was stand there, staring at each other. Then the building started to rumble and the mothwoman looked up in terror. She threw open the door.

"Run!" said the mothwoman. The sound was raspy, like human speech wasn't something her vocal cords should have been able to do.

We didn't argue and sprinted into the parking lot, where we were almost blown down.

Jeanie looked up in the sky and got very pale, even for her. "Black helicopter!"

"That's bad I assume," I said.

"We'd disappear, never to be seen again," said Jeanie.

"What do we do?"

"Head for the woods and try to hide until daylight," said Jeanie.

We ran, but Jones stepped out from behind a car, his gun drawn. He seemed more amused than angry.

"Time for plan B," said Jeanie.

"We have a plan B?" I asked.

Jeanie sighed. "Sadly, no."

Jones motioned for us to move toward the back of the hotel. He had the gun, so we didn't have much by way of choice, so we went. One moment Jones was behind us, then he wasn't. We looked around, but he seemed to have vanished, then his gun dropped from the sky. We looked up and he was fighting with the mothwoman in mid-air. Jones was losing. A moment later, the mothwoman dropped him and his body plummeted to the pavement with a thud. Jones didn't move.

Jeanie grabbed for the gun. The mothwoman dropped to the ground nearby. Jeanie started to lift the gun up.

I grabbed her hand. "No. She saved us. She won't hurt us, will you?"

The mothwoman shook her head.

"I have so many questions, I don't even know where to start," said Jeanie, but the mothwoman seemed to only have eyes for me.

We were all pushed to the pavement as the black helicopter hovered over us, the gust from the rotors trying to pin us.

Jeanie again tried to lift the gun to fire at the helicopter, but this time the mothwoman caught her hand and shook her head no. Then she pantomimed a ricochet bouncing off the helicopter and hitting one of us.

From the horizon, three balls of light suddenly appeared and moved at amazing speeds toward us.

"Foo fighters," gasped Jeanie. It wasn't a rock group, but the phenomenon first described by WWII pilots the band was named after. They had been seen near the bridge disaster almost forty years ago.

Jeanie lifted up the gun, but the mothwoman shook her head again. "Friends," she rasped.

The black helicopter lifted up and took off in the opposite direction.

"It's scared of them," I said.

The mothwoman nodded. "They... will crash it..." She pointed at the motel.

"Why?" I asked.

"Danger underneath," she said. "Evil."

One of the lights cut off the fleeing copter and it came back toward us. The three lights and the helicopter seemed to be having an aerial dogfight.

"When that copter comes down, it'll kill everyone in the motel. We need to get everyone out," said Jeanie, running toward the outside doors on the first floor. "Plus, if there are more witnesses, we have a better chance of the men in black leaving us alone. You take the second floor."

I looked at the mothwoman. "I gotta help. Thank you."

She smiled and pointed to me. "Welcome."

I ran up the stairs and started banging on doors. "Get out!"

I was ignored. "Fire!" I screamed. A couple of people ran out and saw the lights in the sky. I told them to get to the parking lot. A few couples were at the windows staring out, but not moving.

I tried a different tact. "Cops! It's a raid! Get out." That emptied three more rooms. The other rooms had the curtains open and they were empty. I moved toward the stairs but was cut off by Smith. He had his gun drawn now and his face and hands were bleeding from glass cuts.

"Going somewhere?" Smith asked.

I didn't bother to answer. He was fifteen feet from me. I leapt onto the rail and reached up and pulled myself onto the roof. I started running toward the opposite side of the roof, planning to lower myself down. Smith didn't waste any time chasing me. Worse, he fired into the air.

"Hold it right there, Mr. Spenser," said Smith.

I listened.

"Now turn around slowly," said Smith. "That helicopter is going to get rid of those freaks and it is going to land. Then you and your girlfriend are going to get on board."

"And if we don't?" I asked.

"I'll load your corpse on board myself. Now, lets go down," Smith said, motioning me with the gun barrel.

"No," I said.

"Excuse me?" said Smith, more angry than amused.

"According to Jeanie, no one who's ever gotten on a black helicopter has ever been seen again. You want to kill me, do it here where at least maybe someone might see you."

"Okay," said Smith.

I had hoped for a different answer. I got ready to go for his gun, but before I could a shadow dropped out of the sky and knocked him over the edge. Smith landed on the sidewalk, hard. The shadow did a loop and landed on the roof. It was the mothwoman.

"Thanks again," I said, looking at the still form of Smith and realizing I was one push or slip away from joining him.

"Least I could do... after so many years," she rasped.

Down below, Jeanie was shouting. "Kent, you okay?"

I looked over the edge. "I'm fine."

"Everyone's out. Get down quick," Jeanie said.

The mothwoman looked down, then at me. "You love... her?"

"Yes," I said. "You can tell?"

"A mother knows," she said.

I was confused. "You have children?" I asked, trying to picture what they might look like. I pictured little bat creatures.

"Yes," she answered. Then she kissed me on the forehead. "You."

"Me? But that's impossible. It's..."

Before I could say anymore, the black copter dive-bombed us and it was shooting.

The mothwoman grabbed me by the shoulders and leapt up into the sky.

"We're flying!" I said. I could feel her body vibrate from her laughter. We zigged and zagged and I could hear the copter behind us. A foo fighter was coming straight at us. It passed mere feet over our heads. The copter veered off and the mothwoman landed in the parking lot, next to Jeanie. The gathered crowd stared and pointed.

"Get far away," rasped the mothwoman. She bent and whispered in my ear, "We will see each other again." Then she leapt back up into the sky, chasing after the copter.

"You heard the lady, people. Move it," I yelled, grabbing Jeanie's hand and running across the street. The rest of the crowd followed.

When we were a block away, we ducked down in a drainage gully.

The black helicopter was fighting the foo fighters and losing. The night was lit up by the strange lights. I could see the mothwoman who had claimed to be the mother I had never known going up toward the dogfight. I was having problems getting my mind around the concept.

She slipped underneath and removed some sort of shielding near the engine, then gave some sort of hand signal and the three foo fighters sped off into the night.

She waited until the copter was directly over the motel and let out a screech. The copter went dead in the air and fell like a stone. When it hit the building below, the fuel tank ignited and there was an explosion. A second explosion lit up the night sky like it was suddenly daylight.

We stayed with the crowd until the police and news crews showed up. Everyone, even the ones who shouldn't have been at that motel, talked to the police and most of them talked to the media. That included Jeanie.

"From what happened here tonight, it's clear that the mothpeople have never really left Point Pleasant and that the government is involved in the cover-up," said Jeanie to a group of reporters.

I stood nearby and one of the reporters approached me, microphone first.

"What do you have to add?" he asked.

"No comment," I said, walking away. I could barely think, let alone speak coherently on camera.

Jeanie ran up to me. "Kent, what are you doing? We need to document what we saw with the media so the truth can get out to everyone."

"Sixteen other people already told what they saw. One more won't make a difference," I said.

"You're wrong," she said. The reporters were hovering nearby, but I couldn't tell if the cameras were on or not.

"Jeanie, please," I whispered. "Not now."

"Kent, you know how much this means to me. Please, talk to them," pleaded Jeanie.

"I can't," I said.

"I don't believe this," said Jeanie, storming off.

"Jeanie, wait. I can explain," I said.

She turned back. "Then explain."

"Later," I pleaded. "You know I wouldn't do this to you without a reason."

"Fine, but it better be good or that might be the last later we ever have," she said.

I nodded, then noticed a shadow move in the nearby woods. I tried to not appear to be staring as I looked into a pair of red eyes. I watched as the mouth beneath smiled and she nodded to me. Then I heard the flapping of great wings and the shadow was gone.

WORKING GIRL
A Tale of the Daring

Tara sat down carefully. She had to, otherwise, the scarlet ultra miniskirt she was wearing would ride up and end up looking more like a belt. It did go well with the black fishnet stockings she sported, however. The bar was dark, the air smoky and the beer expensive. The place was the kind only neighborhood types frequented and from the looks, this neighborhood was not the finest the City of Rune had to offer. It was just a few blocks from Ruby Town, where any perverse pleasure or pain could be achieved for the right price.

Tara scanned the men in the seedy barroom. Although it looked casual, her assessment was thorough and professional. She was working tonight, like she had every night for the last two weeks, and she let nothing get in the way of a job. Her objective was to find a man, or better yet, let him find her. It didn't take long for one to approach her.

"Hey, pretty lady, can I buy you a drink?" asked the tall, dark haired man. It wasn't the most original line, but this wasn't the kind of place you found something new. It was the type of place old things went to hide from the world.

Tara raised an appraising eyebrow. "Sure." She nodded to the bartender and he brought her a second glass with a pink liquid.

"Pink lady?" asked the man.

"Lemonade," said Tara. It was the man's turn to raise an eyebrow. "I don't drink when I'm working."

"So are you working tonight?" he asked.

Tara sipped her lemonade but didn't bother to smile. "Yes."

"You looking for a customer?" asked the man.

"I'm never short on clients. What did you have in mind?" Tara asked.

"You, me, some whips and chains..."

"This ain't Ruby Town," said Tara.

"Close enough for me," said the man.

"Not for me," said Tara, standing up as if to leave. The man grabbed her wrist.

"Don't go yet. We're just getting acquainted here."

Tara pulled her wrist away.

"I ain't here to make friends. I already told you, I'm working," Tara said through gritted teeth.

"I'll pay you for your time."

"Do I look like a hooker to you?"

"Well, yes," said the man, confused.

"Okay, then. What denomination did you have in mind?" asked Tara.

"Fifty bucks."

Tara laughed and turned away.

"Wait. A hundred."

She turned back. "You're getting warmer."

"Warmer? A hundred will get me any piece of tail in Ruby Town."

"Then go to Ruby Town," said Tara.

"And deal with those freaks? No way."

Rune had its own Daring, super powered men and women, many of whom were referred to as heroes. The guardians of Ruby Town usually weren't graced with that label. The normals called them freaks, so that's what a team of them began calling themselves–The Freaks.

In a lifestyle that practically demanded spandex and leather, The Freaks went far above and beyond the call of duty.

"You afraid of The Freaks?" asked Tara, wounding her companion's male pride.

"I'm not afraid of anything. It's just having powers just isn't natural. Somebody should do something about it."

"About all the Daring?"

"Well, some are okay. Utmost and the Luminary are all right, I guess."

"What about Spike and Dike or the Sex Kitten?" The man shook his head no. "How about the Blow Up Doll?"

"The chick that explodes? She's a freaking hitman. They're all a bunch of no good freaks."

"They protect the innocent," said Tara. It was the man's turn to laugh.

"Nobody's innocent in Ruby Town."

"I'll have to remember that. Well, at least they punish the guilty," said Tara.

"In Ruby Town, that's probably a full time job."

"I'm sure it is."

"Enough about those freaks. Let's talk about us," said the man, inching closer and draping his arm around her shoulders. Tara decided to finally grace him with a glance, but his eyes were so intent on staring down her cleavage, he didn't even notice.

"There's an 'us'?" Tara asked coyly, pulling his arm off her and dropping it at his side.

"Sure there is," said the man, pushing a pair of hundred dollar bills across the bar. Tara reached out to grab them. She pulled, but the man would not let go, so the bills tore in half. "You get the other half after we consummate our friendship." The man stood up, waving his half of the bills like he was dangling a carrot in front of a rabbit. "Coming?"

"Not likely with the likes of you," Tara whispered under her breath, but she stood up and followed him out of the bar onto the dark street. After they had walked a few blocks in silence, he beckoned Tara to a half hidden and deserted alley.

"We're in Ruby Town now. Aren't you afraid The Freaks will get you?" asked Tara.

"I already told you, I ain't afraid of nothing. You coming or not?"

Tara looked at the empty alley and shook her head.

"Mamma told me never to do it an alley, not even for two hundred dollars. Nice girls get taken to motel rooms. Take your money. I'm leaving," said Tara, tossing back the torn bills.

The man reached out and grabbed her wrist again. Tara pulled and struggled, but her hand didn't escape the man's grasp.

"Well, you ain't exactly a nice girl, now are you? You'll get in that alley and like it," said the man, smiling as he forced her into the alley.

"Please. Don't hurt me. Let me go," said Tara. The man pulled a switchblade knife and held it to her throat.

"Too late for that. We had a deal. Take off your underwear," the man demanded.

"I'm not wearing any," Tara whispered.

"That's what I thought, slut," spat the man, as he removed articles of his clothing and hiked up the red ultra mini. It didn't have far to go.

In a timid and frightened little voice, Tara asked, "Are you the man who raped and killed Cindy Waters?"

The man laughed. "Yeah, that was me, although I didn't know the whore's name until I saw her picture in the paper the next day."

"What are you going to do to me?" asked Tara.

"The same thing I did to Cindy, so you might as well relax and enjoy it," said the man.

Suddenly, everything about Tara changed. She was no longer acting timid. It was as if she was another person.

"If you value your life and well being, I'd advise you to stop and just walk away," said Tara.

"You're threatening me? Are you nuts? I'm the one holding the knife here," said the man.

"Can't say I didn't warn you," said Tara.

"Thanks," said the man sarcastically, as he moved in to complete his heinous crime. As his manhood touched flesh, but before he violated Tara, there was a bright light and an explosion between her legs.

The man screamed louder than a banshee and collapsed to the filthy alley, holding his bloody groin with both hands. The shock and the horror at what had happened was momentarily stronger than the pain. The man moved his bloody hands away and looked.

"It's gone," he whined, like a pouty little boy who had just lost his favorite toy.

"Vaporized, so there's no hope of reattachment," said Tara, pulling her skirt down.

"You're one of those Freaks. You're the..."

"Blow Up Doll. Yes."

"Why? I never did anything to you," said the man.

"You call attempted rape nothing? I didn't do it for me. I did it for Cindy. Her family paid me to find and punish you for what you did to their daughter."

The man was losing blood steadily and collapsed onto his side.

"You need to take me to a doctor or a hospital."

"I don't need to do anything," replied Tara.

"But I'll die."

"Maybe, but maybe not. That's more of a chance than you gave Cindy," said Tara.

"But I lied when I said I killed her. I was just bragging to impress you."

"Color me real impressed," said Tara.

"Please help me. I'm innocent," begged the man, reaching a bloody hand up toward Tara. She ignored it. "I wouldn't lie."

"Ever?"

"Ever."

"Well, that settles that." Tara turned and walked toward the mouth of the alley.

"Where are you going?" he said, shivering as shock from blood loss started to kick in.

"Away."

"How can you leave an innocent man to die?"

"Innocent? Look where you are. Don't you remember what you said?" asked Tara.

"What?"

"Nobody's innocent in Ruby Town."

Tara turned and left him in a pool of red. She stopped at a pay phone and called 911, then waited in the shadows until the ambulance arrived. Despite her threats to the contrary, she wouldn't let him die. Tara wasn't the type to let him get off that easy.

TESQUE, TESQUE
A Story of Fugtown

You'd think there'd be easier ways to make a living for a seven hundred pound gorilla, but ever since I became a reluctant member of a different species, I've had to take what I can get. And I can assure you that taking a case and being happy about it are two very different things.

I work out of Fugtown, which tends to be even worse than it sounds, but at least I don't stand out. Not much at least. Konundrum City is about as corrupt as they come and has no problems sectioning those more deformed members of society away from its less disturbing population. Police protection stops south of Robinson Avenue, which is why people come to me. I'm no cop, but I'm big and have a reputation for being honest. Odd that I wasn't considered trustworthy before my brain was put into an ape's body. And maybe I wasn't. Life's funny that way, kind of like a dad who thinks it's hilarious to tie his kid up in a dark closet and leave him there for the weekend. Yeah, I had issues even before I became a gorilla.

I don't think Mildred Maccina much cared about how I got where I was. The lady had big problems of her own. Milly didn't have arms. They'd been replaced with purple tentacles, although replaced implied she got new limbs. Now, rushing to judgment is considered rude, but that don't mean first impressions aren't right. I'd have to guess they weren't grafts, but mutagen retrovirus exposure. Mutizen is nasty stuff. It screws with flesh and DNA, affects the gene pool of any later generations that crawl out of the muck of affected birth canals. A lot of the folks around here, including Milly, have gotten up close and personal with the stuff, which earned them a no-expenses paid trip to Fugtown.

Believe it or not, she's one of the lucky ones. Milly was able to get by. She takes in laundry and can walk without help. If the virus had attacked her legs, she'd be reduced to rolling around on a wheel board or red-lighting it.

Right now I think she'd be willing to red-light if I could solve her problem, which considering my furry physique says a lot. Cash is as rare in Fugtown as a lone flatfoot, so I have to be willing to take things out in trade to survive, but I don't make red-lighting part of my fee. Even I won't sink that low.

"Are you sure it's your husband who took your twins?" I asked.

"Ex-husband," she replied.

"You got a divorce?" I said, thinking maybe I might be able to get some cash out of this case after all.

She smirked and made a dismissive wave of her tentacles. "Yeah, right. I live in Fugtown because of my great wealth."

I started to laugh but caught myself. If I'm not careful, my laughs these days sound too much like animal grunts. Never a good idea to frighten the clients. I should have known better. It's rare for someone to get enough scratch to be able to afford the divorce fees. Cheaper to pay the polygamy fine.

"I refuse to acknowledge that man as my husband. While he's safe at work, me and my two boys were out shopping and some loony let's the mutizen gas loose. I grabbed my babies and ran, for all the good it did me," she said. I'd disagree, but didn't want to offend a client.

She showed me pictures of the boys. They had similar arms to their mother, plus purple heads. Her running with them probably stopped them from having to live riverside because of a total transformation. I imagined she carried a kid in each arm, running through the gas. Her arms probably covered their legs, protecting them from changing. By the same token, their bodies kept the gas from getting her face. Not that she'd want to hear that her kids were living shields.

"When our neighbors found out, my ex abandoned us. Left in the middle of the night and I couldn't pay the rent uptown. Not that the landlord was even willing to give me a chance. Evicted me as soon as he learned my ex had split. I understand why he'd leave me when I looked like this, but to walk out on his kids—that's unforgivable." I couldn't argue, but with my old man, an exit would have been preferable to having him around. "At least if he stayed long enough to help us move, the neighbors and the landlord wouldn't have stolen most of our belongings."

"So if he ran off, what makes you think he's behind your missing children?" I asked.

"Mr. Borroughs…" I had already asked her to drop the honorific so I let it slide. "… Al left me a note telling me he took them."

She handed it over. Seemed pretty cut and dried. Minus the tentacles, she took this to the cops, she'd win hands down. The courts tend to overwhelmingly side with mothers on custody issues with one exception— when the mother's a tesque. It's short for grotesque, which is supposed to be a more polite term than mutant or freak.

"What do you want me to do?" I asked.

"Find them and bring them back."

"I could simply go to your ex's apartment and take the children." But it would be an incredibly stupid thing to do. I've been in the paper a couple of times. Plus, there's not five other talking gorillas that they can put in a lineup with me. Even someone with cataracts would be able to pick me out. "But if he calls the cops, they could come down in force to Fugtown and take them back. Not likely for a couple of tesque kids, I admit, unless your husband has connections. Is he connected, Ms. Maccina?" Al Maccina probably didn't have money or he would have just hid his family, but that didn't mean he didn't have family connections to the cops, the corps, or one of the mobs. Most people lie, but it doesn't hurt to ask.

"Not unless it's happened since he ran off," she said.

"Are you sure?" I asked in a deep voice. The Shade Mob runs Fugtown and has tesque leg-breakers that even I don't want to mess with.

"Yes."

I nodded in approval. "Now if I just take the kids, you may have to go into hiding." Not hard to hide from norms in Fugtown. In most cases, just crossing south of Robinson will do it. If there's nothing visibly wrong with someone, they stick out and probably won't get far without having to deal with a welcoming committee. "He probably won't be able to find you, but he might hire someone who might. Are you prepared for that?"

"You could just see to it that he has an accident, couldn't you?" she said, playing like she was hinting instead of being blatant.

I stood, the unexpected movement of my bulk made her lean back, even on the other side of my desk. "Sorry, we couldn't do business."

"What I meant…"

"I know what you meant. I'm not a killer for hire." I've killed, but I'm not a hitter. I don't kill without reason. Personal gain doesn't qualify at least in my book. "Maybe you should talk to the Shades. Their fee structure might be a little different than mine, but they'd probably help you out." They might let her do their laundry in exchange for a hit, but it's more likely she'll be red-lighting for folks with fetishes. "Good day."

Her face dropped, stunned. I picked up the newspaper and started reading. The tabloid looked like a paperback in my hands.

"I'm sorry," she said. I turned a page, ignoring her. "I'm angry. He took my kids. Do you have kids?"

"There's a couple of chimps I'm not too sure about," I quipped. Milly didn't crack a smile. I put down my paper and looked at her. "No, I don't. And now I won't be able to." My old boss believed in spaying and neutering all his lab animals. Of course, I never expected to be one of them. I was lucky that the silverback had gotten a basic vasectomy. I could still be intimate with any woman willing or crazy enough, or any gorilla for that matter. Not that my mind wanted ape booty, but the body I was in reacted to things that made my mind ill. I supposed the snip and cut is good in a way. I certainly couldn't see myself raising an ape child. Transplanted brains don't exactly carry over to the next generation.

"I might be able to, but after being exposed to the mutizen, I wouldn't want to." I nodded. "But I still want the kids I already have. Please help me get them back. I'll do anything."

"Define anything," I said, putting down my paper and opening negotiations.

Her eyes almost fell into her lap. It didn't take a genius to figure out what she was thinking. "What do you want from me?"

"I understand you take in laundry," I said.

Her head shot up in relief. "I'll do your laundry forever."

"That's a good start," I said. The wariness returned to her eyes. "But I don't actually have much clothing. I can't exactly wear uptown cast-offs." Which made up the majority of Fugtown's wardrobes. "I understand you do some tailoring too."

"Yes." She actually had some fine motor control at the very end of her tentacle by wrapping the tips around things. Not as good as opposable thumbs, but good enough to sew.

"I could use some new suits," I said. Oddly, when I was human, I hated suits and ties. Now I find it makes me less scary. So does the hat.

"I don't have enough material to make something in your size," she said.

"Leave the material to me," I said. A former client had paid me in reams of fabric that had fallen off a truck. I traded the pink and lace for things I needed but kept the blues, grays, and blacks for myself. And one ream of white for shirts.

"I'd be happy to."

"Shall we say two suits and three shirts as a retainer and a suit and a shirt a day plus expenses?" I asked.

"It would take me some time to make them," she said.

"Have the first suit and shirt ready in a week and we'll talk about deadlines for the rest," I said. "Is that acceptable?"

"Yes," Milly said.

I held out my hairy hand and she looked at me. "You don't want me to sign anything?"

I shook my head. "Neither of us can afford to take this to court. We both know what we agreed to. And I can assure you, you don't want to welch on a deal with me."

"Very good, Mr. Borroughs," said Milly, putting her right tentacle in my furry hand. "Bring my babies home."

Like most things, it was easier said than done. Milly had no idea where Al went after he left. I'd start on the assumption that he hadn't left Konundrum. It was a pretty safe bet. Not many people left and came back. Greener pastures I guess.

There are ways of finding people. Those rich enough have phones and are listed in the phone book. I checked and Al Maccina wasn't. It's never that easy.

Finding someone uptown is easier for a flat foot. Everyone has to register and they have clerks to sort through files for them. It rarely takes more that a few days to come up with an address. Since the cops weren't likely to loan me either their files or a clerk, I had to consider other options. I checked the last place Milly knew he worked. It was a chemical manufacturer. Turns out, Al left them about a month earlier for one of their competitors, Pharmzuc. They were sorry to lose him. Apparently, he was a gifted chemist.

My visit to the old employer had gotten me a cold reception and some quick answers to be rid of me. Pharmzuc wasn't so easy.

As soon as I was through the lobby, a pair of guards flanked me on either side. A look was enough to convince the rent-a-cops of the folly of laying hands on me. I simply tipped my hat and kept walking toward reception. They followed on either side of me.

There was a blonde doll working the desk. I wasn't being sexist in my choice of terms. Women subject themselves to surgery to make themselves more beautiful. Dolls went to the extreme, going so far as to have their skin hardened. It slowed aging, allowing women to look twenty well into their sixties. Probably worked longer too, but their bodies tended to start shutting down about then. The same process that grants them lasting beauty makes it very difficult for them to move because the skin loses its elasticity. This tends to make simple things like changing positions difficult and occasionally painful. Dolls tend to get put in one position and left there. The tough skin prevented pressure sores. They probably wheeled her chair out at night to her sleeping quarters and then back in the morning. Having a Doll in your employ was a sign of status because you needed money to keep one.

This one wore opera gloves up past her arms. Means they didn't do the process on her elbows and hands, at least not completely. Gives her some function—typing, writing, answering phones and such. Even so, she can't clean up after her own plumbing. They hook her up to a machine twice a day to clean her out. Most women only agree to get dolled up in exchange for a large amount of money. Usually, the family gets it. Kind of like being voluntarily sold into slavery.

Like I said about Milly, it can always be worse. Even for the Doll. She's helpless, but at least she's looked after.

Her face was locked into a permanent smile. Her pupils widened as I approached.

"Good afternoon, sir," she said in a very polite tone.

"And a good afternoon to you. I was hoping you could help me," I said.

"I'm afraid ceptanze is only available for a cash payment," she said. It was a reasonable guess. The only reason the mad scientists are able to graft and transplant between species is because of ceptanze. It virtually eliminates rejection without suppressing the immune system. Without the drug, the gorilla body would have long ago rejected my human brain. Fortunately, there are other ways of getting it than buying it from the manufacturer. The black market in the stuff is huge and definitely not sold at any of the company's corp sites, but I didn't want to correct her. "And we don't keep any on site."

"I'm actually here looking for an employee. His kids are missing and I'd like to talk with him," I said. "His name's Al Maccina. In research, I believe. Could you tell me if he's in?"

"I'm afraid I can't give out that information," she said, trying to bite her upper lip. It was too stiff to move much so she only succeeded in a mild nip. "Since it involves his children, I'd be happy to relay him a message."

"I appreciate that," I said, reaching over and grabbing the sign-in book for the building.

"Sir, that's privileged. Please put it back…" said the Doll.

"Okay ape, you crossed the line," said one of the guards with unfettered sadistic glee, reaching up to take it from me. I lifted it too high for him to reach, so he grabbed my right forearm, his partner, my left. My arms didn't move, even when they tried to drop to their knees to drag me down. I flipped a page. Each entry had a time in and out and I went all the way back to the previous morning. No Al.

I let my arms fall quickly to my sides so the guards slide off and down to the floor with the momentum. As they scrambled up, I leaned over and put the book back.

"My apologies," I said, handing her a card. I keep a couple in my sleeve. My appearance makes people nervous. Don't want them to panic when they see me reaching in my jacket and mistake paper for a gat. "Please let Mr. Maccina know I can be reached at that number." It was the phone for Bevo, my cyborg landlord. Getting messages was included in my rent. It cost extra, but still cheaper than having my own line. The guards were trying to give me the bum's rush. So far I hadn't moved and was acting like I hadn't noticed them. "My thanks for your help, pretty lady."

The Doll smiled at the compliment or at least her frozen one got a little bigger. Beauty was what was expected of them, so dolls rarely hear a sincere sounding compliment about their looks.

I turned toward the door. The guards were pulled along in my wake. I was leaving, but the loud mouth couldn't leave well enough alone. "You need to leave the building now fur-ball."

"He is," said the Doll.

"Shut it, doll face," shouted the guard. I turned back to see the woman's pupils narrow.

I stopped and turned back to the Doll. "Which way are the rest rooms?"

"I'm sorry, they're only for…" she said.

"I told you to shut your pie hole," said Loudmouth.

Her head turned slightly as she glared at the guard. Her smile all but disappeared. Turning back toward me, she said, "Go right down that hallway and make a right. Second door on the left. Visitors can only use the facilities with a guard, but since you have two, I assume that won't be a problem?"

"Pretty and attitude. I think my heart just did a back flip. Dinner sometime?" I flirted, knowing it wouldn't ever be an option.

"Sorry, I'm sort of a career girl," she said. "And I'm not really into hairy men."

"My loss," I said, standing straighter. The Doll had called me a man. Gave her brownie points as far as I was concerned.

"You know it," she said. The smile was back on her face.

I waved and followed her directions. The whole time the guards tried to slow me down, with no success. Loudmouth pulled his billy club to take a swing, but I pulled it out of his hands and snapped it in two. I shook my head as I handed him the pieces.

"I'm going to take a leak. You both are welcome to join me if you promise not to be too intimidated by what you see," I said.

"I can call a dozen more guards down here," said Loudmouth.

"If you think I'm that impressive, I may have to charge a buck each," I said, walking in the door. Loudmouth put himself between me and the urinal. I pulled down on my zipper and Loudmouth stood fast. "I'm aiming there. If you are in the way, you're going to get wet."

"Do it and I'll call animal control," he said.

"Why? Looking for a date?" I said, moving forward. Loudmouth sidestepped and I took care of business.

After flushing, I washed my hands. As I reached toward the towels, I found Loudmouth again blocking the way.

"I ain't moving this time, monkey," he said. I didn't bother to correct him on the whole ape/monkey tail thing. Instead, I shrugged and pulled his shirt out and used it to dry my hands.

"Thanks," I said.

Loudmouth tried to cold-cock me. It hurt enough for me to rub my jaw, but he wasn't good or strong enough to knock me out. I debated about hauling off and hitting him but decided against it. Uptown and on his turf, the cops would side with him regardless of who was right. Plus, ceptanze is hard to come by. Never know when I'll need to come to the source for enough of the drug to make sure my human brain didn't kill my ape body.

Loudmouth had a key ring on his belt. I pulled until it snapped off.

"Give that back," he yelled. I yelled back, but mine didn't involve words, just volume and something primal. Both guards took a step back, allowing me to get to the restroom door unmolested. I shut it as soon as I was through it. I could feel the pair throw themselves at it from the inside, but my foot blocked it from moving. Luckily it opened out. It took a while, but I found the key that fit the padlock and turned it closed. I took it off and left it in, pocketing the rest of the ring.

As I exited the way I had come, I heard their fruitless pounding on the door.

The lobby now had some workers exiting for smoke breaks, each stopping to sign out at the Doll's desk. There was a floral arrangement near one of the doors. I pulled a red rose out and revisited the Doll, placing it between her hands where she could reach it.

She looked up and saw me and her eyebrows strained to rise.

"Your buddies got locked in the bathroom. Key's in the door if you want to let somebody know to let them out," I said.

"Not particularly," she said, picking up the rose and putting it to her nose, using her elbow and wrist. She strained to inhale deeply, but her ample chest fought her attempting to expand it. "Thanks."

"My pleasure," I said.

"By the way, you best take your card back," she said, her elbow flexing to hand it to me.

"But how will you call me if you ever change your mind about dinner?" I teased.

"I memorized the address and number. And my bosses will just take it from me," she said, flipping it so I could see the back. She had written something down. I reached out and took it. "You better go. I just had to hit the alarm button when you came back without them. Sorry, I can't afford to make my bosses angry at me. If you hurry you should get out in plenty of time," she said.

"Cameras?" I asked.

"Yep, but no microphones," she said.

"Then allow me to thank you while making angry gestures," I said, waving my arms over my head. The Doll laughed and I made my way to the exits. I was out the glass door before any of the backup arrived.

And in all the excitement I seemed to have forgotten to return the keys.

The Doll had written down Maccina's home address for me. It was on the lower Eastside, in a working class neighborhood. I would have taken a cab, but the budget didn't allow. Uptown people pretend not to notice the unusual, assuming it's only there to visit. In the regular neighborhoods, I got hostile glances and things muttered under people's breath, but rarely much more than that. Maccina's block wasn't any different. To make matters easier, I carried a sizeable packing crate so the neighbors would think I was making a delivery.

Maccina lived in a sixth floor walk up. Ape knees weren't made for stairs—the steps are too small—so I took them three at a time. In situations like this, the dilemma was does one knock, pick the lock, or bust the door down? My new hands weren't apt at fine motor control and I wanted in before someone noticed me, which took one option right off the table. The question was did I think Maccina was a danger to his children. I honestly didn't and planned to try to reason with him, so breaking down his door wouldn't be the best way to go. However, I doubted he'd just open up when he saw me through the peep hole.

I put my ear to his door. Someone was inside—there was some pounding and a muffled scream. Someone was getting a beat down. With one arm I shoved the door in and the lock snapped on the first try. I dropped the box after pulling out the baseball bat I had hidden inside.

There were three people inside, none of them Maccina or the twins. There were two mugs in suits. Corporate muscle unless I missed my guess. They wore purple ties with a yellow handkerchief in the breast pocket, oddly enough Pharmzuc Corp. colors. The mooks were smacking around some kid, barely old enough to shave. Tied to a chair, he was spitting up blood and teeth.

This was, of course, the perfect time for a witty remark or wiseass comment, but I've found even the most seasoned professional tends to spook when a seven hundred pound gorilla runs at them screaming and waving a baseball bat.

This pair was more seasoned than most. While the one closer to the window hooked something to the back of the chair, the one closest to me pulled out a piece and started shooting. I had more meat than a man, so it was harder for a bullet to find a vital organ, but I could still be ventilated. I dove behind a couch and the goon kept shooting. Times like this made me wish I could find a gun big enough for my fingers to fit in the trigger guard. I had one with the guard removed, but lost it during a bogus arrest last week and didn't have the scratch to get another one yet. Instead of waiting for him to figure out how to put a bullet in my furry hide, I put down the bat, picked up the couch and threw it at him. The sofa hit the goon and the goon hit the wall, smashing into the plaster and lath. He was stunned, but his eyes were moving rapidly. I didn't have time to wait to see if he'd pass out on his own, so I hit him under the chin and sent him to dreamland. Barely a sound out of him the whole time. I had to pry the gun out of his hand. As I turned to deal with his partner, I watched as he threw the kid, chair and all, over the side of the fire escape. Then he started running down the steel ladders.

I tucked the gun in my waistband and went after him, only I didn't need to bother with the steps. Instead, I kicked off my shoes and climbed down the outside of the fire escape.

He was already at the third floor landing and the kid was on the ground, chair upright. There was a wire and a hook attached to the chair back that slowed his descent enough so he didn't crack his skull on the sidewalk.

The corporate mook reached inside his coat and I doubted it was to offer me a smoke. I leapt to speed my fall. Normally a twenty-foot drop onto the pavement would do even my ape chaises some damage, but I made sure to land on the goon. He broke my fall and by the crunching, I broke parts of him. It seemed like a fair trade to me, especially after I saw the snub nose drop from his hand.

Unfortunately, not only did my act of self-defense not go unnoticed, but it was also misinterpreted by the very human neighbors.

"Get out of here, ya freak!" yelled one, who then threw his beer bottle at me. It missed, no doubt aided by the fact that he had already drunk it and several of its comrades.

After the first toss, others found their courage and started throwing things my way. I figured I was obligated to return in kind, so I threw the mook. I knocked down a few but didn't get a strike. I had nothing left to throw to pick up the spare and I doubted they'd stand still long enough to let me. As they were looking for bigger and better implements of destruction and my bat was still upstairs, I decided a hasty exit was called for. I picked up the mook's piece and tucked it in my waistband with the other. My new feet were pretty close to hands, so I grabbed the kid's chair with my tootsies and leapt up to the fire escape. My hands grabbed rusted steel and I used my upper body to climb the outside of the building while pulling the kid's dead weight. It was tougher than I made it look and my arms were sore by the time I pulled him over the roof.

My first instinct was to untie the kid, but my street sense kicked in first. I just pulled his gag off.

"Thanks," he said nervously.

I nodded. "What's your name?"

"Pete."

"Pete, what were you doing in Maccina's apartment?"

"I was just looking after things," he said cautiously, the realities of being tied to a chair in front of a large silverback starting to sink in. I stood up straight, something my back wasn't thrilled with for prolonged periods, but it made me look bigger.

"Where is Maccina?" I said.

"How should I know?"

"You knew he'd be gone if you were looking after things," I said. "I'm a detective. Don't let the fur and big teeth fool you. And those Pharmzuc goons seemed to think you knew something. They'll be up and around soon. I see them come over that ledge and I'm taking a powder. It'd be a pity if it happens before I got a chance to untie you, wouldn't it?" I walked over to the edge and looked down. "Looks like he's twitching. One of the Good Samaritans is pouring whiskey down his throat." Like they'd waste anything better than rotgut on a stranger.

I turned back to the kid. "Are the twins okay at least?"

"They'll be better than okay when he gets through with them," he said.

"I'm not sure I like the sound of that. What's he doing to them?" I asked.

"He's not going to hurt them. Tentacles or not, they're still his kids," said the kid defensively.

"I don't remember asking you his relationship to the twins. I asked you what he's going to do with them. Remember I'm a detective." I was stretching the truth a bit. Real detectives work for KPD, but they tend to be mean, tough SOB's. Maybe it's different in other places, but in Konundrum interrogations tend to start with a backhand to the face and get rougher from there. Rubber hoses are standard issue. Making his mind draw that connection would only help matters. Not that I was above beating someone to get skinny, but they had to deserve it. The jury was still out on whether this kid did.

"Hey, he's just trying to save a couple of gassers," said the kid.

I smacked him once across the face. "Killing kids ain't saving them, no matter what they look like."

The kid looked more hurt by the accusation than the slap. "Who said anything about killing? They're his kids, man."

"Wrong primate. You must need glasses. Then what's Maccina going to do to them?" I asked.

"He came up with a way to fix…"

He stopped talking when the bullet went through his skull and out the other side, taking bits of brain with it. Damaged the gray matter left in his skull to the point where he stopped breathing.

The corporate mook from inside the apartment had a second gun in an ankle holster and used it to put the kid's lights out. I rushed toward him, hoping to get him before he could get a shot off at me. Inside of taking target practice on my furry hide, he jumped off the roof, holding onto another rope. He hit the pavement feet first, picked up his injured partner and started picking in a pile of garbage. There was a motorcycle hidden under it. Smart move, at least if you wanted the bike to be there when you came back.

I didn't bother to go after them. They'd be around the corner before I even made the street.

Instead, I hid the guns and my bat, then retrieved my shoes to wait for the cops to arrive.

The concerned citizens had used a call box and the flatfoots made it in about twenty minutes. If people hadn't seen me, I would have disappeared right behind the corporate mooks, but the cops would get a description of an ape in a suit from the witnesses and it wouldn't exactly take a genius to track me down.

I searched through his apartment as quickly as I could, only going downstairs when I heard sirens. I stood on the street trying to look innocent when the cops pulled up. I was surprised and relieved when I recognized the detective.

O'Malley's eyes rolled when he saw me. "Borroughs, what had you gotten yourself mixed up in now?"

"A pleasure to see you again too, O'Malley." As cops went, he was one of the good ones. I gave him the run down on what happened as he checked the murder scene and the apartment.

"Purple tie and yellow hanky, huh? What's Pharmzuc got to do with this?" he asked.

"I never said they did." I'd been careful to just mention the colors, not speculate on what they meant. Most corps had lawyers on retainer ready to sue for any hint of slander, especially if it was true. "But Maccina works for them."

"The guy who lives in the apartment." I nodded. "Maybe Pharmzuc has a proactive sick day policy and had those guys come to check on Maccina."

"I wouldn't even bet your money on that," I said.

"Me neither," he said. "What do you think he's doing with the kids?"

I had been forthright with everything except the guns and what the kid said before they popped him. "Not sure," I fibbed. It sounded like the kid was going to say Maccina had found a way to fix the effects of the changing gas. It was a big leap but would explain Pharmzuc's interest. Something like that would be worth enough to buy your own city. Odds are Maccina had a contract with Pharmzuc that said they owned anything he invented. Meant that if he turned it over to them, his kids would never get to try out the treatment, mainly cause they don't pay him enough to afford what they'd charge. At the moment it was just a theory, but it made a lot of sense. "But my client wants her kids back, so I aim to find them."

"Be awful hard to do that from jail," said a voice from behind me.

O'Malley started to roll his eyes, but stopped himself and forced a smile. "Hello, Lieutenant."

Harrison ignored the greeting, instead speaking loud enough that the entourage of reporters following him in his wake couldn't help but hear. "Detective, can you explain to me why this…" Harrison was a known bigot. Probably helped him get to where he was. I wouldn't wish changing gas on anybody, but if I were forced to pick someone, Harrison would be on the top of my list to get a snootful. "Mockery of life isn't in cuffs?"

"We don't have any big enough. And his story checks out with what the witnesses tell us."

"Ordinary citizens obviously strong-armed by this monster to tell us what we wanted to hear," Harrison ranted as if preaching to his choir of reporters. Word was, he was running for city council. Guess he wanted to seem tough on crime and he hardly looked like a bully picking on somebody my size.

"But didn't Mister Borroughs stop Dr. Kronik…" My old boss, the mad scientist who put me in this body. I was a loyal lackey, except for the part about me sleeping with his wife. Some guys would have come after me with a baseball bat. Kronik put my brain in an ape. "From destroying a large part of the city at great personal cost?" This question came from Marty Molson, an old poker buddy who I gave the exclusive to. It also helped me spin things my way so I didn't end up in a zoo or worse.

"We still are looking into those allegations…"

"By we, you mean the police department is still investigating after the mayor gave Mr. Borroughs a commendation?" asked Marty.

The commendation wasn't worth the paper it was printed on. It was just a way for the mayor to get mentioned in the paper, complete with a picture where his arm was around my neck. Not like the guy would take my calls if I needed something. He was being a politician. Fugtown still had the right to vote and we had a higher turnout rate than the city as a whole. We had only one council member out of seven, but it made sure we weren't just forgotten entirely.

Harrison's eyes narrowed but his smile widened. "Of course not, it's just that we like to keep all our options open…"

Which is when the gawker showed up. O'Malley cursed, Harrison went pale and the reporters started making a miniature lightning storm with all their flashbulbs going off.

Gawkers are not exactly rare in Konundrum, but neither are they on every street corner. There are varying stories about what the little metal floating spheres really are. They tend to appear when something interesting goes down, following one of the players around. They've attached themselves to me before. I'm not thrilled about it. The general consensus is they are flying cameras, but who or what they are broadcasting back to is a matter of some debate. One popular theory is our entire world was created for the amusement of those same creators to follow some pre-ordained lifestyle. People don't like to discuss it much. Not many old folks around, but some of them claim to remember being brought here by big headed gray men. Entire religions are built around the premise. Worse,   occasionally we get tourists, visitors living vicariously through a robot who can get greeted as prophets and generally make a nuisance of themselves.

The gawkers are protected at the highest levels. Law enforcement is forbidden to interfere with them. The tourists get treated like everybody else. Of course, they have to be put in special jails as they can bend the iron bars on the traditional cells.

The gawker hovered over my left shoulder and Harrison cursed. As annoying as the gawker's arrival might be, its choosing me to follow around just gave me a get out of jail free card.

"I'll be going now," I said with a smile and a tip of my hat.

"This isn't over, monkey man," growled Harrison.

I held my wrists out. "Then take me in."

The gawker floated between me and the lieutenant, spinning back and forth. He glared at it, then me again. "You got lucky this time. Just don't leave town."

It was a dumb thing to say. As I've said, very few people who left town ever came back.

"Mr. Borroughs, anything to say about this murder?" yelled a reporter.

"Only that the ending of any life is a sad crime. Other than that, no comment at this time," I said.

The reporters wandered off to take some more pictures and interview the neighbors so they could write up their stories for the morning editions.

"I assume I'll get an exclusive?" whispered Marty.

"If there's anything worth telling," I said.

Marty nodded his head toward the gawker. "There will be."

I agreed with him and it worried me.

All I wanted to do was go home and get some sleep. I was even contemplating a shower, which said something. With the furry hide I had, drying off was an ordeal. It took at least a dozen towels and some major airtime in the buff.

Problem was I didn't want to come back empty handed to Mildred. I know she'd be watching my office anxiously and be there before I even took the key out of the lock. Besides, it was dark, which would help what I had planned next.

I had carefully lifted the kid's wallet, memorized his address from his ID and put it back. His name was Wally Millar and he lived about twelve blocks over. The chance that Maccina would be holed up there was slim but was worth checking out.

Being an ape has some advantages. For one thing, few buildings lock their roof access and scaling the side of a building is not as rough as say trying to stand upright for two hours. Millar's building was no exception, so I went to the roof, opened the door and walked down two flights. His apartment was one of four on that floor. There was a time in my previous life's youth where breaking and entering were among my skill sets. With my fingers too big to manipulate the picks well, it takes me two or three times as long to open a lock. Every second a break-in takes increases the risk of being caught and the lieutenant was gunning for me as it was. If he had evidence and a witness, even having a gawker following me wouldn't keep me out of jail so I prayed the neighbors were all sound sleepers.

The gawker had followed me up the side of the building and to the apartment. Luckily, the things have never shared what they recorded with the cops, so I didn't have to worry about it turning stool pigeon.

I heard someone in another apartment and decide to forgo the lock picks. Millar had four decent locks, but a cheap door frame. One good shove was all it took to separate the door from the jamb. I stepped inside and tried to close the door on the gawker, but the little bugger hit the wood with enough force to shove me back a foot and that's saying something. It floated inside and I shut the place up, pushing the wood together. I kept the lights off. Better not to announce my presence. There was a better than average chance the cops would be following up this lead, so I had to get in and out as quickly as possible.

It didn't take a minute to determine that Maccina and the kids weren't here. Millar wasn't exactly a good housekeeper, but at least all his bills seemed to be in the same pile. The street light outside his window was bright enough that I could read. The usual electric, heat and so on, but I found one for renting a single bay garage. Judging by his surroundings, Millar wasn't in the income bracket where owning a car, let alone a place to park it, seemed an option. I pocketed it inside my jacket. I looked around for anything else when I noticed the gawker's lens rotate toward the door. I hadn't heard anything but had been stalked by these things before. They tend to anticipate action before it happens and try to get the best angle. They can act as an early warning system, which meant someone was outside in the hall. It could be a neighbor, but more likely it was a cop. Worse, it might be the lieutenant.

I needed to leave and the door wasn't an option, so I opened the window. A man could have squeezed out, but I wasn't going to fit. I looked around for a hiding spot, but that wasn't going to work either, so I pushed the dead man's couch in front of the door to make up for the lack of a functional lock as I tried to remove the upper half of the window.

Whoever was outside tried the door. It opened slightly before being stopped by the sofa. The door rammed into it a couple of times. It seemed to be holding, so I yanked and the window came free at the same time the door was kicked in. In wasn't entirely accurate. It didn't so much come off the hinges as shatter into kindling. The sound made me turn in time to see a metal foot moving back down to the floor.

It was a damned tourist. I'm several times stronger than most men and a tourist makes me look like a ninety-eight pound weakling. Worse, this one was packing and apparently liked the idea of big game hunting and unloaded his gun at me.

I threw the window at him. The thing with the tourists is they are immune to things shy of large arms fire, but if surprised they sometimes react like they're flesh and blood. Even though the wood and glass couldn't hurt him, the bot flinched and stopped shooting.

It only lasted a second, but it was long enough for me to grab the gawker, careful not to obscure its lens with my fingers.

"I wouldn't shoot again unless you want to risk damaging your audience's window." Gawkers are bulletproof, except for the lens. "And we both know you aren't allowed to damage them." Actually, I tended to do a lot of bluffing with the tourists, but they tended to fall for it more than they didn't. They tend to be a little shaky on the finer points of human nature. "And my ape body is fast enough to use it to block any bullets." A total lie, but the tourist lowered his gun and I noticed his yellow and purple arm markings. "What's your interest in this? Why's a tourist working for

Pharmzuc?"

"Wouldn't you like to know?" it said in a male baritone with a metallic echo.

"Obviously or I wouldn't have asked," I said. Tourists tend to like to banter, although sometimes they aren't very good at it. "What's Maccina got that you want?"

"Wouldn't you like to know?" it repeated.

I rolled my eyes and turned the lens toward my face. "Not very bright, is he?"

"You're not allowed to do that!" the bot shouted. "No talking directly into the camera!"

"Not only can't he banter, but he whines a lot," I repeated into the gawker.

"Stop it!" he yelled.

"Okay, but do you really need two of you bots to get me?" I asked, pointing my chin over his shoulder. He actually fell for it and I leapt out the window and prayed the lamppost was close enough for me to grab.

It was and I managed to slide down to the sidewalk. A car was driving toward me. A mook in a tux had a blonde in a red sequined gown in his rumble seat. He was doing his best to make time, so he didn't have his entire attention on the road, which let me jump on his passenger side running board.

When the mook turned to make goo-goo eyes at the cupcake, he saw my ugly mug instead and screamed, slamming on his brakes.

"Not the best way to impress a dame. Hello, miss," I said and tipped my hat.

"Get off my car," he ordered, slamming on the brakes.

"I'd be glad to, say in a few blocks," I said. "I'd advise putting pedal to the metal unless you feel that you need to be ventilated."

"Huh?" he said.

"Drive unless you want to be shot by a tourist," I said.

"Why should I help you?" he asked.

"Because it'd be the right thing to do," I said as a gunshot rang out. "And because since I'm holding on to your car, if you don't floor it, you and this lovely lady are just as likely to get hit by a slug as me. Go!" The mook did as instructed. I figured I'd put some serious distance between me and the bot, find a place to hide for a few hours then check with the garage management when they opened. Last thing I needed is a gun totting machine following me to where the kids might be. A block later the gawker flew in the car window. "The mosquito's with me."

"Ooh," purred the cupcake. Some consider being followed by a gawker impressive, a sign of importance or celebrity. They've obviously never had the pleasure. Cupcake started making goo-goo eyes at me, putting one perfectly manicured hand on my furry arm. "I know you. You've been in the papers. You're Borroughs the man-ape."

"Just Borroughs is fine," I said.

She ran her hand up my jacketed arm to my shoulder as the car sped along the night streets. "Wow, you're so big and strong." She leaned out the window and looked down below my belt. "Are you this big all over?"

"Like you wouldn't believe." The mook realized not only was I making time with his date, but she was also supplying the hands for the watch, so he slammed on the brakes again.

"Get off," he shouted.

I looked at the cupcake and winked. "I'm trying."

The dame giggled and leaned forward so her arms were crossed on the window, giving me an unobstructed view of her balcony. It was impressive enough for Romeo to have dumped Juliet for.

The mook realized he was steady loosing control of the date and tried to remedy things. He climbed out of the car and stomped over to my side.

"I must insist you depart immediately and leave my date alone," he said.

I had just been flirting, but I hadn't had the best night and I hated this guy's type. Has more than a little money and thinks he's better than everybody. Never had to do a hard day of work or fight for anything in his life. Assumes that I'll leave just because he tells me too.

"Jamie, you're being rude," said the cupcake. In a whisper, she added, "He's famous!"

I didn't think being in the paper a few times qualified me as famous, but I didn't argue with the pretty lady.

"Shut up, Lucy," he hollered.

"I don't like your tone," I said, stepping off the running board. I had been bent almost in half to make a smaller target, so when my feet hit pavement, I instantly got taller. To add to the merriment, I made myself stand straight to really look big. "Didn't your Momma teach you to be nice to ladies, especially the gorgeous ones?"

Jamie was now considering the wisdom of his actions and had stepped back. The cupcake had stepped out of the rumble seat, excited by the prospect of two men fighting for her favor. Well, a man and an ape-man.

"Lucy, get back in the car," he yelled.

"I will not," she pouted.

"Don't make me…"

Jamie stopped short when I cleared my throat. "Don't touch the lady or I'll touch you. Hard." I emphasized my point by slamming my right fist into my left palm.

Jamie screamed like a child and turned and ran back to his side of the car. He got in and screamed, "Lucy, get in."

"In a minute…" she said to the sound of squealing tires as her date sped away. "Jamie, you pansy-waisted coward! What if he's planning to carry me off and ravish me?"

Jamie didn't even slow down.

"I can assure you, I'll do nothing of the sort," I said.

Lucy turned toward me and wrapped her arms around my right biceps and leaned against me. "Not even if I said pretty please?"

I smiled. "There'd have to be sugar on top."

"I'll give you sugar wherever you want. My apartment is just around the corner," she said.

"Lead on," I said.

She did. It was a nice part of town. Apparently, Jamie hadn't given up on his date yet, because he was parked and waiting across the street when we got there.

"Lucy, c'mon and run over here and I'll take you to my place," he shouted.

The cupcake dismissed him with a wave, but he kept calling her name.

"Jamie, go away," she said. "I'm not interested."

"What are you going to tell me you're interesting in that… thing?

Lucy laughed and reached up to pull my face down to hers. Boy, the cupcake could kiss and wasn't at all put off by the species thing. My kind of dame.

She pulled out a key to open the vestibule door. "I'm still interested in you carrying me off. My apartment's 3A. I'm done walking for the night, so the quicker you get me up there, the quicker you can get to the ravishing part."

"Your wish is my command," I said picking her up bride style.

"Too nice," she purred.

I hate to disappoint, so I threw her over my shoulder, just as Jamie came running up the steps.

"I'll save you, Lucy!"

"Go away. I don't need saving," she said.

I stepped inside and slammed the door with my foot, but Jamie got his tootsie in before it shut. Lucy let out a shriek of excitement as the wood hit his toes. It takes all kinds. I decided to ignore the stairs, instead climbing the rails and floor to go straight up the middle of the stairwell. The noises coming from my passenger made me think she had started without me.

I put her down so she could put her key in the door. It was a good neighborhood, so only two locks. We were inside before Jamie even made it to the second floor landing.

As soon as her door was closed her lips were on mine. I started to bend down. Instead, she pushed me back and leapt up. She was every bit as flexible in her limbs as she was in her choice of lover because she managed to wrap her legs around my waist.

Problem was, Jamie had made it to her door and was banging on it, begging her to give him another chance.

Lucy disengaged from me. "Would you mind getting rid of him while I change into something more comfortable?"

"Sure," I said, opening the door slowly, making sure not to give the rich guy enough room to weasel his way inside. He stopped in mid-bang. "Go away."

"Listen, I took her out to dinner and dancing at the most expensive club in Konundrum. If you think I'm going to let her take you home after that kind of investment…"

He stopped as the red sequined gown Lucy had been wearing landed on my head. It was soon followed by a matching brassiere and panties. I turned to see the cupcake standing in all her naked glory.

"I'm comfortable now," Lucy said.

I turned back to see Jamie's jaw dropped down to his chest. I grabbed his shoulder. "I'm not going to bother explaining to you how long it's been for me. Suffice it to say, if you don't leave now, I will drop you down the three flights. Head first." I shoved him toward the stairs and shut the door. It was stopped an inch from closing. I yanked open the door expecting to have to hurt the rich guy. Instead, the gawker flew in.

I shut the door as Lucy watched the floating metal ball taking in her apartment, then stopping to focus its attention on her.

"Is that thing going to watch and broadcast everything we do?" she asked.

I sighed and got ready to hit the pavement. I knew this was too good to be true. "Yes."

Lucy wiggled over to me and my trousers became far too tight. "Good," she said grabbing hold of my necktie and pulling me into her bedroom.

I woke the next morning happier than I'd been in a long while. I tried to sneak out without waking Lucy, but the creaking of her bedroom door woke her.

"You weren't going to leave without saying goodbye, were you?" she asked.

"You looked too pretty to wake." Lines like that worked when I was a man, but Lucy's creased brows told me the effectiveness was dramatically decreased by my built-in fur coat. "Bye." I waved meekly.

Lucy grabbed my tie and pulled me in for a kiss. It was short and sweet, nothing like the lip locks of the night before.

"Come back and see me," she said. Her apparent sincerity took me back, but her next statement cleared everything up. "And make sure the gawker comes with you."

I left, the gawker floating behind me as I hit the sidewalk. "Most of the time I can live without you little guys, but thanks." The gawker made no reaction and I headed to the garage management company, which turned out to be nothing more than a granny in a knitted shawl with a fancy business name and a seven bay garage. The withered fossil was all of ninety pounds and needed a wooden cane to answer the door. It became pretty clear that she hated freaks.

"Monstrosities like you should have the decency to stay down in Fugtown away from real people," she said, waving the cane at me. Spotting the gawker, she proved to have a quick swing as she managed to swat it. "And that goes for floating cameras filming good folks for your gray masters."

"Some people are only monsters on the outside while others are pretty ugly inside," I said.

"I don't care what the gas did to a tesque's innards," she spat, entirely missing my point. "And I ain't going to tell you which one of my spaces is Mr. Millar's."

I peered into her backyard. Her rental space company consisted of some old industrial space that had been converted to seven car slots. Her neighborhood was several steps above mine, but still, nothing that would allow the neighbors to own autos, so she probably rented to people for storage. One had a light peering out through a crack in newspapers that had been taped to the windows.

"Well, I certainly have learned my lesson. I will return to Fugtown, with my head held low in shame for having met you," I said.

"At least you learned something," she said, slamming the door.

I stepped down but knew enough not to go directly to her backyard. The old biddy was watching me through a crack in her curtains, so I walked down the block then doubled back through the neighbors' backyards and hid for a few minutes to made sure the biddy wouldn't be watching. I used the time to pry off the trigger guard on the snub nose to make it useable for my oversized fingers.

Each garage of the seven garage doors had a regular door cut into it, with the same sections so it could lower and raise or open. I pulled on the one with the light. It was locked but cheaply made. Shoddy workmanship is so helpful in my line of work. A quick yank was all it took to force open the door, but what I saw stopped me short.

I found the kids, unless there was another set of twins with tentacles for arms. Each was strapped to their own examination tables. Maccina stood between them, enough chemistry beakers and glassware to make a mad scientist jealous behind him, a large syringe in his hand.

I was shocked. I really hadn't thought he'd hurt his kids. He was a mid-level chemist—there was no way he came up with a real cure. No telling what the concoction would do to them and if it was going to help them, why'd he strap them down? "Maccina, put the needle down." I had the snub nose out and pointed between his eyes.

"Stay away! I'm doing what's best for my boys," he said.

"Hurting them isn't best," I said.

"I'm not hurting them, I'm giving them back their lives."

I didn't buy it. I could hit the broadside of a barn, but might not get the plank I was aiming at. A shot may stop him, but it might hit Timmy or Tommy.

A second latter I was knocked to my knees. The tourist had found Maccina too and hadn't bothered to try the little door, kicking in a whole section with its metal legs.

"Maccina, give me the syringe," bellowed the tourist through its mouth speakers. Its gun was now trained on the man and I was going to guess the possessed bot was a better shot than me. I suddenly realized this was a different tourist. For one thing, it was all silver, no purple or yellow markings. For another, it was like an older beat up bot version, popular when I was a kid.

With a revving engine, the Pharmzuc mooks showed up. One put a link of chain around the bot's metal chest, the other end of which was attached to their motorcycle. The driver took off pulling the tourist behind them. He was the mook I had fallen on and he moved like his ribs were taped.

The lassoing mook threw a grenade into the garage. Maccina and I both saw it. I could see him start to throw himself on it, but then he realized it wouldn't do any good. It was a gas grenade. Maccina injected the entire contents of the syringe into the boy he was closest to, then went back to the bench and tried to refill it from a test tube as the purple and yellow marked tourist clanked in and charged him.

The grenade started to leak green mutizen gas. I'd like to say I rushed the bot and got the man and the boys out, but it'd be a lie. I did try to pull the boy closest to me out, but the table was bolted to the floor. As the cloud of green gas grew larger, I ran out. Holding my breath wouldn't have done any good—it could seep in through skin pores.

I did grab the granny's hose. The corporate mook who had stayed behind tried to jump me. In the open spaces of the yard, the advantage was mine and I simply grabbed him in mid-leap and spun, tossing him into the mist-shrouded garage. It was a nasty fate, but he had been the one tossing the grenade.

The gas becomes inert when it comes into contact with water. As much as I hated getting wet, it beat growing a second head or worse, so I hosed myself down and poured as much water down my mouth and nose as I could stand. Not too hard. Gorilla nostrils aren't designed to block water. An ape could actually drown just from having his head under water. Luckily I learned to cope somewhat, but swimming would always be dangerous for me. I turned the hose on the garage at full blast, using my thumb to spread the spray. I guess granny was too cheap to buy a nozzle.

As if summoned by the thought, Granny ran out of the house toward the open garage bay.

"Don't go in there," I shouted.

"Freaks shouldn't be seen or heard," she said. The glasses that earlier were on the tip of her nose now lay on a string around her neck, so I was guessing she couldn't see the gas clouds, but she saw well enough to rap my knuckles with her cane as she went by. The unexpected blow made me drop the hose and a cloud of the gas drifted up toward her face. Her next inhalation made her collapse, about five feet from the door.

I didn't much care for the old biddy, but even she didn't deserve to be gassed. I picked up the hose and turned the water on her. It may have helped some, but it was too late. Her skin started turning into something somewhere between the consistency of onions and feathers.

I turned the hose back on the garage, aiming for where the grenade had been. Inside there was much screaming and the sounds of glass breaking. The lights went out and the screaming got worse. As the cloud started to shrink I turned the spray on the twins, hoping to spare them. I had no idea what a second exposure would do, but I doubted it was anything nice.

The tourist came out of the mist, one metal hand stained red, laughing at me. Our eyes locked.

"Don't go anywhere," I said.

"We both know how this will end Borroughs, so you have a choice. I'm sure I still have traces of mutizen on me. Ever wonder how a different primate would react to the changing gas? It'd be interesting. So you can let me go or try to stop me. Life or death, what will it be?"

"The kids still alive?" I asked.

"Don't know. Didn't check," it said, walking past me

"This isn't over, tourist," I yelled, aiming more water at the boys.

"It isn't? How ever will I sleep tonight?" it said. "But we will see each other again."

"You got a name?" I said.

"Why? You want to whisper sweet nothings in my ear?"

"Nope. Want to make sure I kill the right pile of gears," I said.

"But I'll still be fine. You can call me Sava."

The bot pumped his metal legs and disappeared. I stayed where I was, making like a firefighter for another twenty minutes until I didn't see any trace of the gas, making sure my furry hide or suit never got dry.

I tried to get up the nerve to risk going inside. Before I could, I heard metallic footsteps behind me. I spun expecting Sava. Instead, I got the second tourist.

"Damn, I'm too late," it said.

"For what?" I asked.

"To save the cure," it said, stepping up to the edge of the dark garage when something dark and scaly ran out. It stopped to glare at me, before heading to the street. It had the remnants of a purple tie around its neck.

The bot walked inside, its eyes lighting up like twin flashlights. Its first stop was the back of the garage where it knelt next to the body of Al Maccina. At least I assumed it was. It was hard to recognize, not because of the effects of the mutizen, but because his head had been ripped away from his body, which stayed strangely human. The gas can change even the flesh on corpses so long as they weren't too long dead.

The tourist turned its eyebeams on the twins. The one on the left was now a mass of tentacles, his entire body purple, his face barely recognizable. As horrible as that was, it was near as shocking as his brother. His tentacles were gone—he was entirely human.

"How…" I stuttered.

"Did Maccina inject him with anything?" the tourist asked.

"Yeah, a syringe." The bots eyebeams turned on a mess of glass shards scattered around a plastic plunger. "He got it out of a test tube."

The tourist scanned the remains of the chemical lab. The glass had been ground to powder and any chemicals had been washed away down the drain in the cement floor from the constant stream of water.

"I'll never figure out how he did it," said the bot.

"Did what?" I asked.

"Al Maccina developed an antidote to mutizen. It was supposed to be impossible, especially for the controlled science of a playworld. Mutizen was outlawed, but playworlds fall outside the treaties. This could have helped so many instead of just one boy." The tourist looked right at the gawker. "If you would have spared one of your little eyes to follow him, we'd all know the cure, but no, science isn't exciting enough unless it goes boom."

The gawker was unimpressed and the tourist left. I unstrapped the boys. Turns out Timmy was the one that got worse and Tommy got cured. I took them outside and hosed them down some more. I took all our clothes off and burned them with enough kerosene that they lit despite the water. I wrapped Tommy with a shirt from the old ladies house. Timmy tentacles did the job sadly. His eyes seemed unaffected if all his tears were any judge. I wrapped myself in an old bed sheet toga style. As we left, the old biddy had gotten to her feet. My squirting her must have helped because she wasn't too bad, just her face and one arm got changed.

She was looking at her twisted limb, screaming and crying.

I stepped over to her. "If you need help, come to Fugtown. Unlike so called real people, most of us try to help each other."

Her screaming only got worse as I took the boys home.

PUT YOUR DEMON ON MY SHOULDER

A Little Insanity Featuring Lunay

"**D**octor, do you think I'm crazy?" asked the frazzled blonde, leaning in the chair and trying to scoot away from her own left shoulder. The shoulder, unwilling to be left behind, followed her. So did the thing perched upon it like a bird from Hell. Cindy's eyes twitched involuntarily as they fell closed from exhaustion. She forced them open. Sleep had eluded her much more successfully than she had her shoulder.

"Cindy, what's more important is do you think you're crazy?" asked Dr. Hill. Hill was the type of shrink who would have sported a carved pipe if his work environment hadn't prohibited smoking, not because he enjoyed the effects of burning tobacco, but because he thought it made him look sage. A pipe lay in his top drawer waiting for him to get the courage to try it again after the last time, although in retrospect trying it out on a woman who was trying to cope with the death of her father from smoking a pipe in bed and her own narrow escape from the burning house was probably not the wisest choice. Sadly, Hill hadn't realized the extent of his error until the patient emptied an entire fire extinguisher on him and his pipe. He lost two patients that day, the one he was treating and the one who got nervous by the woman running screaming from his office, followed by him rushing after her, his body and clothes made white from the chemicals in the extinguisher. It turns out he was coming because he thought he was seeing a ghost and thought Hill was mocking him. He tried to pass both incidents off as aversion therapy, but that day nobody was buying what he was selling.

Cindy's eyes rebelled against her strict orders to avoid looking directly at Gaz, in hopes that if she ignored him the winged and horned creature with the Buddha belly would go away. So far the way of the ostrich was failing her miserably because he was still sitting on her shoulder and now he was smiling and waving.

"Don't look at me. I think you're perfectly sane," said the shoulder demon. "Of course I think disaster videos are funny. You just have to remember that crazy is just a state of mind. Or in your case 'mine.'" The doll-sized creature's laugh sounded forced, and his elbow nudging her neck didn't exactly lend him an air of sincerity. Then again, few who knew him would lend Gaz anything they ever wanted to see again. Even among his fellow shoulder demons, he was hardly considered popular, although it still stopped short of being ostracized. Gaz didn't much like his job, but the nether world had a shortage of demons, so they had to make do with what they had. Gaz was mean-spirited and annoying but was far less evil than his fellows. Not that this was any comfort to Cindy as the tiny demon put his feet up on her neck and pulled her collar around him like a blanket. "Sheesh, you'd think with all his hot air I wouldn't be cold."

"Yes, I do think I'm crazy," she answered, yanking her collar back. Cindy was a very private person and having this creature with her constantly was overwhelming. Although she could grab things that he tried to move, she had yet been unable to touch the demon. He was too fast. The first few times it was like a cartoon, with Gaz maneuvering so when he dodged, she would hit herself. The demon found this hilarious, his human hostess not so much. Cindy had never believed in violence, but she wished for just one good shot to wipe the smirk off his little face.

This time was no different. Cindy tried to swat the demon, but he leapt over her hand and landed in her hair.

"Oh no, I'm stuck," he said. Cindy knew he was faking it, but the anger inside her couldn't take the chance that he really was immobilized. As fast as her limbs could move, she smacked at him with both hands, but no matter how swiftly or hard she hit, Gaz wasn't there. The demon evaded each swipe with artful moves reminiscent of a rhino ballerina. Cindy ended up hitting herself in the head repeatedly and messing her blond strands.

After viewing this display, anyone else would have concurred with her belief in her own insanity. However, Dr. Hill merely sat and waited until her little fit passed, choosing to ignore it as if nothing out of the ordinary had happened. Hill's philosophy was big on not making his patients feel out of sorts. If a client came in with a bloody cleaver and a severed human head, he'd offer them coffee and chat about the weather until they felt comfortable discussing why they were subscribing too literally to the two heads are better than one philosophy. "Well, I think we've found part of your issue. If you were crazy, you probably wouldn't know it. I think it was Poe who wrote something to the effect that the only difference between a genius and a madman is the genius knows he's a madman."

"This quack's not playing with a full deck himself if he thinks you're a genius," mocked Gaz. "You can't even balance your check book."

"That's because you keep hiding it on me," whispered Cindy. "I'm sorry Dr. Hill. You were explaining to me why I know I'm crazy."

"Actually, we don't like to use terms like crazy anymore. I prefer judgment impaired or troubled."

"Apparently the quack thinks crazy is like ice cream. There's all kinds of flavors," said the shoulder demon. "Think of me as Rocky Road."

"I'd prefer if you were ice cream," whispered Cindy.

Dr. Hill had let the first statement slide but decided to address the second. "Why would you prefer I was a frozen confection?" Hill loved reading into odd things his clients, or people in general, said. He envisioned himself a vast intelligent, able to glean vast and arcane knowledge from simple statements. More often than not he was wrong, but this didn't shake his grasp on his reality or his absolute conviction that he was always brilliant and insightful. Hill didn't even have an inkling that more often than not he was projecting his own views onto someone else's words and then loading his questions to get the answers he wanted.

"Not you, Doctor," said Cindy, glaring at her left shoulder and wishing she could detach it from her body and run away from it. Sadly, he was convinced the demon would only pick up the limb and chase after her, reattaching it when he caught her. "Him."

Hill did her the courtesy of looking at her shoulder, but he saw nothing, not realizing Gaz was real and invisible to others. On the way back he stole a look down the cleavage of her blouse, two buttons of which had come undone while she was swatting at her hair. Hill debated about telling her, deciding against it, telling himself that she must want him to look otherwise she would redo the shirt. The idea that she was unaware of her exposed skin because she was too distracted by her problem never occurred to him.

"Your shoulder demon is talking to you." Cindy nodded. "He thinks he's ice cream?"

"Yeah, baby. Somebody double dip me in chocolate and lick me clean," shouted the demon. It was loud enough that the doctor thought he heard something but quiet enough that the feeling passed without a second thought. The doctor didn't bother much with thoughts of the second variety anyway, which may have been a blessing of sorts since his first ones tended toward the vapid and self-serving varieties.

"No, he thinks you're just using words to describe mental illness as ice cream flavors. He also thinks you're a quack," said Cindy. "And he wants to be licked."

The psychologist bristled at the criticism. "Judgmental for a figment of your imagination, isn't he?" And kinky he thought. Hill wasn't above sleeping with a patient, but he only did it if he was certain it was for her own good. He was a licensed professional after all. Because of that, he always knew his judgment was right. Plus it saved him money at the Honey Shack; especially since he convinced Jiggly she needed very special therapy. Hill claimed to be able to read her unconscious desires from watching her dance routines, which he insisted she do for him, one a session. Hill also had the stripper convinced he could read her psyche by observing up close and personal the nuances of her lap dances. And since Jiggly had no insurance, he charged her for each session. It never bothered him that she paid in singles. Of course, he often used role reversal and had her pay for his services by dressing up in one of her outfits and dancing for her. He claimed that this exercise was about empowering her, giving her back what her job took away, but the truth was he rather enjoyed it. But the therapy didn't end there.

Jiggly often shared when she was thinking of sleeping with one of her generous or good-looking clients. Hill always convinced her it was always a bad idea for anyone to sleep with a client and that it would also take away from her the empowerment they had worked so hard on. Hill went so far as to suggest that Jiggly not sleep with any men because so much of her self worth was wrapped up in being a sex object that the actual act would weaken her entire psyche. Jiggly went on to explain that she still had needs, so Hill said he was willing to let her satisfy those needs with him, in the safe place they had made together so she could go to work and through life with a clear mind. Jiggly had a lot of needs. Sometimes they had to do emergency sessions at three in the morning when she got out of work, but Hill never complained or addressed the issue of why he was breaking the no sex with clients rule that he insisted she enforce on herself.

Hill turned his attention away from visions of Jiggly and back to the woman in front of him. His eyes went directly back to her cleavage. Cindy was attractive, although not quite as overly top heavy as Jiggly. More perky, though. Still, if things worked out, maybe he could convince her to pay a visit to Jiggly's plastic surgeon. The man did amazing and gravity defying work. Hill wondered if the man added helium to the implants to give them that extra lift.

Unbeknownst to Hill, Gaz continued to mock him. "Judgmental isn't he? At least I'm not a quack. Hey, Cindy honey, you should knee him in the balls and walk out. Then lick me."

"No," she whispered.

Dr. Hill raised an eyebrow and became angry at the rejection, forgetting for a moment that he hadn't suggested out loud that sleeping with him might help her delusions. But his self-espoused professionalism came through again as he realized what she was responding to and jumped back into the conversation with both feet, barely avoiding a social verbal banana peel. "No, he's not judgmental?"

Cindy turned back to the doctor, feeling like three of her five-fingered grasp on reality had slipped down. She wanted to apologize and have Hill tell her she was going to be all right. Cindy strained to have sanity spill out through her eyes while holding back her tears, but what she got was embarrassment radiating out through her cheeks. "I wasn't speaking to you."

"That seems rather rude. Especially since I'm here trying to help you," chided Hill. He could abide a patient in parts of a corpse, but not being dismissed as anything less than the most important person in the room.

"Ha, at two hundred an hour he's in no hurry to help anyone but his bottom line," said Gaz, licking his arm first and then his leg. "Phooey. My tongue's not big enough. And there's no chocolate sauce."

Cindy hadn't yet mastered the art of having two conversations at once; especially since only one of the other parties was even aware there were three of them involved. It was even harder when the smaller of the two started licking her ear and something deep inside told her the other one wanted to do the same.

The tiny demon ran his tiny forked tongue around her stud earring again. "See what I mean? It's not the same as a big tongue like yours. I think I have tongue envy. Maybe I should see someone about that? Think Hill has an opening later today?" The demon leapt off and started riffling through the appointment book on the windowsill behind the shrink. "Hmm, you know this guy's got no male clients. And he consistently blocks out two slots for someone named Jiggly."

With her shoulder briefly uninhabited, she leaned forward. "How can you help me if you don't believe me?"

Hill held out a pen, which was proportionally the size of a broomstick to the demon. Gaz jumped to the shrink's chair then leaned all the way back like he was going to go under a broom at a kid's party, before leaping the eight feet back to his shoulder perch.

"Limbo time," he said. "Your turn. How low can you go, toots? Well, lower than limbo is hell. Been, there, done that. Incinerated the t-shirt."

Cindy struggled to ignore her shoulder demon as he started singing the limbo song.

"Dr. Hill, if you don't believe me, why should I even bother coming?"

"You tell him, toots. If you're too squeamish about the groin thing, give him a Moe, Larry, and Curly special right in the eyes. If you manage to poke one out, I'll even eat it for you. Better than ice cream. Good licking there no matter the size of your tongue. Still not as tasty as chocolate, but sometimes one has to make do."

"I believe that you believe there is a demon on your shoulder," said Dr. Hill, unaware of how patronizing his tone actually was.

"But not that's he's really there," said Cindy, her face dropping faster than the stock markets on a bad news day.

Dr. Hill gave her his number seven smile, designed to project empathy, totally unaware of the design flaw that ensured it came across as condescending. "Demons are a part of the Judeo-Christian mythology. Many people draw on them for their psychos… judgment impairments."

"Impairments my scaly ass. He was going to say psychosis. I love hypocrites," said Gaz. "He doesn't care about you. Quacker doesn't want to help you, just string you along until the insurance and your cash run out. And I think he's got the hots for you. He keeps looking down your blouse. Who can blame him? I mean, that little taste of boobage is nothing. I've seen you in the shower and you've got it going on." The demon did indeed follow her into the shower. For a time, she bathed in a bikini, but he was still there when she took it off to change into dry clothes. Cindy took to trying to dress under a blanket, but Gaz burrowed underneath it, claiming to have a flashlight. It had gotten to the point were she only showered when the smell got to her, and then only in the dark. Luckily she had recognized the feel of the feminine hair remover and not used it instead of her conditioner. The demon denied switching the bottles, but she knew better. Fortunately, she had caught the switch the time he swapped out her hemorrhoid creme for the toothpaste.

"But demons are not real," lectured Dr. Hill, still secure in his delusion that he was far smarter than any of his patients. It actually shocked him that some of them didn't recognize it from the get go. "The idea that demons cause injury or mental illness went out during the dark ages."

"And don't think we don't appreciate it, Doc. Makes my job a helluva lot easier," said Gaz.

"But why don't I have a shoulder angel to counter him?" asked Cindy.

"An excellent question. Why don't you tell me?" asked Dr. Hill.

"Cause I ate him. Tasty and the feathers tickled my throat," said the shoulder demon, not bothering to explain that the side of the angels was having an even worse personal shortage than his side. And rather than leave someone neglected like Hell did, they shifted one angel around between several people. Each one had hundreds of people to watch out for. The shoulder angels were overworked to the point of exhaustion. It was nothing for Gaz to duck away during the angel's inspection time. Otherwise, the feathered killjoy would be forced to stay and combat Gaz directly.

"You're supposed to tell me," pleaded Cindy

Hill leaned forward, putting his hand on Cindy's knee. Gaz ran down, jumping and pointing. "He's making his move. Don't worry, I'll stop him."

The tiny demon bent over Hill's index finger and opened his jaws as if to bite him. Cindy slapped at Gaz in an attempt to stop the demon, but he leapt away so she ended up hitting Hill's hand. The shrink pulled back, feeling like a kid caught trying to put his hand up the cookie jar's skirt.

When in doubt Hill stuck with what worked, so he ignored what he thought was a rebuff. "That's not how this works. I'm here to help you find the answers inside yourself."

"He's not supposed to be getting inside that," said Gaz.

"Let's try something else. What does the demon say about the lack of an angel?" asked Dr. Hill.

"That he ate him."

"I see. And why would he eat your angel?"

"Cause I was hungry, you quack," said Gaz. "And he wouldn't lick me. I need a good licking."

"Because he was hungry," said Cindy.

"Splendid! Hunger is a need. So your evil id…"

"Here comes the psychobabble," said Gaz. "Bah, bah, bah."

"Devoured your good super-ego," said Dr. Hill.

"Who's secretly a mild mannered idiot shrink who hasn't looked at any new theories since Freud," said Gaz.

"But he's really there," insisted Cindy.

Dr. Hill looked deep into her eyes with what he thought was equal parts compassion and sex appeal. What he achieved was far closer to creepy. Fortunately for him, Cindy was too concerned about keeping an eye on Gaz to notice. "If he was there, I should be able to touch him, no?"

"Why? I can't. He moves too fast," said Cindy, unable to accept Hill's logic.

"May I?" said Dr. Hill, holding his right hand up. Cindy nodded and he reached for her left shoulder. The demon jumped, flipped and ducked, totally avoiding any contact with the doctor's hand as it passed back and forth over her collarbone. "Nothing, see."

"He moved," said Cindy. Dr. Hill nodded, but there was no compassion or understanding in the motion, just annoyance that his patient wouldn't just take his word as absolute truth. "Why won't you believe me? He's constantly telling me to do bad things, hurt other people."

"But that's nothing but your id rising up and demanding to be heard. Just because a little voice tells you to do something doesn't mean you have to listen."

"But he's always talking. I can't sleep. I can't hold a normal conversation…"

"Not like your conversations were that normal to begin with," said Gaz.

"You're doing fine with me," said Dr. Hill.

"But he keeps interrupting," she said.

"Is he telling you to hurt me? Or lick me?" he added hopefully.

"Not now, but earlier…" Cindy hesitated.

"He wanted you to lick me? Maybe we should confront this licking obsession head on. Sometimes doing something can make it seem less frightening," suggested Hill.

"Not me, he doesn't want me to be licked. He wants to be licked," she said.

"And by he, you mean you," Hill said. "As I said, I'm here to help you confront this head on and if that means helping you lick your problem or licking you—wherever your demon demands—I'm willing to go that extra mile."

For the first time during their session, Cindy ignored Gaz to turn her full attention on her psychiatrist and she didn't like what she saw.

"Hey, the quack's trying to hone in on my action," said the demon. "If anyone's getting licked, it's going to be me."

"Whatever it is he said, you can tell me. This is a safe place. Our place," said Dr. Hill.

"He said I should kick you in the balls." The psychiatrist crossed his legs protectively.

Hill smiled. "You seem to be awfully focused on my groin area."

"It's not me!"

"Of course. What did he say next?"

"He suggested I poke out your eye."

"Why? Did he give you a reason?" asked Hill.

"He wanted to eat it. Said it was better than ice cream. And he keeps yelling that he wants someone to lick him. With chocolate sauce."

"Again with the licking. I think I see the root of your problem. How is your sex life?" asked Dr. Hill, wondering if he had any chocolate syrup anywhere in the office.

"Nonexistent. Too hard to get in the mood with him going on."

Hill remembered a chocolate bar in his desk, but how to melt it down and make it seem therapeutic was stumping him. "Perhaps the yelling about being licked…"

"Don't even go there," said Cindy warned, finally noticing Hill's eyes looking into her cleavage. Realizing her blouse was undone, she quickly buttoned it.

Hill frowned at the closing of his private peep show but wasn't giving up on his patient, or his fantasy, just yet. "Okay. Is he telling you anything now? Like what flavor of ice cream I am?"

"No," said Gaz. "But I will make a suggestion about what you should do to the quack." The shoulder demon leaned in to whisper in her ear, pointed to a large crystal award on the shelf that came to a very sharp point and moved his arm in an animated fashion.

By the time Cindy finished relaying the rest of Gaz's intentions, Hill was already on the phone to Tumult to arrange for a twenty-four hour observation and commitment.

Cindy was an administrative assistant. At her job she knew the ins and outs better than anyone, which was how she was still able to function. She liked a certain amount of control of her environment, but that was now gone. Hospitals were a foreign land that her only guide to was her memory of medical television shows. Asylums were more akin to an alien world, although Dr. Hill had corrected her when she read the sign over the wrought iron gate "Tumult Asylum" Hill told her not to use that term, that she should call it a "judgment readjustment center".

It was an imposing stone building built over a century ago. Cindy had barely arrived on the grounds before she regretted coming. True, she had agreed to go, but only because Hill assured her that it was the best place to get help.

It was too late to undo the decision because she had signed the paperwork. Dr. Hill said she was a danger to herself and others and that he would commit her with or without her consent. Hill told her it would look better for her if she went voluntarily when in truth he was more concerned about himself. Hill could get in trouble with the state board for refusing to see a patient and he couldn't pawn her off on a colleague without disclosing why. By having her committed to Tumult Asylum that problem became moot. Dr. Termagant had no issues taking over cases of those committed to his facility, even the extreme cases. In fact, he often insisted on it. Dr. Hill had mentioned on multiple occasions to Termagant that he should change the facility's name to something less harsh than asylum, but the director always ignored his comments.

Hill introduced Cindy to the director, wished her well, but stopped short of running for the door although he could have been mistaken for a race walker as he made his exit.

"Welcome to Tumult, Ms. Hanford," said Termagant. "I hope you enjoy your stay with us."

"Like you have a choice," said Gaz. Termagant turned his head slightly so his eyes were pointed right at the shoulder demon. The doctor's sudden turn toward him caused Gaz to become quiet. There were those who could hear him without him making an effort, but none could see him unless he let them. He was just going to have to watch himself around Termagant.

"I just want to get better," said Cindy.

"And break up our special friendship," Gaz whispered, still aware of the doctor's proximity, unwilling to risk being heard. The revelation that another could hear him would weaken the demon's hold on his host.

"I know you do and that's half the battle," said Termagant. "I'm not sure if Dr. Hill explained to you, we tend to be a little unorthodox in our practices. We still utilize things like electroshock therapy." Cindy pulled back. Gaz climbed to the top of her head and convulsed as if a strong current was surging through his little body before falling to the ground. Cindy let her eyes dart down, hoping to see a tiny and unmoving corpse, but Gaz had brushed himself off and was climbing her pant leg.

Unaware of the drama unfolding in front of him, Termagant gave a comforting laugh after seeing Cindy back away. "It's not for everybody, but it is almost like a restart button for some of our bipolar patients. We also believe in medication, as well as eastern herbs. We'll do whatever it takes to make our patients better. If traditional methods fail, I'd even be willing to try an exorcism."

Cindy's pupils became very wide. Gaz chuckled. "Would that work? It's not possessing me, just annoying me."

Termagant shrugged. "It might, although due to the validity of the procedure or your belief in it I can't say, but if it solves the problem, it doesn't matter does it?"

"No, it doesn't," Cindy agreed. "So you believe me about the shoulder demon."

"To paraphrase the bard, there are more things in heaven and earth than are dreamt of in my philosophy. While I find it highly unlikely, I do not dismiss the idea because there is a chance, however slight, that what you think is the reality may, in fact, be true. What I would like is to try and convince you that the problem is indeed in your mind, while still giving you a chance to convince me otherwise. Sound fair?"

"Yes," she replied, hopeful for the first time in ages.

"Let me take you on a tour of your new home," said Termagant. "You'll be limited to your ward, including the dining and rec areas."

As they passed a heavy steel door with a small but thick window, Cindy looked inside. A woman with long black hair noticed her and started to struggle with her straightjacket. "You have padded cells?"

Termagant nodded. "They are necessary sometimes. Come, let me show you the rec area."

As they walked away, Cindy looked back to see the woman at the window waving, the now undone strap trailing from her covered arm and a goofy smile on her face. Dr. Termagant took Cindy's arm and led her around the corner so she missed seeing the woman jimmy the cell door to open it, her straightjacket straps trailing behind her as she skipped through the corridors.

"I have an appointment, so I'm going to leave you here. Please feel free to join in any of the games, watch TV, read or just sit. I'll send someone for you in two hours to bring you to our appointment," said Termagant.

"Ooh, he's leaving you in the loony bin. On the plus side, the rest of them are crazier than you," said Gaz.

Cindy looked around the room nervously. There was a man who was pulling his hair out and eating it, yet didn't seem to have a bald spot. A woman in the corner was talking to a potted plant and explaining to it that the world was going to end. Another male was covered head to toe in aluminum foil. An old woman was beating a teddy bear with a toothbrush.

"I'm not sure about this," said Cindy. "I think I'd rather wait in my room."

"I'm sorry, but your room won't be ready for a while. And because you were admitted as a possible danger to yourself and others, we have to keep you under observation, so you have to stay here. But don't worry, you'll be fine. And you have Biff," said Termagant, indicating a very large man dressed all in white who stood next to the only open door with a look on his face that not only made him look constipated but angry about it.

"Don't sweat it toots. You're among your people now," said Gaz. "Let out your inner crazy."

Termagant left without noticing the woman in the straightjacket who had ducked behind a silver medicine cart until he had passed by. As soon as the coast was clear she stood and went to the door and reached to Biff's far shoulder. He turned and she rushed past him, which somehow he seemed not to notice.

The woman looked around and sat across from Cindy. "Hi, my name's Lunay."

"Loony?" asked Cindy, trying hard not to stare at the straightjacket.

"Lu-Nay," corrected the woman.

"I'm Cindy."

Lunay held her hand up to be shaken. Cindy stared at the long sleeve that covered her fingers.

"Oops, sorry," Lunay said, writhing and quickly pulling the straightjacket over her head, revealing a green t-shirt with a yellow star on it. "It's just so comfortable I forget I have it on."

"What a loony," said Gaz.

She turned and looked straight at the shoulder demon. "I already told you it's Lunay."

Gaz's jaw dropped open. So did Cindy's.

"You can see him?" she said.

"Little brownish red guy, horns, wings, big beer gut, not terribly attractive?" said Lunay.

"Hey!" said Gaz.

Lunay leaned forward, her index finger over her lips. "Shush! This is girl talk here."

Too stunned at being not only seen but dismissed, Gaz found himself speechless for the first time in centuries.

Which is when a man dressed in yellow came over, bobbing his head up and around Cindy, who cringed away.

"Don't worry about him. That's Cannibal Pete. He's harmless," said Lunay.

Cindy's pupils got almost as wide as her irises as she leapt up and ran five feet away to cower behind a support beam. "How is a cannibal harmless?"

"Easy, Pete thinks he's a chicken," said Lunay. "As long as you don't have feathers and a beak, you'll be fine."

Pete clucked by way of confirmation and strutted away.

Clutching her chest, Cindy hesitantly sat back down. "I don't like this place. I want to leave."

"Crazy is as crazy does," said Gaz.

Lunay's hand shot out before Gaz could react and grabbed the tiny demon so only his head and wings stuck out above her fist.

"What part of girl talk didn't you understand?" Lunay reached over with her other hand and made pinching motions at the level of Gaz's groin. "Unless you want to become a lady?"

"No," squeaked and stammered Gaz. "I'll be quiet."

"Good," said Lunay, putting him back on Cindy's shoulder and brushing off his shoulders.

"You can catch him! And hold him! I've been trying for months and couldn't," said Cindy.

"It's all in the wrist. Sometimes it leaks out and I have to wash my hands," said Lunay.

Torn between fear and hope she asked, "Could you get rid of him?"

"I'm not a hitman. Or hitwoman. Although for a while I may have been a hitmaker."

"You don't have to kill him. Can you just get him to leave me alone?"

"You don't like having a friend with you constantly? It seems great. I'm alone a lot of the time, locked away in my room. I talk to myself, but sometimes I forget to answer and get mad at myself so I stop speaking to me which makes me sad because no matter where I go, there I am, stuck in my cell."

"You got out okay," said Cindy.

"I can do that when I remember there's stuff outside of the padded walls. I forget sometimes. Unfortunately, I have trouble multi-tasking," Lunay said. "And when I'm not speaking to myself, I can hardly remind me, now can I?"

"I guess not, but trust me, I rather be alone," said Cindy. "Would you take him away from me, please?"

Lunay turned to Gaz. "Would you like to come stay with me and talk to me when I won't speak to me?"

"Lick me!" said Gaz defiantly.

"Okay." Lunay leaned forward, her tongue brushing up along the tiny demon from belly to face like a puppy.

The demon suddenly felt lightheaded and happy. "What was that? I feel different. What did you do to me?"

"When I touch people, things change, especially their perceptions. Not their underwear though. I have to draw the line somewhere. Like right there," said Lunay, pointing to the wall where a blue line squiggled across the sheetrock.

"Like what?" asked Cindy.

"I think she drew the line over there," whispered Gaz.

"Exactly. Not my best work, but it is from my blue and 2D period. But I am an artist and I have to draw what the muse demands of me." Lunay leaned in close and whispered, "Otherwise she hides my crayons. For some reason, they don't like me to have pens and pencils. Or scissors."

"I can't imagine why someone would want to keep sharp and pointy objects away from you," said Gaz.

"Me neither," said Lunay, jumping up so she spun in the air. Stopping in front of Cindy, she put her finger over her lips in the universal shush position, making pinching motions at Gaz's demonhood. He quickly crossed his legs and covered himself with his hands.

The little dance was enough for Biff to finally take notice that she was in the rec room. The supervisor stomped over to her.

"Lunay, what are you doing out of your room?" Biff demanded.

"I hoped to be rumba-ing but there's no music," said Lunay, when the wall speakers started to blare music. She grabbed the orderly and dragged him around for a few dance steps.

"Stop that," he said, slapping her hands away from him.

"How's the constipation? The prune whip working?" asked Lunay.

"No," grumbled Biff. "And don't change the subject."

"Okay," she said, pushing the orderly's belly button with her index finger. "Beep."

Biff's face quickly changed expression and Cindy could actually see his buttocks clench. The orderly sprinted to the men's room. Gaz trailed after him, disappeared inside and came back out a few moments later.

"His butt is now the Niagara Falls of crap. That was awesome!" said the demon.

"Just trying to help. There's a trigger point in the rectus abdominis muscle that can cause diarrhea," said Lunay, suddenly turning her head and running off. "What pretty butterflies."

"We're indoors. There are no…" Cindy stopped speaking when she saw butterflies flocking around the crazy woman, including purple and yellow zebra stripes, and metallic gold colors she had never seen before. She realized a woman at the crafts table had been cutting them out from different types of paper and had blown them up into the air. "Oh, they're paper."

"I've never seen paper move like this before." Lunay held her finger up like one would to a parakeet and the oddly colored zebra stripy one flapped its wings and landed on the offered perch. "Polly want a cracker?" The butterfly seemed to be straining to answer.

Cindy realized that there was a large netted enclosure filled with butterflies which the woman who was cutting the paper seemed to be taking care of.

A nurse, brimming with self-important authority, marched over with two tiny paper cups of pills and handed one to Lunay and the other to Cindy. The nurse obviously dreamed of military discipline, at least in terms of others obeying her.

"I'm not on any medication yet," said Cindy.

The nurse rolled her eyes and got another two. "These are Dr. Termagant's special herbal supplements. Everyone takes them."

"They're all the rage," said Lunay with a wink. The crazy woman turned to the nurse. "She's new. I'll take care of it."

"See that you do," said the nurse and tried to walk away with purpose, but purpose stayed behind, not wanting anything to do with her. In truth, it was a little embarrassed to be seen with her after her behavior at the last Christmas party.

"Do I really have to take those?" Cindy asked.

"Nah," said Lunay as something brown and furry climbed up her leg, ending up perched on her shoulder. She scratched the rodent behind his ears with her index finger.

"There's a rat on you!" screamed Cindy.

"Where!" said Lunay, spinning and looking directly at the rodent. The rodent also looked around and neither seemed to notice anything unusual.

"On your shoulder," Cindy said, hesitantly pointing out what appeared to be the obvious, not realizing that in Tumult the obvious often came in disguise whether it wanted to or not.

Lunay looked first at her empty shoulder, then at the one with the rodent. "Oh, that's Moonbeam. He lives here."

"Is he a patient?" asked Cindy, backing away slightly simply because she was expecting a yes.

"No, the staff doesn't even know about him." She held up a pill and the rat took it and nibbled on it like it was a nut. "Moonbeam helps me get rid of this nasty stuff. He loves it. Also most of the stronger meds." Lunay leaned forward and whispered, "Confidentially, I think he's addicted. We tried two interventions, but it didn't make any difference. I guess he doesn't want to change yet. Want me to give him your pills?"

"Okay," said Cindy handing the pills over. Lunay juggled them. "I just want to know can you help me get rid of the demon?"

"What's your name little guy?" asked Lunay to the shoulder demon who had been watching with interest, but keeping quiet, with both hands still over his groin.

"I can't give you my name," he said.

"But what about all those gifts I gave you for your birthday?"

"What gifts?" said Gaz.

"Oh, so that's how you're going to play it. Fine, see if you get anything from me this President's Day. How do you like them cumquats? But still, Gaz, if you won't tell me your name, what will I call you?" she said.

Gaz puffed himself up; raising his arms up in what he hoped was an intimidating fashion. "I'm rather partial to The Destroyer of … wait a second how did you…"

Lunay stroked her chin. "I'll need to give you a nickname then. How about Pudgy? Or Little D? I know, I'll call you Gaz, okay?"

"But I never told a human my real name…" The shoulder demon slouched and shrugged his shoulders, realizing he was not only in over his head but also his wings. "Sigh… Whatever."

"So, Gaz, would you like to come live with me?" asked Lunay.

"What, and give up Cindy here? Not a chan…" The glare the crazy woman gave him made his stop mid-word. "I don't have a choice here, do I?"

"Sure you do. We always have choices, but we don't always like them. Cindy doesn't want you anymore, so you can't stay with her," explained Lunay.

"So what are my other choices?" asked Gaz.

"Would it be that bad spending time with me? After everything we've meant to each other, all the good times, all the bad times, you're just going to toss me aside like yesterday's aardvarks without giving us a chance?" Lunay asked, her voice wounded like a deer in drunken hunter crossfire. The matching expression hit Gaz with the force of a bullet, making him experience something new—guilt.

The demon searched deep inside himself, also a new experience because he had never felt he had anything beneath his brash exterior before. There was a spark that hadn't been there before the lick and it made him feel good. The spark got dimmer when he considered doing something that might hurt the crazy woman. It gave him a gut full of happy which he only hated slightly. "Do you do stuff like that crapfall trick a lot?"

"It depends on my mood," she answered.

"How can I tell what your mood is?" said the demon.

"I used to wear a ring, but then it tried to wear me, so I had to get rid of it," said Lunay. "So you want to be roomies?"

"You never said what my other choice was," said Gaz.

"You wouldn't like it much," said Lunay. "Although it would be really funny in a sad sort of way."

"I suppose it might be interesting," said Gaz.

Lunay jumped up and down, clapping her hands excitedly. Stopping, she reached out her open palm and Gaz walked up her arm to her right shoulder, totally ignoring his former host.

"Don't be rude," said Lunay.

"But that's kind of my job description," said Gaz.

"That's no excuse," said Lunay. "Maybe she'll throw you a cell warming party, although we'd have to be careful. The foam on the walls is actually very flammable, trust me. Maybe we can just have hot chocolate with little carrots in it."

"Even I find that thought disgusting," said Gaz.

"Do the right thing and say goodbye to Cindy."

Gaz looked meekly at his former host and gave a half wave. "See ya."

Cindy wanted to smile but was still in shock that what she had longed for, prayed for was finally happening. Instead, she gave a palm-closing wave in return. "So long."

"Now apologize for driving her crazy," said Lunay.

"Fat chance," said Gaz.

Ignoring him, Lunay looked at Cindy. "What kind of car did he use? Which of you was making the payments? Do we have to work out a custody agreement and visitation? Or auto support payments?"

Cindy and Gaz looked at each other. "Um, he can keep it?" said Cindy.

"That's very good of you," said Lunay. "Gaz, say thank you."

"Not a chance. She can kiss my browny red…"

"If you don't, I'll never lick you again," said Lunay.

Gaz shivered involuntarily. "If I say thank you, you'll lick me?"

"No, but if you don't I never will again."

The demon muttered under his breath. "Thank you."

"Was he the only reason you came here?" asked Lunay.

"Yes," said Cindy.

"Do you want to stay and make some arts and crafts? Or have dinner? We're having macaroni and cheese."

"Not particularly," Cindy said.

"Then I guess you can go," Lunay replied.

"I can just leave? I thought I had to stay for twenty-four hours. Hill said…"

Lunay listened as Cindy told her all about what Dr. Hill had done, with Gaz adding commentary. The crazy woman smiled. "Come with me."

The crazy woman grabbed her hand and pulled the woman off the secure ward by waiting until someone opened the locked door and holding it slightly ajar until the coast was clear. They ended up outside the office Hill had brought Cindy to.

"Wait here," Lunay said, dropping to the floor and crawling around the office. The paperwork Cindy and Hill had signed was on a clipboard near a secretary's arm. Every time the crazy woman would reach up to try to grab it, the secretary would turn so she had to drop down. She pulled the woman's cell phone out of her purse that was under her desk and dialed. The phone rang, making her turn her body to answer it.

"Tumult Asylum, can I help you? Hello, is anyone there?"

Lunay leapt up, grabbed the papers off the clipboard and replacing them with a smiley face drawing. Next, she grabbed the clear plastic bag they had put Cindy's possessions in when they admitted her.

Lunay made it out unnoticed, giving Cindy the papers and bag. "Here you go. Take these with you and you should be fine."

"How do I get out?"

"I recommend the window. Go out and make a right out of the parking lot. There's a strip mall about a mile away. You can call someone from there."

"I don't know how I can ever thank you."

"You can lick me goodbye," said Gaz.

"Be good," said Lunay.

"It's against my nature."

"We'll work on that."

"We will?" said Gaz.

"If you want to thank me, could you send me a bouquet of fish. I'm partial to religious ones."

"Holy mackerels?" said Gaz.

"Yes!" said Lunay, jumping up and down while clapping her hands.

"I'll keep it in mind." Cindy's hands and eyes started to twitch. "I better go."

"I guess we better," said Lunay.

"We?" said Cindy nervously. "You're not following me home to live with me or anything, are you?"

"I wasn't planning on it. Why, are you offering?" asked Lunay.

Cindy shook her head frantically. "No, no, no."

"I think it would be therapeutic for all of us to go pay a visit to Dr. Hill. Especially him," said Lunay, folding and twisting her straightjacket until it became a white trench coat.

Lunay climbed out the window, then helped Cindy out.

Gaz looked at them for a moment and Lunay beckoned to him with a sideways nod of her head. "Oh, what the heck." The shoulder demon fluttered his tiny wings and flew the short distance to Lunay's shoulder. He landed, huffing and puffing. "I'm out of shape."

"I could help," said Lunay.

"Like what, personal trainer?" asked Gaz.

"No, just change the shape you are in. I'm good with my hands. How about a triangle? I'm partial to triangles," said Lunay.

Gaz swallowed nervously. "I think I'll stick with the shape I'm in."

"Okay. Let me know if you change your mind," she said. "I'm good at octagons too, but my decagons need work. The angles are supposed to add up to 1440 degrees, but I can't get the oven past 550 degrees, even the time I added moonshine. I would have tried sunshine, but couldn't get it to stay in the jar."

"Okay," said Gaz, drawing out the symbols and wondering if she'd be able to find him if he just wandered off.

"Yes, I could," she said and the demon startled at having his unspoken question answered.

Lunay motioned Cindy to follow her across the lawn, although the sun was only just setting so they could have been seen if someone was watching.

When they reached the high iron fence, Cindy got nervous. It towered up fifteen feet, a remnant of a bygone age. "Do we have to climb that?

Maybe I should just check out the normal way…" She stopped when Lunay pulled back a section of sod, revealing a tunnel.

"I dug it with a spoon. I'm a traditionalist," said Lunay.

Gaz jumped down into the hole and popped back up with a two-foot long spoon, easily the size of a small shovel. "Who'd you rip this off from?"

"It was a gift from a baby," said Lunay.

"A baby what?" asked Gaz, but Lunay was already crawling through the tunnel.

Cindy and Gaz exchanged looks, actually commiserating.

"After you," said Gaz.

"Why? So you can make comments about how big my butt is?" she said.

"Fine, I'll go first," said the demon, shocking his former host, but she followed him through.

They emerged from under a utility cover on the outside and followed Lunay down the road for about a half mile. Once out of sight of Tumult, Lunay put her thumb up in the air. Several cars sped by without even slowing.

"I'm not sure about hitchhiking. It could be dangerous and nobody is stopping," said Cindy.

"You're not doing it right," said Gaz, motioning for her to show a little flesh.

"Gotcha." Lunay waited until she saw a pair of headlights and leapt in front of them.

Cindy screamed, but brakes were hit. What stopped wasn't a car, but two bikers on Harleys. They were decked out in leather vests. One's head was shaved bald and he sported a Fu Manchu. The other had shoulder length bushy brown hair and a beard that matched. Their arms sported tattoos and their faces fought to remain somber, probably beating any other expressions into submission.

"Hi," said Lunay. "We need a ride."

There was nobody else on the dark road. Fearing bodily harm or worse, Cindy started to back away slowly.

The biker with the Fu Manchu looked the crazy woman with the long dark hair up and down, smiling at what he saw. "I'll give you a ride if you give me one first."

"But I don't have a vehicle," said Lunay. Cindy frantically searched for someplace to run that a motorcycle couldn't follow.

"Lunay, honey, that ain't the kind of ride he's talking about," said Gaz.

"You got all the vehicle in those jeans I need for a fine ride," said Fu Manchu, his bushy companion laughing.

"I don't understand," said Lunay. Gaz leaned in and whispered in her ear. "Oh, I get it." She walked over and grabbed the biker's belt and pulled it forward and looked down the front of his pants, then frowned. "No wonder you have such a big bike. I always thought that was a myth, but even if you hung a horse and choked a chicken I wouldn't want to ride you or your barnyard, except for your pig. You didn't even offer to take me out for chicken wings and peanut butter first."

"Huh?" replied Fu, not following any of what she said.

"So, the only ride you're going to get is if you let me drive your pig," said Lunay.

"It's a hog," corrected Gaz.

"Actually, it's a bike, not an animal, but he should be proud that he doesn't have any training wheels," said Lunay looking at the demon on her shoulder.

"Who is she talking to?" Fu Manchu asked Bushy.

Bushy shrugged. "Beats me."

"Not yet I haven't," said Lunay. "I'm not into violence. Most of the time anyway.

Cindy hadn't yet figured out an escape route saw that the bikers were looking at her for a better answer. Reluctantly she answered. "Shoulder demon."

"What's wrong with you two?" asked Fu.

"They probably escaped from that asylum back there," said Bushy Beard.

The biker had been just trying to get a rise out of the women, never expecting the answer he got.

"Who told? It's supposed to be a secret," whispered Lunay. "I want to be back in time for mac and cheese."

"So you're crazy?" said Bushy.

"No, Lu-Nay," she said. "Why does nobody seem to get that? It's simple really, just like you two. So, what are your names?"

The bikers looked at each other and a pair of evil grins pushed the somber expressions off their faces and over a cliff.

"Crazy chicks aren't reliable witnesses," said Bushy.

"No DA would prosecute on their testimony," said Fu Manchu. The pair stepped off their bikes and each unfastened his belt. "It's a get out of jail free card."

"Lunay, you two need to get out of here fast," said Gaz.

"Nope," she said. "So are you going to be nice and give us a ride on your bikes?"

"First, you have to be nice to us," said Fu Manchu.

"I thought I was. This relationship is just too high maintenance for me, so no thanks. We'll walk," said Lunay, turning to go. "Ta, Ta."

Fu Manchu grabbed her shoulder and spun her around. "I'm afraid you can't leave the party."

"Why not?" asked Lunay.

The innocent and naïveté of the question caught the biker off guard. He lifted up his knife. "Because I'll cut you."

"If you had said we'd be playing pin the tail on the jackass, I might have stayed and stuck you with that, but I don't like your attitude, mister. Are you so ugly that you can't have sex without forcing yourself on someone?" she said. Cindy started to wet herself and ran toward the trees.

"The strong dominate the weak. It's the way of the world, baby," said Fu, unaware that the shoulder demon was now near his feet.

"Ain't it the truth, infant," said Lunay, stepping backwards. "By the way, your shoe's untied."

"Like I'm going to fall for that," said Fu, who took a single step and tripped over his inexplicably tied together bootlaces.

"Looks like you did fall for it," Lunay said, picking the knife right out of his hand. "And I guess that's my fault. Tied, untied, I get them confused. And this knife is for cutting, right?" Lunay spun and pointed it at Bushy who was trying to sneak up behind her. The biker quickly backed up. "Since you're being lead astray by your little wee-wee, how about we cut it off and then you won't be bad anymore? There used to be a mohel in the cell next to me. I think I could handle it. He gave me a couple of tips and boy were they disgusting. I could get you the tips and you could use them to bet on a horse. There's one in the sixth race tomorrow called Circumcised Lightning."

"You're insane," said Bushy.

"Odd that when you thought it was a helpless kind of insanity it was a turn on. What's the matter? Can't handle a strong woman with a knife and several psychoses who's not afraid to use them?" Lunay started waving the blade like she was a swashbuckler with a sword. Bushy and Fu slowly backed away. "You're lucky I don't have a chainsaw. I can turn a block of ice into a swan, a log into a bear, or a rapist into a eunuch."

"We didn't rape you," said Bushy.

"Not for lack of trying, but I was referring to that cheerleader a month ago," said Lunay.

"That wasn't me," lied Bushy.

"But it was you on a night away from your buddy. You can deny it all that you want, but I can tell when you're lying. Your lips move," said Lunay.

"How could you know? I wore a mask," said Bushy.

"I hear voices and they tell me things," she said.

"Lunay, behind you!" yelled Gaz.

The crazy woman spun, slamming the knife hilt into the bridge of Fu's nose, breaking it. "Tu pid itch."

"I don't know how you learned about the pom pom whore, but you just signed your own death warrant," said Bushy.

"I guess it's my own fault for signing stuff without reading it, but that's enough of this. We really have to be going," said Lunay.

Fu lifted up his pants and pulled out a .22 pistol. "Geth again."

Lunay shook her head. "I wish I could share the love, but all I can do is share the insanity."

"I'm just going to share the lead," said Fu, pulling the trigger, but Lunay had already moved to the side and the bullet missed. Unfortunately, she stepped in front of Bushy, who grabbed her in a bear hug from behind.

"You ain't going nowhere, missy," said Bushy.

"But I am. And I'm taking your bike," she replied, sticking out her tongue. "Nah, nah, nah, nah, nah."

"Like hell you are," said Fu, who leaned in to lick Lunay's face. Instead of pulling back, she kissed him full on the mouth and his eyes glossed over. Fu blinked a couple of times and Lunay stomped on Bushy's instep hard enough to loosen his grip and let her pull away.

When Fu refocused his eyes, he was looking at Bushy and pointing his gun. "Well, where'd you come from? Ain't you a pretty thing. I think you'd better get naked so we can get better acquainted."

"Dude, what the hell are you talking about? It's me, Bear," said Bushy.

Fu lashed out and pistol-whipped his partner in crime across the face. "Don't sass me bitch, or I'll put a hole in you. Now off with them pants."

Lunay grabbed Cindy out from behind her tree and dragged her over to Bushy's bike. Cindy couldn't take her eyes off the scene unfolding as Fu forced himself on his friend, not seeming to realize who he was.

"How did you…"

"Just sharing the insanity. I can change people's perspectives. It tends to turn the wicked against themselves. Speaking of which, we have to go see your Dr. Hill," said Lunay, jump-starting the motorcycle. Cindy numbly got on the back, torn between turning away and watching the brutal drama unfold.

Gaz had stayed behind to take everything in, only fluttering away toward the ladies when the hog started to drive away.

"Damn girl, you sure you aren't from the Pit? That's some fine evil back there," said Gaz.

"Evil was what they were trying to do. This is more like a taste of their own medicine," said Lunay.

Gaz's reply regarding exactly whose medicine he'd be tasting was drowned out by the roar of the engine as they sped away.

"I doubt Dr. Hill is there. His office hours ended forty five minutes ago," said Cindy.

"He had a Jiggly in his appointment book," said Gaz.

"And his lights on, which means he's home. Although people always tell me my lights are on but nobody's home. Which I guess right now is true cause I'm here," said Lunay.

"Should we take the elevator or stairs?" asked Cindy.

"The stairs. The elevator is too small to turn around in," said Lunay.

"What?" said Cindy, who had mistakenly assumed they'd be getting off the bike.

Instead, Lunay drove up to the door, paused long enough to hit the automatic opener designed for wheelchairs and drove inside. The door to the stairwell was propped open and she went right up the steps, ignoring Cindy's screams to stop. Somehow Lunay managed to make the narrow turns between flights to the third floor.

Lunay stopped on the landing. "Open that, will you?"

Happy for the chance to get off, Cindy complied and Lunay roared her way through. Cindy watched as her former shoulder demon held on and gave a rebel yell.

By the time Cindy stepped out of the stairwell, Lunay had already gotten the motorcycle into the waiting area. She rushed after her, considering if perhaps she would have been better off having stayed in the loony bin.

She rushed in expecting to have to explain to Dr. Hill what was going on. Instead, she decided that she was the one in need of an explanation.

Hill was on top of his desk dressed in a white leather corset, thong, fishnet stockings and six-inch pumps. The borders of the corset and thong had dozens of dollar bills stuffed in them.

There was a woman who was so top heavy she looked like she could topple forward at any moment, dressed in a lacy black bra and matching panties with a handful of dollar bills.

Gaz couldn't stop laughing.

Hill stood aghast at the motorcycle in his office until Lunay grabbed a dollar bill from Jiggly and waved it in the air squealing. "Take it off!"

Hill grinned, figuring Jiggly had arranged for a friend from the Honey Shack to join them. Enjoying the attention, he spun doing a little dance, shaking his moneymaker.

"No, really take it off. Looking at you is making me nauseous," said Lunay.

"This is a private office. You need to leave or I'm calling the police," demanded Hill, realizing that Lunay was not there for a threesome.

"Please do. You can explain to them exactly how this is therapy," said Lunay.

"And this is the guy you came to see to get better," said Gaz to Cindy, holding his belly from laughing so hard.

"Dr. Hill, what the hell is going on?" said Cindy, furious because she found herself embarrassedly agreeing with the demon.

Realizing Cindy was there too, Hill jumped down and put his desk between them. "You escaped! Did you come back to violate me with my award?"

"I was never going to do that. The demon wanted me to," said Cindy.

"Like he wouldn't have enjoyed it," said Gaz. "Look at this freak."

"Doctor, is this some kind of new therapy?" asked Jiggly, confused and embarrassed.

"No and neither is what he's been doing to you," said Lunay, looking the exotic dancer up and down. "Look, in a nutshell, you're father didn't love you, but he was an ass. Trying to find another father figure is a dangerous proposition. Many men will take advantage of you and you are letting them. You are more than a pair of implants and your body shouldn't be the end all and be all of your self-esteem. Nothing will change until you decide to make it happen. It'll be hard, but so much better than what your doing now."

"So you're saying I should stop dancing?" asked Jiggly.

"No!" shouted Hill.

Lunay shot him a look and made a zipping motion over her lips. Despite himself, Hill found himself listening. "For money? Absolutely."

"Then how am I going to pay my bills?" Jiggly asked.

"Cindy, is there a job opening at your job?" asked Lunay.

The question caught Cindy off guard. "Yes, we need a receptionist."

"And Jen is very obviously a people person," said Lunay.

"How'd you know my real name?"

"It's not important," said Lunay. "So Cindy, would you be willing to give Jen a reference?"

"I don't know," Cindy said nervously, worried about her own job security if it didn't work out.

"Jen's had a rougher time than you have. Besides, I'll vouch for her," said Lunay.

"You?" exclaimed Cindy before she could stop herself.

"What, my word's not good enough for you? You want Gaz back?" she said.

"Hey!" said Gaz. "I'm right here."

"I guess I could put in a good word," said Cindy, not wanting to risk getting her demon back.

"Then it's settled. Jen will start Tuesday," said Lunay.

"But I don't own the company and I'm not in charge of hiring…"

"No worries. It'll be after her interview on Monday," finished Lunay. "And no more seeing this quack."

"Excuse me? Where exactly did you go to medical school?" said Hill, having thrown his sports coat over his woman's lingerie.

"I've been on the other end of therapy for a long time and you are hurting more people than you help. You are betraying their trust to satisfy your ego and libido. And you drove Ashley Hanover and Marjorie Jacobs to suicide instead of helping them."

"That's nonsense. I'll have you know that I trained at…"

Lunay shook her head. "All that opportunity for knowledge wasted. I'm going to open your eyes."

She took the dollar bill in her hand and placed it over his eyes, her hands touching his temples.

Hill yanked his head back, slapping at her. "Get your hands off of me!"

"Guess you gotta be wearing a G-string for him not to mind," said Gaz.

"Who said that?" said Hill.

"He can hear me now?" said Gaz, fluttering up.

"Yep," said Lunay, as Hill backed up in fear.

"More sharing the insanity?" said Gaz.

Lunay nodded. "He now has every symptom of every patient he ever hurt. Not only can he see you, but he thinks you are twelve feet tall and following him because you're out to get him, because the voices in his head are telling him and…"

"I get it. He's bonkers," said Gaz, landing on the desk. His head perked up as he processed the information. "Twelve feet tall you say?"

"Yep."

"Heh." Gaz moved purposefully and slowly toward the psychiatrist, stomping with each step. Hill cringed and jumped back each time. The tiny demon lifted his arms up high and yelled "Boo!"

Hill screamed and ran out of his office.

Gaz looked at Lunay. "Do you mind if I…"

The crazy woman smiled. "Go, have fun, but I'm leaving in ten minutes if you want a ride."

"That's five more minutes than I'll need." The little demon ran after the doctor who sprinted faster toward the stairs, screaming all the while.

Cindy looked on in a combination of shock and gratitude. "What'll happen to him?"

"He's going to be at the other side of therapy for a long while," said Lunay.

"This has all been very weird, but you helped me. Thank you."

"Happy to. Just make sure Jen gets that interview," said Lunay.

"What if I can't?" asked Cindy.

"Then I'll have to come visit personally," said Lunay.

Cindy shuttered. "I'll make sure. What about going back to the asylum?"

"I wouldn't worry about it. The paperwork's gone and the admitting doctor's loony," she said.

"I thought it was Lunay," said Cindy smiling.

"Finally someone gets it," she said.

"I guess this is goodbye," said Cindy.

"I don't like to say goodbye," said Lunay.

"You prefer 'Until we meet again'?" asked Cindy.

"No, I'm rather partial to keep a banana in your pocket so if we meet again I'll know you're happy to see me."

"I'm going to go with bye," said Cindy.

"To each their own or the next best thing. See ya," said Lunay.

"Really?" asked Cindy, trying unsuccessfully to stop her voice from going up an octave.

Lunay just smiled, hopped on the bike and sped off down the stairs again.

"Who was that crazy woman?" asked Jiggly.

"A friend. A crazy friend, but a friend just the same," said Cindy. Turning to look at Jiggly, she added, "I think we should discuss wardrobe for your interview."

As the motorcycle sped past the spot where it had been stolen, a squad car was stopped, lights flashing. Fu and Bushy were sitting it the backseat. Bushy had tried to run once Fu had tired. The bald man gave chase and caught him in the middle of the road. A patrol car had come upon them. They arrested Fu for the crime they had witnessed and Bushy because he matched the description of a suspect in a cheerleader's rape. A witness had seen a masked man leaving the football parking lot and watched him take off the mask and ride away on a motorcycle. The cops had already called in for a warrant to test his DNA as soon as he was booked.

Lunay waved and honked as she went by. She ditched it in the woods around Tumult and snuck back in the way she got out, Gaz riding on her shoulder the whole way.

"Let's head back to the rec room," said Lunay.

"Sure, I'm just along for the ride," said Gaz.

When they got close, Dr. Termagant was yelling for Biff. Cindy had not shown up for their appointment and he couldn't find her. Biff was telling him the last time he had seen the new patient she was with Lunay.

"Trouble?" asked Gaz.

"Yeah. I think it might be best to put off going back to the rec room until later. Want to see my room?"

"I guess," replied Gaz.

Lunay skipped back through the halls until she got to her cell where she pulled out a key and used it to open the door to her padded room.

"You have a key?" Gaz asked.

"Yep, but it only works from the outside," she said.

"So the lunatics are running the asylum," said Gaz.

"It's Lunay. Cindy got it, why can't you?" she said, shutting the door. Lunay waved her arms as if she were showing off a palace. "So what do you think?"

Gaz leapt off onto a padded wall, then plopped to the padded floor. "Cushy."

"Yeah, it's great, isn't it?"

"So what did you have planned for the rest of the night?" asked Gaz.

"A nap before a late supper," said Lunay, putting on her straightjacket and curling up in a corner.

"Seriously?" said Gaz.

"They're having mac and cheese," said Lunay.

"That's what I hear," said Gaz. "But I thought maybe we could…"

Lunay had already closed her eyes. A patch of padding lifted up revealing a classic mouse hole and Moonbeam the rat came through, his tiny feet scraping across the thick floor. He stopped and nodded to Gaz, which caught the demon off guard. The rat climbed up and curled into the crook of the crazy woman's elbow, closed his eyes and dozed off.

Gaz sighed and climbed up to her right shoulder, forgetting again that that was the side his feathered opponents were supposed to take.

"If you can't beat 'em, join 'em I guess," he said, settling down for a snooze as the sounds of the screaming doctor drew closer demanding an explanation, but Termagant would only find her asleep in her own little padded corner of the world.

CARDIAC ARREST

A DMA Casefile of Agent Karver

In my line of work, shootouts are terrible. Don't get me wrong. I'm sure shootouts are bad for anybody, but they tend to be worse for DMA agents. When the Department of Mystic Affairs gets involved, there are times when bullets are about as effective as spitballs.

Mervin Ketzel was the perfect example. He had robbed fifteen banks in the last eight months. Ketzel didn't wear body armor and he had been shot at in six of the robberies, including two headshots, yet he walked away.

The FBI got called in and when they saw the video, they passed the case onto us. The sad part is we knew what was happening within seconds.

"He did what?" asked Agent Pine of the FBI. The profiler and I had a long history, although he didn't know it. I was once possessed by a demon. I did lots of bad things. Pine brought me in, although it took everything I had to control the demon long enough to allow him to do it. We've worked together before and he doesn't recognize me. For one thing, I'm supposed to be dead. For another, a lot about me has changed, not the least of which is my face.

"Took his heart out and hid it," said Mandi Cobb, my partner. There's nobody else I'd trust as much to watch my back. To be honest, there's almost no one else I trust period.

"Then why isn't he dead?" asked Pine.

"Old time mage trick. Mystically remove the heart and as long as it remains hidden, you can't be killed," I said.

"Karver, tell me you're joking," he said.

I shook my head. "Wish I was."

"How does he survive without something to pump his blood?"

"Magic," said Mandi.

"If it's such an old trick, how did this guy learn it? Everything we've found out about him points to the fact that he's a geek with no real skills."

"Internet," I said.

"The internet?" he said.

"Yep. There are plenty of idiots who post old grimoires online. With all the translation sites available, it doesn't take a genius to make the text readable. We've had a rash of these lately," said Mandi.

"So to stop this guy, we have to find his heart?" he said. I nodded. "How the hell do we do that?"

"And here's the rub," I answered. "The only thing in our favor is these people weren't bright enough to learn this on their own, so they don't always think through the hiding of the heart part. We found one in a shoebox under the guy's bed."

"So does this heart thing mean you couldn't catch this guy if we knew where he was?" he asked.

"We didn't say that," said Mandi, raising an eyebrow.

Pine wasn't one to ask questions out of idle curiosity and Mandi was obviously picking up some empathically. "Where is he?" I said.

"Bar outside of town. We have him under surveillance, but after seeing the type of punishment he can take, we didn't want to engage him near civilians," he said.

"Smart move," I said.

"Can we gas him or poison him?"

"Nope. Got to catch him like a rat in a trap," I said. "And since it's a guy, guess who gets to be bait?"

Mandi rolled her eyes. Pine chuckled a little too loudly for my tastes.

"Actually the gentleman lives an alternate lifestyle, so he wouldn't be interested in the lovely Agent Cobb," he said. "He might, however, find the dark and brooding Agent Karver strangely titillating."

"You're kidding," I said.

"Nope," said Pine.

"Oh joy."

"I'm sure we can dig up a nice leather outfit for you," he said.

"Only if you want him to make me as a cop," I said.

Pine looked at me sideways. "I expected you to put up more of a fight."

I wanted to, believe me. There was a time where the thought of trying to entice a man by pretending to come onto him would have me heading for the hills. It was a lifetime ago, before I had been an unwilling party to perversions of a much higher and deadlier caliber.

I shrugged. "I'm secure enough in my manhood, but I'm decking him if he even tries to get to first base." That's not so much homophobia as touch phobia. Simple human contact was how the demon helped lull and lure our victims. Intimate touch gives me nasty flashbacks.

I discarded my suit in favor of blue jeans and a red t-shirt. That made up the extent of my undercover outfit. I had a couple of accessories. One was a watch, which had a transmitter in it, and the second was a small speaker deep in my ear canal where Mandi could feed me any information I needed. Usually, she just used it to make wisecracks. Not that I wouldn't do the same if our positions were reversed. Undercover, my ankle usually sported a holster, but it wasn't like a gun of any size would do anything to Ketzel except tick him off. Or tip him off. For the same reason, I left a pair of blades behind that I normally carved under my suit jacket. The simple act of touching my back and feeling metal could alert him that I wasn't actually looking for love in all the wrong places.

I was expecting the place to be a dive, but it was nice in a middle class suburb kind of way. I paused for a deep breath before going in. The seriél demon that took control of my body had had its way with me in more ways than one. It modified my flesh in order to better do its dark deeds, including giving me an ability to attract people sexually and it wasn't limited to the opposite sex. I kept it reigned in most of the time. I let it loose before I walked in the door.

I played it cool, but all the covert stares made me uncomfortable. One of the not so covert stares was from Ketzel. I parked myself on the stool next to his.

The lady bartender was in front of me before I sat down. "What can I get for you?"

"Beer," I said. She poured and put it in front of me.

I pulled out a five, but Ketzel beat me to it. He had a hundred in his hand.

"Let me get that for you," he said, leering at me.

"That's my partner, the love machine," broadcasted Mandi in my ear.

For obvious reasons I ignored her and feigned interest in Ketzel. "That's neighborly of you."

"I'm Merv," he said, putting his hand out.

I shook. "I'm Jim," I lied, but it sounded nice and normal, something I'd never be again.

"Well, Jim, tell me did you hurt yourself when you fell from heaven?"

"Ask him if he's from Iowa. With a line that corny, he'd have to be," said Mandi.

"Just a sprained ankle, but I stayed off it for a couple of weeks and I was fine," I said. Ketzel laughed. "You going to ask me my sign next?"

Ketzel's cheeks turned red. "I've never been good at this kind of thing. I came into some money lately and I'm just looking to celebrate."

"Tacky lines and bragging about money you may or may not have isn't going to do it for me," I said.

"It's a lot of money," he said, raising his eyebrows suggestively.

"How much?" I said.

"According to the file, $875, 312," said Mandi.

"Enough to cover your naked body," Ketzel said. "Including some really big bills for those special places."

"Ick."

"That's a lot," I said, leaning closer in. I feigned interest. "Look, I've got to be honest with you. I haven't done this kind of thing a lot. It would kind of be bad for me and my reputation back home. I drove two hours to get here so nobody would recognize me. I have a fiancé, so I'm not looking for anything long term."

"Me neither," Ketzel said, putting his hand over where his heart should have been. The pressure made a mild indent in his shirt where I guessed there was a hole in his ribcage. "Honest."

"You can be discreet?" I asked.

"It's my middle name."

"According to the FBI file it's actually Lloyd," said Mandi.

"There is a motel not far from here."

I made a worried face. "They have security cameras and clerks." I took a deep breath. "I borrowed my future brother-in-law's van. He has it all set up to score with the ladies, so I figured..." I paused. "It has a bed."

Ketzel laughed. "Sure. It sounds fine."

"The van is ready and waiting," said Mandi. "You're doing good, partner."

We stood and he tried to hold my hand. I pulled away before I could stop myself. I looked around feigning embarrassment. "Not yet," I whispered.

"Tease," Ketzel whispered back.

"Don't forget to put a wiggle in your walk," teased Mandi as we went into the parking lot.

The van was a classic from the eighties. I walked to the back door and opened it. To make sure he didn't get suspicious, I went in first. He followed, a little too hot on my tail.

There was a mini door connecting the front seat to the back. I opened it. "I got some protection up front."

He grabbed my wrist. "I don't need any protection." Which was true enough.

"I do," I said. He pulled. The hidden heart made him strong, but I was no weakling. I yanked at the weak point between his thumb and index finger.

Ketzel looked at my free hand. "You're pretty strong."

I didn't answer. I moved backwards through the mini door. Ketzel lunged at me, but he was a second too late. I was through and had the door shut and locked.

"What the hell is this?" he screamed.

"Department of Mystic Affairs. Mervin Ketzel, you are under arrest," I said and read him his rights.

He started wailing and smashing into the walls and the partition, but even the windows were built to withstand much more than he could dish out.

After a few minutes, he was tired and breathing heavy. He began to get the idea that he wasn't going to be able to bust out. "This is entrapment!"

"Nope, just plain, ordinary trapment," I said. "Now I think it's time for a heart to heart talk. It would help if you could tell us where yours is."

The interrogation didn't go great, but I really didn't expect it to. Ketzel knew he couldn't be seriously hurt or killed, just bored. He didn't even lawyer up.

We couldn't force him to take a lie detector test, not to mention polygraphs are unreliable. The only thing they're good for is intimidation, maybe fooling someone into thinking they'd get caught in a lie so they tell the truth. If someone can keep a cool head, they can beat a polygraph as often as not, despite what the experts will tell you. I've done it.

We could, however, use Mandi's empathic powers to gauge his reaction to questions. When we asked him where his heart was, he said, "I left it in San Francisco. You might as well give up. You'll never find it."

"I bet it's in Mobile," I said, which is where most of his heists were. Mandi's hand signal told me no.

"No, it's in Clearwater, the town where he grew up," said Mandi. Ketzel's pupils got wide, but otherwise showed no reaction, but Mandi's smile told me we hit the jackpot.

However, some jackpots are harder to collect on than others. Clearwater was a small town compared to New York or Boston. Only nine thousand residents, give or take, but that left a lot of hidey holes. We had a warrant for his parents' and sister's house but found nothing.

We touched base with the local police department to alert them to what we were looking for. As it turns out, the Clearwater PD had already found the heart.

"Jon Gunther's dog dug it up in Van Dover Park about three months ago," the sergeant on desk duty informed us. "Our ME verified it as human. We've had no luck in finding the body it was taken out of."

"We actually have it," said Mandi.

The sergeant got that look cops get on their faces when they hear about a death. Somewhere between that's too bad and not another one. "Was it a local?"

"Used to be. It's now in custody awaiting trial in Philly at ESP Federal Prison," I said. Stands for Eastern State Penitentiary, the Alcatraz for mystically inclined convicts.

The sergeant's eyes went wide. Our story was outlandish enough that he actually called the home office in DC to verify we weren't a couple of wackos impersonating federal agents. It's supposed to be standard protocol, but rarely gets done. Badges impress people, even other people with badges.

The long and the short of it was at the end of the call he knew we were the real deal and was trying to get his mind around it. "How is that possible?"

"Dark magic," I said. "Didn't you guys ever notice the heart was beating?"

He shrugged. "It only did it every couple of hours. At least I thought it did, but I knew it wasn't possible, so I didn't say anything."

And that was the advantage those that used the darker side of magic depended on. It doesn't exist, so don't speak up or you'll be judged mad. That's why the DMA has a policy of openness in regards to our cases. It's not our fault most people choose not to believe us.

"Where is the heart now?" Mandi asked.

The sergeant looked sheepish. "We don't know."

"Why's that?" I asked, not liking where this was going.

The sergeant seemed to shrink down on himself. "It kind of got lost."

"From out of your evidence room? How's something like that happen?" I asked, unable to hide the disapproving tone from my voice.

"Technically, it was out of our morgue. Doc Boshson, our ME, thought it was best if we kept it refrigerated. We only noticed it missing about a month ago."

"What did your internal investigation reveal?" I asked. I had been a fed long enough to know it would have been checked out and the results kept in house, especially if the issue wasn't solved.

"Nothing. We don't have video surveillance. Never needed it before. The last person to have signed it out was Boshson, but he only works an eight-hour shift, Monday to Friday. Anyone could have gone in after hours."

"Great," I muttered. Without that heart, there was no way to control Ketzel shy of reinforced walls. One screw up at ESP and he'd get free. I doubt even my demon-carved good looks would get him in a trap van again.

"Why would someone take a human heart?" Mandi asked.

"Snack for some sicko?" joked the sergeant. "They say it tastes like chicken."

"More like dried pigs feet," I answered before I could catch myself. The sergeant looked at me oddly. "That's what I hear, anyway." It was a poor cover, not that it mattered. "It wasn't eaten or our prisoner would have died. Ditto for being destroyed."

"I wonder if the heart itself has any innate magic?" asked Mandi. "The traditional spell doesn't give it any, but these mage wannabes tend to change things around. Think something could have empowered the heart?"

I shrugged. "No idea." I pulled out my cell phone and hit "1" on my speed dial. It wasn't technically a call, instead connecting me with a web address for a fellow DMA agent who calls himself the World Wide Spyder.

A man's face in a finned sci-fi helmet appeared on my screen. Spyder changed his appearance frequently. Being made of sentient electrons, it wasn't difficult. "Hey Karver, what's up?"

I brought Spyder up to speed. "We need to find the site Ketzel used for his spell, see if there are any major differences between it and the traditional one. Assuming he was able to follow directions and any changes weren't made in his execution of the spell."

"I'm on it. I'll have the conjuring lab see what they can figure out."

"Thanks, Spyder." I hung up.

"Any unusual activity in Clearwater recently?" Mandi asked.

"Lots. About five people have dropped dead in the last month. Last one was yesterday. The lot of them from no apparent cause "

"Says who?" I asked.

"Boshson, the ME. At least on the first four. He's autopsying the fifth today," answered the sergeant.

Mandi and I exchanged a look. "The dead have anything in common or unusual about them?"

"Not that we've been able to find, although…" The sergeant hesitated.

"What?" asked Mandi. She had been exuding trusting emotions since we started the conversation. Now she turned them on high in order to cash in on them.

"I really shouldn't say anything, but the first victim was Rudy Daniels. Word was he was doing Doc Boshson's wife. Don't think he knew and since there was no evidence of foul play..."

"You let a man who was a suspect do the autopsy on what was possibly his own victim?" I said.

The sergeant shrugged. "He don't have an assistant. Nobody else was qualified."

The guy who is sneaking around with the wife of a man with access to a magically removed heart conveniently drops dead. I believe in things that go bump in the night, but I don't believe in coincidence. "I think we need to talk to your ME."

"He's in the morgue," said the sergeant. "I'll take you down."

For whatever reason, morgues are usually in the basement. Maybe it's because they're underground which is where we as a society put dead people. Or it could be because basements flood easily and nobody else wants their office there.

The Clearwater City Morgue was pretty typical. A bunch of metal exam tables and about a dozen coffin sized coolers built into the wall. It was also dark. No one ever seems to want to give these guys good lighting.

The man we had come to question was elbow deep in a body.

"Doc, got a couple of feds here who wanna talk to you about the missing heart."

Boshson froze. It was half an instant, but I caught it. Mandi used a hand signal to let me know the subject made him very nervous.

Mandi turned to the sergeant and shook his hand. "Thanks for your help. We can take it from here." The cop stood, debating whether or not to stay. It would be easier if he left, so my partner sent out feelings of unease and revulsion–normal enough around the dead. It was enough to convince him to make his exit a hasty one.

We introduced ourselves. "Dr. Boshson, I was hoping you could tell us everything you know about the missing heart," said Mandi, again making with the trust mojo.

The ME paused and removed his gloved hands from the victim's chest cavity. "Not really much to tell."

I moved alongside him and peered inside. He had most of the organs from the abdomen out and weighed. Everything except the heart.

"Really, doctor? I think we all know that isn't true," I said.

"I really have no idea what you're getting at," said Boshson.

"Right," I said. "We can play it your way for now." Which is when my phone rang. The tone let me know it was Spyder. "Excuse me."

"Doctor, when is the last time you saw the heart?" asked Mandi.

"When I put it in the freezer. Number eleven. When I checked a month ago, it was gone."

"Don't you lock the morgue?" she asked.

"Sure, but there's a key upstairs on the pegboard. Anyone could grab it and put it back when they were done," suggested Boshson.

"Did they dust the key for fingerprints?" asked Mandi.

"I have no idea. Would that help catch whoever did this?" he asked.

"Probably not," I said, hanging up the phone. "Agent Cobb was asking to see your reaction." I put on a pair of gloves that went up to my elbows, tucked the end of my tie into my shirt and moved over to the body. With the information Spyder had dug up I now had a working theory. It was time to test it. I reached inside the corpse.

Boshson freaked. "You can't interfere with my autopsy. You may destroy evidence."

"Don't worry. I know my way around a body." Better than I'd like to. "I can't seem to reach what I need. May I borrow this?" I said, taking the Stryker saw next to him. I turned it on and he started screaming reasons at me as to why I had to stop. By revving up the saw, I drowned out his commentary. It was a good saw, better than the one I had back in my demon days. It cut through the ribs easily. I reached back inside and found what I was looking for. When I pulled my hand out, a shriveled human heart was in it. Boshson seemed shocked. I put it on the scale. "Interesting. I'm no doctor, but I think the average adult human heart weighs in the neighborhood of 300 grams. This poor guy was well over two hundred pounds, but his heart only weighs 87 grams. Agent Cobb, do you think this sliver of wasted cardiac muscle could possibly have kept this man alive? Ignoring, of course, the obvious state of necrosis it's in."

"No, Agent Karver, I don't think it could," said Mandi, moving so she was between Boshson and the door.

"That means that whatever killed him was able to kill his heart from the inside. Any idea what could cause that?" I said.

"I'm going to take a wild guess and say the very heart we came down here searching for," said Mandi.

"You are good, partner. That call was from one of our fellow agents.

Turns out our conjuring lab was able to test the spell Ketzel used. Due to a scanning error on the part of the owner of the website, it combined the invulnerable spell with a decay spell. The missing heart can feed on the living variety. Unfortunately, that tends to kill their owners," I said.

"I don't have any idea what you're rambling about. You're talking crazy," said Boshson.

I didn't need Mandi's hand signals to tell me he was lying. "Boshson, it's over. The agent I was speaking to is already getting a warrant to search your home and car. We're going to find the heart."

Boshson smiled. He probably sucks at poker. "You won't find it."

"That's what the last guy said. Who knows? You may be right, but we will also be checking DNA. You yourself took the samples," said Mandi.

His smile got bigger.

"We will, of course, be double checking your samples against the prisoner's," bluffed Mandi. There was no way we could get a tissue sample from Ketzel without risking someone's life.

Boshson's smile lessened.

"And we will get a court order to have an outside examiner check the bodies of the four other deaths you've ruled natural. My guess is they will find hearts just like this one in each of them. Then we'll find proof that your wife was sleeping with Rudy Daniels. How hard will it be to convince a jury that you knew about it?"

"Like a jury would believe a magic heart could kill somebody," he smirked.

I walked over and wiped my gloves on his lab coat, then took each one off, making sure I snapped them, before putting them in his pocket. "Our jury pool pulls from those who not only believe in magic but have it as part of their lifestyles. Plus we have nice footage of Ketzel being shot during the bank heists and not being hurt. Not to mention video of him walking around with a gapping hole where his heart should be. It won't take much for them to convict. And using magic in the commission of a crime makes it a federal offense. Using it to kill gets you the death penalty."

Boshson's smile was as dead as the people he worked on. He was looking for a way out. We gave it to him. "The Attorney General looks favorably when someone works with us to prevent further crimes. The incidences where the death penalty is asked for is greatly reduced," offered Mandi. It was the truth. The death penalty was saved for the more extreme cases like demon possessed serial killers.

Boshson didn't take our way and opted for the highway. "I want a lawyer."

"Fine. You're under arrest," I said.

There was another interrogation. This one was less successful than Ketzel's. Lawyers tend to have that effect, especially when they are pointing out little things like lack of a murder weapon, even if it was an internal organ. The search warrants hadn't turned up the heart, but we had some trace evidence. It would be some time before we got lab results. We had put the locals sifting through video surveillance. So far they had found footage from a bank camera that put Boshson near the second body twenty minutes before it was found. With luck, there'd be more. According to Spyder, the heart had to be close to each victim, touching them in order to kill them.

Mandi pulled me outside. "I think he's good for the first four victims, but not the fifth."

"Why?" I asked. "Guy lives right behind him. Maybe he played his music too loud and that upset the good doctor."

"No. I felt total shock when you pulled that shrunken heart out," she said.

"It was an unusual thing for a fed to do," I suggested.

"That wasn't what the shock was at. When we asked him about Rudy Daniels he felt smug and vindicated. The next three he felt significant guilt, but no personal attachment. The last, Andrew Leon, there was much confusion. The other guilt seems to be eating him up. When we asked him where the heart was, there was more confusion. My hunch is he ditched the heart and someone else found it."

"And that someone used it to kill Leon," I said. "Think he'd be stupid enough to stash it in his backyard?"

"The dogs smelt human remains in the backyard and there was freshly turned dirt there, but nothing we were able to unearth," said Mandi.

We ran a check on priors on Leon. He had no convictions, but he had been charged with molesting his ten-year old son. The kid was removed briefly from the house, but when the investigation turned up nothing concrete and the kid recanted, they sent Andy Jr. back. Kids tend to be curious. If he saw Boshson bury something, he might have dug it up. And Leon was found dead in the boy's room.

school was still in session and Andy Jr.'s mother had sent him in rather than have him underfoot while she was planning her husband's funeral. Her words, not mine. Not a pleasant woman. Spent as much time as we'd give her complaining that she didn't know what would happen to her now that her husband was gone. She had never held a job and the pair married right out of high school. Despite myself, I felt some sympathy for her. I couldn't decide if she knew whether Leon had hurt her son or had been broadsided. If she knew, I'd love to bring her in, but there was nothing to charge her with. Nothing we could prove anyway. I felt for the kid. We offered to let her come with us when we questioned her son. She declined, signing a consent form rather than make the ten minute trip to her son's place of learning. Said she was too depressed and Mandi backed her up. I know I shouldn't judge, especially given my circumstances, but I can't help it. I despise anyone who cares more about themselves than their kid.

When we got to the school the metal detector went off, but our badges got us in to see the principal. We told her we were investigating the death of Andrew Leon Sr. and showed her the consent form. She called the mother to double check, then led us out to the playground. Andy Jr. was a small kid and three larger ones were pushing him around like a pinball.

When they saw the principal, the trio of bullies stopped. She seemed happy to leave it at that, letting them move a short distance away.

"You aren't going to reprimand or suspend the bullies?" I asked.

The principal smiled the type of grin that I remembered adults in authority using when I was a kid to try to beguile someone. "It's just boys being boys."

"Odd attitude for a principal to have, especially toward a kid who just lost his father," I said. "Which tells me one or more of the boys has a parent you're afraid of professionally."

Mandi brushed an imaginary something from her eye, our signal for bull's-eye.

"I'll thank you to leave the running of my school to me, Agent Karver," she said with all the indignity that she could muster. It was considerable. "Room 101 is empty if you'd like to talk to him there." Then she left in one of the finest huffs I'd ever witnessed.

Mandi walked over to the kid. "Hi, I'm Agent Cobb, this is Agent Karver. We'd like to ask you a few questions."

"What'd you do now, Andrew?" asked one of the bullies mockingly. I hate bullies.

"It's none of your damn business. Now drop and give me twenty," I said in my best disciplinarian voice.

"You ain't a teacher. I don't gotta listen to you," he said.

"Really? I just saw you assault Andrew. How about I arrest you for it? Andrew wouldn't even have to testify since you were dumb enough to do it in front of two federal agents," I countered. I knew it'd never hold up, but I wasn't about to take crap from a 'tween. He did the push ups.

The classroom was a kindergarten room. The class that usually occupied it was on a field trip.

"We'd like to ask you some questions about your father's death," said Mandi.

"Okay," he said meekly.

"How did he die?" asked Mandi.

Andy shrugged his shoulders. "I don't know."

I sat down across from him. "Andy, was he trying to do something he shouldn't?" Mandi was broadcasting trust at full blast.

His nod was barely a movement, but the tears spoke volume.

"You dug the heart out of Doctor Boshson's lawn and had it in your room, didn't you?"

Another nod, this one less meek.

"When he tried to hurt you, you used the heart, didn't you?"

A third nod. "It told me to. Not in words, but with pictures inside my head. My father told me he'd kill me if I told, but I finally did. Then he told me he'd kill my mom if I didn't say I made the whole thing up. I said I did, but I didn't. I had to lie or he would have hurt my mom."

"I know," I said and I did. Mandi didn't bother with signals. Tears were falling down her cheeks from the kid's inner turmoil. He did this for a woman who couldn't be bothered to get past her own self-pity in order to take an hour out of her day to be there for her son.

"Am I going to have to go to jail?" he asked.

"Even though you killed him, it is pretty clear it was self-defense. You saw Doctor Boshson bury the heart?" I asked.

"Yeah," he said.

"Would you be willing to say that in court?" I said.

"I guess."

"I think I can get the Attorney General's Office to make you a deal if you are willing to testify. You won't have to go to jail. And you'll have to give us the heart. Is it a deal?"

"Yeah, sure."

I made a quick call and got lucky. They wanted Ketzel more manageable ASAP, so in less than fifteen minutes we had the deal.

I told Andy and he led us to his locker. The heart was in an insulated lunch bag, wrapped in aluminum foil. I put it in a warded evidence bag being careful not to touch it.

"So that's it?" he said.

"Yes," said Mandi.

"I have to go back outside?" he asked, obviously reluctant to go.

"You worried about the bullies?" I said.

"Yeah."

"You were planning to use the heart on them, weren't you?" I said.

"I thought about it. I brought it to school, but I didn't bring it out on the playground, even though I could tell it wanted to go."

"You did the right thing. Let us help you out with your problem. The only way to stop a bully is to stand up to him and beat him down," I said.

"I can't fight," Andy said.

"Anyone can fight, it's just a matter of doing it well," I said and proceeded to give him a very abridged self-defense course.

"Now you are going to go out and take care of them," I said.

Mandi gave me a questioning look. I whispered in her ear. "Give him confidence." With her powers, it would be easy. "Give the bullies so much fear that they won't be able to fight back. Make it enough so they won't forget it."

"You sure about this?" she asked. "They're just kids."

It was my turn to nod. "Andy had enough inner strength to save their lives by not feeding them to the heart. Least he deserves is to not spend his days tormented and in fear because of it."

We went back out. "Go over there and demand an apology."

Andy did. They laughed and pushed him. Mandi upped his confidence and poured on their fear. The fight was lopsided, lots of hitting and pushing, but when it was done the three bullies ended up running away in front of all their other classmates. One wet his pants.

Andy ended up being brought into the principal's office. Mandi and I went in with him.

"Agent Cobb and Agent Karver, this is a school matter and doesn't concern you," she said.

"Wrong. We're witnesses. You allowed the first attack to go unpunished, so Andy had to defend himself the second time," I said.

"I have three boys blithering and crying in the nurse's office. He had to have done much more than defend himself," said the principal.

"Actually, he didn't. We saw the whole thing and it was self-defense. If we have to file a report, that's how we would write it up," said Mandi.

"And the fact that had the principal dealt with the earlier fight instead of ignoring it, this wouldn't have happened because those boys would have been suspended," I added.

"We'd send copies to the local police and the school board of course," said Mandi.

"Maybe even the State Education Board. And any attorneys Andy's mother wanted brought into the matter," I added.

We got glared at, but the principal caved. Needless to say, things went relatively well for Andy. He was suspended for the next three days—it was mandatory in the school's zero tolerance policy—but he would have had one of those days off for the funeral anyway. We also managed to get him some counseling with the school shrink. He was hurting and needed it.

His mother was called. She asked if we could bring him home. We stopped for ice cream on the way.

When we got to his home, I handed him my card. "If you need anything just call. I don't want to hear you turned into a bully like those other kids."

"I won't," he said and went inside walking a little taller than he had earlier that day.

"Think he'll be okay?" I asked my partner.

I wanted to hear yes. What Mandi said was, "Maybe." She's honest to a fault sometimes.

Once we showed Boshson the heart and told him we had an eyewitness linking him to burying it, he started to sweat. He broke in less than an hour, even with the lawyer. The heart offered him the chance to kill his rival, but he didn't have to take it. It seems the heart suggested the other three victims and Boshson had gotten a guilty rush from the murders. They were people who had done Ketzel wrong and Boshson figured they'd never be traced back to him.

Ketzel was more manageable after that. We tried to get a court mandated mystic surgeon or fleshsmith to put the heart back in, but he got a lawyer who contended that it was a violation of his civil rights to have surgery forced on him. The matter is pending an appeal. Until then, they had the heart in a separate section of ESP with electroshock pads on it. Ketzel gets out of line, his heart gets a jolt. The invulnerability doesn't pass to the heart and anything done to it causes him some serious discomfort. If he gets the death penalty, they'll probably have to administer the injection directly into his heart. That or hit it with a sledgehammer. Considering all the loved ones his victims left behind, there won't be any shortage of people volunteering to do it.

There certainly wasn't for my execution.

BARBARIAN SUMMER
A Chronicle of Mog & Mikki

It is a rare thing that can throw an entire city into the depths of fear, especially one the size of Philadelphia. Although in truth, it wasn't the entire city, but a small and powerful portion of it that found itself suddenly at war with an unknown foe.

It was known as the Summer of Fear. It is still spoken of, albeit usually in whispers especially in the shadows where human predators still hide waiting for prey. Traditionally the darkness is a safe haven for those who make victims of the weak and downtrodden, especially if they have some muscle and ill-gotten gains to help them hide. All the cash, all the guns, even the gangs and hitmen weren't up to the task that July and August. For that briefest moment, the streets of Philadelphia were safe to walk, even in the dead of night. The dealers, pimps, and muggers were all hiding in the deepest holes they could find, trapped in a sweltering Midsummer's Nightmare. For the rest of the city, the war in the shadows was a dream come true.

Some holes weren't dug as deep as others. Three wannabe gangstas were huddling scared in a burnt out building and praying for September. In their high school, they ruled the halls. Teachers feared them and whatever security wouldn't take their bribes, they beat bloody. They were learning the hard truth that in all too many ways high school just doesn't prepare you for the real world.

"I hear it's a secret task force, made up of all these Green Berets, Special Forces, and Navy SEALS guys. The government is doing it on the down low because they don't want to deal with arresting anyone," said Ill Will.

"I heard it's a guy possessed by a demon from Hell," said Low Joe.

"One guy doing all that? No way. Gotta be at least seven, maybe a dozen," said Ill Will.

"Nah, I heard it was one guy too. Didn't even use a gun. Slices everyone up. Tells the ones that he lets walk away to make sure they tell everyone what happened. Guy with a body count like that, you don't disobey," said Def Jeff.

"Lots of guys have been hit. Mob businesses, a dozen crack houses. He even hit Cra-Z Nat," said Low Joe.

"The psycho arms dealer?" asked Def Jeff. Low Joe nodded. "That loony has his whole place booby trapped and has enough firepower to hold off the army."

"You heard about that fire over on South Street?" asked Low Joe.

"Yeah. Took every fire department in the city all night to put out," said Def Jeff. "You could see it from here."

"That was Cra-Z's entire weapons stash going up in smoke," said Low Joe. Def Jeff let out a long, slow whistle.

"See? There's no way one guy did all that damage," said Ill Will. "And those special forces guys better not show their faces here or I'll bust a cap in 'em."

Hidden in the shadows above the trio, a grin of white appeared for an instant before fading back into darkness.

Mog enjoyed the stories of his exploits and savored the fear. They were right. He was only one man and the fear he was instilling in the criminals of this city was only helping him. It assured the barbarian's foes froze for a second when he attacked, as the visions of all his previous deeds flashed through their minds and, for Mog, a second was all that was needed.

Despite the fear and the damage he had done, it hadn't been enough. The stolen object he had started the war over still eluded him, even after two months. The thought that it was forever gone was too horrible for even a barbarian to contemplate. The icy fingers of fear gripped his heart and he dealt with it the only way he could in this new world. He fought on.

The time for hiding in the shadows was done. Shifting his weight carefully among the ceiling timbers, Mog moved until he was behind the one called Low Joe. He dropped silent as a panther and put his palm over Low Joe's mouth, lifted him off the ash-covered floor and dragged him kicking into the shadows until his struggling stopped from lack of air.

Neither of his companions noticed his absence until Low Joe dropped from the ceiling headfirst. The unconscious gangbanger swung like a pendulum on a rope tied around his ankles.

The remaining pair jumped, screamed a long string of obscenities and sprinted for the only door like their lives depended on it. They hit the wooden door at a fast run and bounced off.

"Open the damn door!" yelled Def Jeff.

"It's jammed!" said Ill Will, yanking frantically on the knob.

"Shoot the frigging lock!" said Def Jeff.

Ill Will took out his .38 and fired three shots at the lock, blowing off the metal pieces. Shifting the gun to his other hand, he pushed again, but the door wouldn't budge.

"What's the problem? Let's get out of here," said Def Jeff.

"It still won't open!" yelled Ill Will.

"Then bust it down," said Def Jeff, an instant before a huge hand hit him on the back of the skull with the hilt of a knife. He crumpled and was dragged away.

Ill Will rushed at the door as hard as he could and succeeded only in hurting his shoulder. Angry he turned to yell at his companion. "You gonna help or not?" That was when he realized he was alone. "Jeff? Where you at? This ain't funny. Don't be messing with me like this dawg or I will hurt you."

Ill Will took some courage from his gun and started to search the room, leading with the barrel of the .38.

"Whoever you are, you picked the wrong gangsta to mess with. I'm gonna kill you, then I gonna kill your family and anyone you ever cared about. The last fool who messed with me got every trace he ever existed wiped off the face of the Earth," boasted Ill Will with bravado, only part of which was false. He had indeed killed a teacher and his wife when the man threatened to flunk him in freshman English. Ever since, he had carried a straight A average, even in the classes he didn't attend, which was most of them.

He shut up when he saw Def Jeff unmoving, pinned to a support beam through the sheet rock by a hunting knife through the crotch of his jeans.

"Holy sh..." said Ill Will, backing away. A noise in the shadows to his rear caused him to spin and fire blindly.

From behind him, a deep voice boomed in an accent he had never heard before. "I have questions."

Ill Will spun gun first with every intention of shooting but was cut short in a most literal fashion. The behemoth behind him slashed out with a short broadsword and sliced clean through to the bone of his index finger and out the other side again. As that was the finger poised on the trigger, the gun tumbled from Ill Will's hand. It was helped along by the slick blood that poured along the handle. The spasms from the twitching fist made sure it got some extra momentum.

Ill Will screamed. "You cut off my finger!"

"You should not have pointed a gun at me," said Mog the barbarian, although this day he wore jeans and a flannel shirt that entirely failed to hide his muscular build.

"I'm going to bleed to death," whined Ill Will, holding the bloody stump that was his finger.

"Not until I am done with you," said Mog, pulling the do-rag off the gangbanger's head. "Tie this tight at the base."

"I can't man. You've gotta do it for me."

Mog shook his head. "Then it will not be done, so we better start my questions." The barbarian put the point of his sword beneath Ill Will's Adam's apple.

Ill Will gulped. "Wait. I think I can get it." The gangbanger quickly managed to secure the makeshift tourniquet. "What do you want from me? I've never even seen you before. What'd I ever do to you?"

Mog moved the point of his sword up to Ill Will's lips. "Just so you are clear, I ask the questions and you answer them. If I do not like the answer, I cut off a part of my choosing." The sword moved down to Ill Will's groin. "Am I clear?"

Ill Will tried to speak but squeaked instead. Deciding some answer was much safer than none, he nodded his head at breakneck speed.

"You deal in stolen goods."

"Yeah," said Ill Will.

"That wasn't the question," said Mog. "I've been tracking down some things that were burgled two months ago. I understand they were sold to you for drugs. Where are they?"

"I don't know what you mean," said Ill Will. The sword flashed and stopped part way through Ill Will's earlobe. New blood flowed down his neck to his shoulder. "What I mean is we get a lot of stuff. When was it?"

"You received it the middle of the week before last," said Mog.

"We moved everything we had on Monday to a pawnshop on Spring Street," said Ill Will.

"Take me there," ordered Mog.

"Sure, but shouldn't we put my finger in ice? So the doctors can sew it back on," said Ill Will.

"If what I am looking for is there, you can come back for it," said Mog.

"And if it's not?" asked Ill Will.

"Then you will not have any need for that finger or any other," said Mog.

The barbarian dragged the gangbanger to the rooftops and they made their way a few blocks over to the pawnshop in leaps and bounds.

"It's closed. Guess we'll have to come back in the morning after I go to the hospital," connived Ill Will, thinking that would get him what he wanted. He was wrong.

Ignoring him, Mog used his sword to slice through wires connected to the building

from an electric pole. The few lights in the building went dark. The wire danced and sparked in the starlight. Ill Will had an idea and grabbed the insulation on the live wires, fully intending to hit Mog with them. One glare from the barbarian was enough to discourage the idea from attempting in any way to become reality.

Throwing Ill Will on his shoulder, Mog dropped from the roof to a fire escape and then onto the cement alley walkway. A window overlooked the alley, covered by steel bars bolted into the window frame. Ill Will smiled. The man with the sword would be stuck. He had no crow bar to even try to pry the metal barrier off.

Mog moved Ill Will to the dead end side of the alleyway and slid the sword into a belt sheath. Then he put his mammoth hands on opposite sides of the bars, his left foot on the wall beneath the window and pulled. Ill Will actually had to stop himself from chuckling at the futility of the effort, that is until small chucks of cement popped loose from around the bolts. The barbarian shifted his weight; first left, then right, followed by up and down. With each moment, the bolts became looser until the entire frame burst out from the wall. The barbarian stumbled but did not fall or even drop the protective frame. Instead, he placed it gently on the ground and slid a knife blade through where the upper and lower parts of the window met. The lock rotated open and the barbarian pushed the window open, then shoved the gangbanger through headfirst and followed close behind.

In fierce, whispered, tones Mog demanded, "Where is it?"

Ill Will panicked. "I'm not sure, man. We give him the stuff, but I have no idea what he does with it. I..." His words were cut short by the palm of the barbarian's hand clamping over his mouth.

A door at the far end of the shop opened and an overweight, unshaven man stepped through it holding a pump action shotgun.

Ill Will didn't even realize the hand was taken off of his face until he saw the owner drop to the floor. He didn't even see Mog knock the guy out.

The barbarian started tearing through the shelves and under the counter, tossing aside jewelry and gold worth thousands. Somehow he even opened the safe but left the piles of cash untouched. Then in a box that looked like it was destined for the dumpster, the barbarian stopped and pulled something out.

"Yes!" he exclaimed. "Thank Prow!"

Curiosity temporarily overwhelmed fear and Ill Will moved forward to see what could have driven a man to cause this much destruction.

"What was it, man? Diamonds, cash, drugs?"

Mog turned, tenderly holding the object of his quest.

Ill Will's jaw dropped. "All this was for that?"

Mog grabbed him by the collar and lifted him off the floor. "It was here, so you may live with some stipulations. Should I ever see you again anywhere —on the street, at the mall, at the supermarket —I will kill you. If I ever hear one word of what I found here get out, I will hunt you down and slay you, slowly and painfully. Can you live with my conditions or shall we just end this now?"

"I can do it," promised Ill Will. Mog threw him one handed out through the open window. By the time the punk got up and looked back in, the barbarian was gone.

He collected his finger and a talented emergency room surgeon was able to reattach it. Ill Will then left town and was never heard from in Philly again.

Mog unlocked the door to his apartment as quietly as the decrepit door and floorboards would let him. The barbarian used all of his stealth skills in an attempt to not wake his daughter Mikki, who was asleep in his arms. The door creaked open on its rusty hinges and Mog held his breath, praying to Prow that the sound would not disturb the bundle in his arms. He considered oiling the hinges, then dismissed the thought as a moment's foolishness. It had taken him a week to get it to be that loud. Otherwise, an intruder might be able to sneak up on him while he slept, which even he had to do. It wasn't as if he could have his toddler stand watch, although Mikki would have been willing. The problem was she was more likely to play with an intruder than gut them and that wouldn't do.

The months following their flight from their home world after the razing had been especially rough on the little girl. Mog had wandered their world as a soldier and mercenary before meeting her mother, so learning to live in a new land was old hat to him, even if Philadelphia had been more of a challenge than any other city he had been in. The buildings were larger, the weapons more deadly, but human nature was the same on Earth as it was at home.

Mikki had lost almost everything. Their home was destroyed and her mother slain before her eyes. Mog only managed to save Mikki through Prow's grace, arriving too late to save Naela, the love of his life. Her killers paid for their crimes in blood, pain, and gore. Mog had been going to fight the source of the razing when his wife's screaming had turned him back.

Mog had only the slightest of chances of beating the enemy, but that was nothing new. But now there was Mikki to consider. Mog could leave her with others to raise. It made sense. He could never storm the foe's stronghold with a child in tow. The idea itself was ludicrous. But when Mog thought about abandoning his daughter to fight the good battle, he found he couldn't. A barbarian always had something to fight for. It varied—revenge, honor, power, pride or money—but Mog had stopped fighting for those things the moment he had met Naela. From then on he fought for love. Mog had been leaving to head off the threat to his family when it found them anyway.

There hadn't been time to take much. Mikki had grabbed what meant the most to her, a doll her mother had made for her. It had been her favorite companion before and since. It was the only thing she had left of her mother. Then some petty thief broke into their rattrap apartment and stole most of their few meager possessions that had been out in the open. He missed completely the hidden compartment under the floorboards that held their money and Mog's weapons.

Mog had been working at a new mundane job and had told Mikki she had to leave the doll behind while she went to the babysitter. The barbarian father had been trying to wean his daughter from dependence on the toy. From the moment they returned to find the doll stolen, Mog had regretted leaving it, even before his daughter's tears began. Anything that could take the smile from her face and the twinkle from her eyes was easily the most horrible enemy the barbarian had ever faced. Mog fought it the best way he knew how, by cutting a swath of destruction through the criminal element of his new city in order to regain Mikki's dolly.

It took far too long, but it had been a successful campaign.

As he tucked his daughter into her bed, she awoke briefly. Mog slipped the doll under her arm and Mikki's sleepy face lit up.

"Daddy found Dolly," she said, hugging her stuffed friend.

"Yes, dear. Daddy will always do everything he can to make you happy," Mog whispered and kissed her on her forehead. "Go back to sleep, my sweetheart."

"First kiss Dolly," Mikki said, holding her up.

"Okay," said Mog, making a loud kissing noise. Mikki laughed then rolled over. The barbarian stood watch until his daughter drifted back to sleep, a satisfied smile on his weathered face.

And outside the streets of Philadelphia slept as well.

DYSENCHANTED

A Hell's Detective Mystery

The dame wore red. It looked good on her, better than flames on a serial killer, but she may have been overdoing it a bit. The dress was tight enough for me to know that she was an outie and had tastes that ran towards the most exotic of the latest nipple piercings, the kind that moved under their own power. It wasn't the dress that put her over the top in the red department. No, it was the rest of her, from her cute button nose down to her pointed tail. Even her lips glistened with a darker form of crimson. Considering Avon ladies don't exactly have the Pit on their routes until after they take the big sleep, I was guessing her lipstick was made from the blood of the damned. Most everything in Hell was crafted from the souls condemned here. It was Hell's one great unnatural resource.

The only parts of her that weren't rouged up were the whites of her eyes and their black beady center as well as her painfully white teeth, no doubt bleached from crushed bones. It's hard to get that shade down here. Its not that we don't have dentists, its just we don't let any of the deceased human ones practice and a demon with a pair of pliers hardly helps one's smile. She brought attention to her pearly whites by licking them and her pouty lips with her forked tongue. It was her warm up to get my attention. It was followed by soft moans and strutting that would make a dead man stand up at attention.

I yawned. The gesture first stunned, then pissed her off. A succubus is not used to being ignored or dismissed lightly, especially the queen of them all. Yeah, I knew her, although not in the biblical way. Oddly, most other biblical ways were frowned upon in the Pit, but that one was still okay. As head of Hell's police, our paths had crossed more than once.

My gesture of boredom had thrown Bambi off her game and it took her a moment to recover.

Yes, her name was Bambi. Not exactly the type of name one would think would strike fear into the human souls in the Pit, but it did. The name seemed to fly well with the mortal men she was entrusted to lead down the slinky path to damnation. It wasn't the act of sex that damned them. No, it was because they chose to have a hot, wild and steamy time with this sexy succubus instead of honoring their other commitments, whether it was to wife, friend, country, or church.

In the Pit, sex was a brutal weapon. Without love, how could it be anything else? When demons fell, they became a lot like humans in all the dark ways. Especially ironic when you consider it was jealousy of the same humans that led to their fall.

Bambi recovered well, but I expected nothing less. The demon in red was unusual among the succubi and the incubi for that matter. Most of the demons involved in the sex trade for souls business were subservient to another demon, a hellish pimp if you would. Sometimes even a pimpette. Red answered to no one less than the boss, not even demon lords and it was even rumored that she was being considered for such an exalted position. Personally, I think most of the rumors were started by her, but one never knows in the Pit.

"Negral, I need your help," said Bambi in a voice husky enough to win the Iditarod. I was sitting behind my desk with my feet up. I leaned further back in my chair putting my hands behind my neck, careful not to knock my fedora off my head. Hell doesn't have a dress code other than the damned souls aren't permitted to have clothing. Or names for that matter. Demons can dress however they like. Many pick themes or time periods. Although I'm an almost forgotten god stuck with a hell of a job, I'm not that much different. I'm rather partial to old black and white PI movies, and I dress accordingly.

"I hadn't realized that word of my prowess had spread that far and wide to the red light district," I said.

That stunned her. Bambi saw herself as more of a high-class call girl than a whore on the corner. Didn't matter much which way to me. Both did pretty much the same things, but we each have our illusions and things we tell ourselves to get through the day. Or in Hell's case, an eternal night.

"Actually I've heard no tales of your prowess. It's as if you're celibate," said Bambi, her tone snide and a smirk across her pouty lips as if she had gotten one up on me by listing one of my sins. Although, by definition, there's not really any sins in hell. All the horror done is to punish the sinners so, therefore, how can it be sinful? That's an argument for philosophers, not me.

"Lets just say I'm particular and leave it at that."

Bambi threw her head in the direction of my reception area. "Apparently not too particular. After all, you are keeping a rather adequate looking female soul at your beck and call, but I suppose maybe you enjoy simple things." The succubus was referring to my secretary, a human soul whose husband had perhaps unjustly sold her into eternal damnation. I took her into my employ, which in Hell is about as far as damnation you can get. Still, you're close enough to touch it and have it paw all over you then rip you to shreds if you're not careful.

"No, if I was into simple I would have paid you a visit a long time ago." I smiled when I spoke, but Bambi literally had fire burning out of her eyes. Being a sun god back in my day, I was hardly impressed.

Still, Bambi wanted something and wasn't so foolhardy to throw it away over a couple insults. Instead, she turned on the charm and I literally watched her proportions swell as she stepped closer, careful to put her hands on my desk at an angle that made sure I got a nice show.

"I need you to do something for me," she purred. "I'm willing to offer you a thousand souls."

There's no true money in hell. I guess the Devil's worried that if it is the root of all evil he might be upstaged and have some competition. Instead, Hell works on a very complicated barter system in which souls are used as currency. A thousand souls is the equivalent of offering to make someone a millionaire.

Since it worked so well the first time, I yawned again. "Not really interested. I have such a back log of souls owed to me that a thousand would just be a drop in the bucket." Truth is, I wasn't interested in owning souls. I had a few that I kept on staff, mostly former cops who were more crooked than they were honest, but still had their uses to me. And the occasional soul that I wanted to make sure got what was coming to it.

This seemed to shock Bambi.

"I'd be willing to make them all female, each one prettier than that thing you're keeping out there," she said, irritated but still trying to close the deal.

"Nah, I'll pass," I said. "What else you got?" Now her smile became real as she thought she had me. Part of the hellish magicks that fueled a succubus's power made them damn near irresistible, emphasis on the damn. She thought I was holding out for her. She walked around to my side of the desk and sat herself in my lap. She started playing with the buttons on my shirt and then let her hand wander south. Deep south. I was only male, so I reacted to her closeness and her touch, but when her hand reached inside my trousers to grab hold of something she hadn't been invited too, I let loose a little something in my nether regions.

Red yelled and when she pulled her hand out of my pants, it was on fire. As a former sun and fire god, I can make any part of me burst into flame at will, and since my flame is powered by the sun, things of the dark don't like it much. Hellfire she could have ignored and maybe even gotten off on. This hurt her.

"Why you son of…" She reached out with the flaming hand and tried to slap me across the face, but the dame was too slow. I caught Red's hand in my own.

"Now, now. You're getting what you deserve. You didn't say may I," I said, blowing on her fingers to extinguish the flames.

The rejection had thrown her very off balance. "What do you want?"

"That all depends on what you want me to do," I said, pushing her back to the front side of my desk and adjusting my trousers and boxers. Just because I wasn't stupid enough to take her up on her offer didn't mean I was happy about it.

"I need you to find something for me," Bambi said coyly.

"That doesn't help me much. What is the something? Was it yours to begin with? Is it in or out of Hell? Why do you want it? And what are you willing to do to get it back?"

Bambi decided to try and answer the last question first, getting herself all revved up. I put a hand up indicating she should stop the theatrics.

"That's enough of that. That wouldn't be how I chose my payment." At least not all of it, I added silently. There was a risk in laying with any succubus. Sure they provided the most intense sex imaginable, but they took something away in the process. More than one man had been left an empty husk after lying with the demon whores. Bambi was supposed to be the most powerful of them all and even demons had been known to be made subservient by her succubusian wiles. I had no interest in becoming a plaything of anyone. "Now answer my questions."

"I will do pretty much anything you want me to if you find it. I don't know where it is, but I don't believe it's left the Pit."

"Why?"

"Because I think I would sense it. What I've lost is my virginity."

I burst out laughing. I know it wasn't the gentlemanly thing to do, not that it matters in Hell. Still, Bambi wielded a lot of power and influence in the Pit and antagonizing her would undoubtedly cause me no end of grief.

"You're a succubus. Whatever you claim you had to virginity was gone a long time ago." I said.

Bambi squirmed and for once there didn't seem to be any sensuality in it.

"After the Fall, I soon realized what was happening and what would be my lot. I took my virginity magically, much in the way a mortal mage might take his heart and hide it to achieve immortality. As you know, the first demon to lie with a succubus forever has power over her." Actually, I hadn't known that, but it explained a lot. It explains why the so-called demon pimps had such influence over their succubi. "I did not want anyone to have power over me. That was the whole point of the rebellion and I wasn't about to hand it over to the first scumbag who could overpower and force himself on me. This also made me very powerful. I've kept it well hidden over the years, but now it's gone and I have no idea where it is. I want it back." For an instant, all the sex and games dropped from her face. "I need it back."

Then she was back to working her wiles on me and I had to admit she was good at her work. It took a conscious effort on my part and the occasional digging of my fingernails into my palm to remember what she was and what she was trying to do.

Still, she had shared something with me, something probably no one this side of the Devil knew about. In Hell, that was pretty much everyone. That showed a significant amount of trust, something totally alien to the Pit. It worried me because if I did find it, I'd be forever dangerous to her. Red wasn't the type to let anyone hold power over her. She'd quite possibly try to have me eliminated. Demons and damned can't die in hell. It was still unclear if I could. In a sense, she had almost assured I would take the case by telling me. She had to know I'd realize she'd most likely come gunning for me once I found it, but if I turned her down now, there'd be no reason for her to put off a campaign against me. She wouldn't even have to do it herself. Bambi had throngs of admirers, any one of which would do pretty much anything to weasel their way into her good graces and other parts.

Taking the case would at least buy me some time because she wouldn't want anything to happen to me until after she got what she wanted.

I wasn't going to make it easy for her though.

"What does your virginity…"

Bambi cut me off with a little sweet smile. "I prefer if we could refer to it as my treasure."

"You can call it your Aunt Sally for all I care, I call a spade a spade. And a whore a whore."

Her hand rose to take another swat at my face, but I let my inner fire burst out through my eyes, mouth, and hair. "Do we really want to go that route again? Although, I'm always up for barbecue." Actually, the custom of the demons eating the damned was one even I had trouble stomaching. I got my food elsewhere, but Bambi didn't know that. "So what does your virginity look like?"

The succubus held her index finger and thumb about two inches apart. "Round, about this big and red. Very red."

I couldn't help but smile. "So it looks like a cherry?"

If looks could kill, I'd be dead. Fortunately, that was a rare gift, even in Hell. Instead, the succubus gave me a curt nod.

"So will you take the case?" she asked.

"I don't have much else on my plate, so I might as well. If the price is right."

"Well, what do you want?" she asked.

"A blank check." The succubus gave me a confused look. As I mentioned, currency here is in souls, not cash or the promise thereof. "I want to be able to name my price, no matter what it is, and have you pay it."

"I can't agree to that," said the succubus.

I shrugged. "Pity. Then I can't take the case. I trust you can show yourself out."

In Hell, position equals power and the more powerful one is the more they are used to having their egos stroked. In Red's case, a lot of other parts were probably stroked first though.

"Do you know who I am!?" she shouted, her body growing in size and in dangerous pointy parts.

"I'd be a piss poor detective if I didn't know at least that much, and you wouldn't have come to me to hire me."

"I'll go to Lucifer. I'll make him make you find it."

"Nick and I have a deal. It's all in writing. I can turn down any case I want to. What we have works, so he's not going to break our contract. Not for the likes of you anyway."

"I'll…" With my hand, I waved her to silence.

"Don't try and impress me with what you're going to do or who you're going to send after me. I haven't lasted this long by being a pushover. You can have someone else go after it or you can have me. I've already stated my price. Either pay it or don't. I don't much care either way."

Bambi was literally shaking in fury. I pulled out a piece of paper — the real stuff, not made from the hides of the damned — and wrote down basically that I could ask whatever I wanted when I had found her virginity. Opening her mouth she pricked her right index finger with her sharp fangs and used the blood to sign her name. I picked up the paper and put it in my inside coat pocket.

"Very good. I'll let you know when I know something more. Now, where was the last place you saw your virginity?"

Turns out the succubus had hidden her cherry in the Western Lava Pits. Direction really doesn't have much meaning in Hell, but they use it to further confuse the damned because whatever direction they name something has nothing to do with its location in relation to anything else. A lot of people think Hell is all souls burning in rivers of flames and lava. It's much more than that, but there are still a lot of traditionalists. The Western Pits are one of the oldest sites and its been full for some time, so it doesn't get a lot of new souls and is not considered an attractive post for a lower demon. Also since it's from a time when there were much fewer living souls to become damned, it's much smaller than the more modern Happy Holiday Lava Pits, which stretch on as far as the eye could see. Western was the size of a small lake and was watched over by a single demon. There should have been more, but demons can shirk their job responsibilities every bit as much as humans.

Not that it was that hard a job. The lava of Hell has adhesive properties and it had proved almost impossible for a soul to extract themselves, as least without help. Making matters even more difficult is the intensity of the lava was set about even with the healing properties of a soul. That meant it would burn away flesh at about the same rate it grew back. Most souls haven't moved beyond the idea that they didn't have a corporal body anymore and have other options for mobility. Nobody's going to tell them either. It's much easier for the keepers of the damned that way.

Traveling through Hell is a challenge. I know short cuts and quicker ways, but I didn't take any of them. I had picked up a tail and I didn't mean the pointy, wiggly kind. I didn't want to lose him. It was safer for me to know where he was.

I guess Bambi didn't trust me. Big surprise there. Since I hadn't succumbed to her charms, she had no way to control me. I was guessing the big bruiser lumbering behind me was no doubt wrapped around her little finger. He was an asphat breed and they tended to be big, not that smart, but not stupid either. Still, lust can turn any rational male into a blithering idiot. The asphat thought he was being stealthy, but I picked him out as soon as I left my office.

There was a hunk of a mountainside missing and I surmised that had been the cherry's hiding place. Back when the Fallen were first condemned to Hell, there were no damned souls just some imposing countryside like the lava pits. Much in the same way a candle is made from wax, Bambi had tied her virginity by a strand of her hair and dipped it into lava continuously until it was the size of a small child. She then put it into the mountain and diverted a flow of lava to cover it further. Bambi figured this would be as safe a place as any in Hell, and for millennia she'd been right.

There are many different ways to learn things, though I've found basic police procedure tends to work well, although perhaps my methods can get a little more brutal than my mortal counterparts. Witnesses are always helpful, although in Hell sometimes they need a little prodding or beating.

I looked again at the lone guard demon on the outskirts of the lava pit, making sure there weren't others hiding nearby. There should have been a good dozen, but to my knowledge, a soul had not escaped from this pit in a few hundred years. That made the lower level demons in charge of it sloppy. They took shifts, leaving their charges unsecured, at least as far as I was concerned. The last demon standing was bored out of his gourd. Occasionally, he poked the damned with a pitchfork, but his heart really wasn't in it. And as far as the pitchfork goes, it was stereotypical, but it worked.

There's always been a big problem with Hell's security. It's entirely geared to keep people from getting out, not in. I've had huge security issues with a Buddhist monk who goes by Phra Malai or Ksitigarbha depending on the day. The punk's immortal and refuses to move on to heaven until all the damned are saved. He's actually managed to get a few out. Luckily, the security of Hell doesn't fall into my jurisdiction, only catching and tracking down those that do escape. A lot of demons, even the Devil himself, try to make out like they're all knowing, but it's a big bunch of hooey. The Devil has the power to know anything that's going on in Hell, but even his mind is only so big. Hell is too large for him to keep track of everything, otherwise, he wouldn't need me.

Of course, I didn't want to suggest that out loud. Those who speak out against Nick find themselves on the receiving end of some tender torture. I consider myself a scary guy, but in Hell, I'm only a mid-weight. Still, I had my methods and they usually produce results. I snuck up behind the single demon and stood there silently. It actually took him a couple minutes to even notice me and when he did, he spun around with his pitchfork at the ready. When he realized who I was, the pitchfork went down but his crimson skin paled two shades.

"Chief…" That's what they call me down here more often than not. "What brings you here?" The demon was respectful which only made sense. My rank was equivocal with that of a demon lord and this schmuck was pretty low level.

I pulled out a cigarette, the real kind from earth, and lit it with my fingertip. I took a puff and blew three smoke circles before I answered. "Several things."

"I didn't do it," said the demon, lowering his pitchfork even further. You could tell he wanted to raise it up to use for defense but didn't have the balls to piss me off.

"If you don't know what I'm here for, how do you know you didn't do it? Guilty conscience?" The demon laughed at that one. Demons didn't have much by way of consciences. It's tortured out of them at a tender age.

"Doesn't matter what it is. I keep my nose clean and I follow the rules."

"Yeah, sure you do."

"You don't believe me?" he said.

I didn't believe him. He was a demon. Only an idiot takes a demon at their word without some kind of enforcement. "So then you reported the rest of your fellow guards for dereliction of duty? I don't remember seeing any report to that effect."

"Yeah, well, they're just on a quick break. They'll be back any moment," lied the demon.

"And there's those few other matters which you thought you'd gotten away with, but we haven't bothered to follow up on." Like I said before, I didn't know everything, but I knew everyone in Hell was guilty of something, so I bluffed. Judging by the narrowing of his eye slits, he was filling in the blanks for me quite nicely. "I might continue to keep those matters on my to do list, if my questions get answered satisfactorily."

"Sure, Chief. Whatever you need," he said.

I jerked my thumb back over my shoulder. "What made that hole?"

At this, the demon's face literally almost froze up, so I didn't believe a word when he told me, "No idea. It's always been like that."

I took a step closer. "I'm not one for giving second chances, so you want to change that story or are you as dumb as you look and going to stick to it?"

"What story?" he answered.

I grabbed the demon's pitchfork with one hand and with the other I grabbed him by the throat. I don't trust demons as far as I can throw them, which in this case was a good twenty-five feet. The sentry flew across the pit, landing on top of the lava. Where it sucks humans under quickly, demons it takes its time with. Gives the home team an advantage against a rebellion of the damned.

Demon hide is a bit tougher than the dead soul variety, so he just began to sizzle and smoke where he touched the molten magma. If the rest of his detail was there, they would have easily been able to get him out. They weren't, so the damned stood on top of each other's backs and shoulders, working together for the first time, just to get at him. Dozens of hands reached up out of the lava and pulled him under. His scream was lost amongst the rest of cries in a few moments.

This may seem like a foolish interrogation technique because it wasn't likely I'd be getting him back any time soon, but he wasn't the only witness. There was a molten lake full of witnesses. Most demons tend to overlook the fact that the damned are not pets or pieces of furniture simply there for their tortured amusement. A lot of very good information can be gleaned from the tortured humans.

Strutting up the shore I called out. "Is there anyone here who can tell me what made that hole?"

I was greeted with choruses of voices speaking to me, most of them asking what was in it for them, but one lone man managed to get his hand up and simply say, "I can." Problem was he was just about in the middle of the lake and there wasn't exactly a rowboat nearby. Fortunately, the lava was hot enough to make flames. While I couldn't directly control the magma, I could make use of the fire it created. Checking to make sure there was enough to get me to where I was going and back I stepped up onto the flames, striding from one tongue of fire to the next until I reached my stoolpigeon. Seeing my interest, his fellow damned attempted to pull him under, but I used the embers of fire within the lava to make a current that pushed them away. I poked my commandeered pitchfork into the lava. The stoolpigeon soul was bright enough not to have to be told to grab on. I turned and pulled the damned behind me over the lake of fire until we were on the shore.

After a couple hundred years of being constantly burned, there wasn't much more than a mess of charred flesh and bone, so I gave him a moment to literally pull himself together. This was a kindness, one he was not likely to have found elsewhere in his time in the Pit. It also allowed the flesh around his throat to start to stitch so he'd be more easily understood. Plus, it gave him a taste of what not being boiled and burned alive felt like. It's my experience that most damned would do pretty much anything to avoid going back to their tortures.

The stoolie rolled on his side and gave me a curt nod by way of thanks. He was smart enough not to make me ask the question again. "It was ripped out by a giant pink demon with bat wings."

Since even most of the lower demons have some control over how they look, pink tended to be a rare color among the keepers of the damned. Most of the people found it soothing, a happy color. Neither of these was something the average demon wanted to inspire, so this narrowed it down to a few dozen suspects.

"Was the demon wearing anything?" I asked.

"Yeah, a pink tutu," said the soul, realizing how odd that sounded as he actually said it. It narrowed my list of suspects down to one.

"You've been most helpful," I said.

A good portion of the damned's muscles had reformed, so the skin would start soon. "Do I have to go back in there?"

"Depends," I said, holding up the pitchfork. "Are you willing to replace the demon on guard duty?"

"Oh yeah," said the damned, taking the pitchfork from my hands.

"That means no wandering off, no unauthorized breaks, letting no one out of the lava," I said. A quick look was all that I needed to tell that the demon I had thrown in had managed to swim his way to shore. He'd gotten a taloned hand on solid, cool ground and was slowly pulling himself out.

The skinless human soul took the pitchfork and rammed it straight into the demon's face. It was enough to make him lose his grip on the ground and fall back where the souls he had tortured were more than willing to drag him back under the lava.

"Then I'll leave the Western Lava Pit in your capable hands," I said, turning my back to pretend I didn't see that my asphat tail was sneaking up on me. This schmuck was obviously overstepping his instructions, having gotten the idea from someone that Red would be happy if I was no longer in the picture, despite the fact I hadn't yet nailed down where her cherry was.

I was waiting until the last moment so I'd have the best chance of flipping him into the lava pool without getting hurt in return when Skinless yelled, "Watch out!" He lunged behind me, leading with the pitchfork and impaling the asphat on the triple spikes. Asphat are big and tough and take injury extremely well. The chest wound only ticked him off.

I grabbed hold of the shaft of the trident and used it like a catapult to launch my tail into the air toward the lake. I used my power to reach out to the fire in the magma and had a geyser of flame that greeted him, making sure he was dazed and weak when he hit the lava. In that condition, he was no match for the hungry hands of the damned that dragged him under.

"Thanks for the help," said Skinless.

"Back at you," I said. The last thing I expected was for one of the damned to be watching my back. "If any of the other guards show up, tell them I left you in charge. Any of them don't like it, tell them to take it up with the Chief. Watch your back, front and sides."

"I will," said Skinless.

I nodded and headed out to see the Lord of the Dance.

Pitiable is rarely a term associated with the denizens of the Pit however it can be one that's quite fitting. I know most mortals would not consider demons pitiable, nor for that matter do most demons. I think perhaps my point of view as an outsider in Hell gives me a unique perspective.

Better to rule in Hell than serve in Heaven is a popular catch phrase these days thanks to Milton. That was, however, the general consensus at the time of the rebellion even though Hell didn't truly exist at that time.

Because of that, the rebellious angels had no idea of what they were getting themselves into, except for maybe the Devil. Sometimes I wonder if he knew. These poor slobs were literally in paradise. Not some cut-rate deal like the afterlife I once ruled. This was the real deal, eternal bliss. The kind of thing that tells even a bad man to try and live a good life in hopes that his acts will buy his way into Heaven. And these demons were there just as a gift. I can't imagine what that kind of paradise would be like, even though I've talked to several who had had it and lost it.

These idiots actually thought what they were fighting for would give them something better than paradise. Let's just say the lot were more than a little disappointed after the Fall. Every one of the Fallen still remembers what they lost. Worse, they realized they didn't lose it at all. They threw it away. It tends to make them permanently pissed off with a hate on for anything human. Humans make good scapegoats for their own stupidity. It's what still fueled them after all this time to punish the damned. Of course, not all demons are Fallen, but even those born in the Pit are tortured and taught nothing but hate, so few of them are actually any better than their sires. Some are even worse.

Few of the Fallen are as pitiable as Balchain. Humans who keep track of such things refer to him as the Lord of the Dance. It's a title also given to Shiva, but he's not on my beat. For Balchain, it's somewhat of a mocking title, whether they realize it or not. There are stories about angels dancing at the throne of God, forever praising the Creator. Before the Fall, Balchain choreographed those visions of angels and their praise. After he fell, the body he was left with was not capable of the type of moves he had once done with ease. Never again would he see or perform the type of dancing that he once helped create. I think Balchain misses that as much as paradise itself.

Whenever he is summoned to the mortal plane, the first thing on his mind isn't death and destruction, but seeing his favorite art form. I once had to escort him back sobbing after a performance of the Moscow Ballet. That is not to say he doesn't enjoy his death and destruction. He once wiped out an entire disco in Des Moines after having witnessed their version of the hustle.

Despite his idiosyncrasies, Balchain was still a Lord of Hell and thus not someone to be taken lightly, despite his choice of frilly pink outer wear. As I walked near his domain, I was greeted with a sound very much like rhythmic thunder. There wasn't any hellish storm, but there were damned lined up farther than the eye could see, forced to do synchronized patterns, the accuracy of which would make any mortal general proud. From my vantage, it looked like they were line dancing.

It may not seem like a very hellish experience to some, although just the thought of it gave me shivers down my spine. One has to realize that Balchain made his damned do it ten million times in a row and severely punished those who missed a step before one can begin to have some grasp of what was involved.

Of course, none of that takes into account the biggest problem with dancing in Hell —there's no music allowed in the Pit. Music speaks to the soul. In kabala they even speak of a part of the soul reserved just for music and they're not far from the truth. Music can stay with you long after the song is done. It's why certain pop songs will offend people to such degrees. Deep inside, everyone has some appreciation for good music. They know what it is and what it's not.

Any music in Hell would lessen the pain in the ranks of the damned and kind of set back the whole punishing process.

That did not, however, mean there were not ways of keeping a beat. Balchain would pull out a damned dancer and tear him or her apart, starting with the pinkies and working his way through the fingers and the toes, until reaching the limbs before moving on to the torso. The Lord of the Dance finally ends with the parts of the face such as the ears, nose, and eyes. Balchain makes sure to leave the mouth until last so that their screams could keep the beat until the very end. This befell any of the damned that caught his attention. It forced them to try to ignore that their naked feet were doing their fancy footwork on terrain terraformed to be sharper than broken shards of glass. Those who missed a beat got much worse. I stood on the outskirts watching as the pink tutued demon dove in and out of the masses a few times. I wanted to make sure I was noticed before I approached, so I stuck my left foot inside his borders and took it out, hoping he didn't think I was doing the hokey pokey. No need to spook him. I certainly didn't want him to focus his more violent attentions on me.

The Lord of the Dance handed off a fresh damned soul to one of his underlings, who was currently decked out like a Vegas showgirl. Not a good look for him. Once Balchain was sure the beat would continue, he flew to me.

"Hello, Negral." Demon lords tended to not bother with such trivial things as titles. Being able to ignore them was a show of power in a place where even the perception of disrespect could end with being flayed alive.

I didn't get hot and bothered by things like that and had no problem using someone's title. In fact, I often found it useful. "Hello, Lord Balchain."

"What brings the police to my door?" asked the pink demon, fixing his frilly skirt. It was splattered with blood and what looked like fat and tendons. Balchain was trying to fluff it back up.

"An act of vandalism," I answered.

Balchain raised an eyebrow and looked at me funny. "Vandalism? It seems with all that happens in Hell, vandalism would be pretty far down on the list of things requiring investigation."

I shrugged in a casual way. "Not so much the act itself, but there was a piece of the landscape taken which has sentimental value to someone who has asked that I see it returned."

The demon laughed loud and hearty. "I thought it odd that Crone wanted a piece of dry magma. I find it even odder that someone else wants it back."

That was too easy. No one gives away information for free in Hell, but I hadn't figured out the catch–yet. "Not that I don't appreciate your cooperation Lord Balchain, but you proffer The Crone's name rather easily. May I ask why?"

The pink demon smiled. "Of course. She offered me something in exchange for my delivery of that hunk of rock, as few others could break it apart. It's something I think you would appreciate." From a pocket of his tutu, he pulled what looked like a music box with a ballerina on top. Of course, the machine could not actually produce any tunes and the female figure on top was no statue, but a soul shrunken by hellish magiks to fit. "Do you recognize her?"

It took me a moment, but I did. "The ballerina from Moscow."

"Yes. Quite possibly the greatest mortal dancer ever. I hated and loved her ever since that night I saw her perform." Her performance had moved the Lord of the Dance to tears. I was so shocked I let him finish watching. She had been amazing. "But then less than two years later she gave it all up, walked away from the dance for the love of a man and to produce offspring. To throw away her ability to make such beauty for such trivialities, it killed any love I might have had for her."

It made sense, especially considering the effect of watching her had on him. Still, it seemed an awful long fall.

"What'd she do?" I said, pointing my chin at the tiny, damned ballerina who was trying to do a piqué and not succeeding. It looked like her feet had been crushed and ground up, so standing on her toes was an act of futility.

"Turns out the guy she married, the man she gave up dancing for, lost interest after a few years and a few kids, then started screwing the babysitter. She walked in on them and snuck out before they noticed her. She took her time planning every last detail and slipped both of them a slow acting poison that took weeks to kill them, every second of that time putting them in more and more agony. Got away with it too." Balchain let loose a sad laugh. "At least in the mortal world."

That kind of thing was certainly enough to get someone into Hell. Taking another life for anything other than self-defense can pretty much be a one-way ticket to the Pit.

"None of this explains why you gave up The Crone so easily," I said.

"Nothing easy about it. The bitch promised me this soul would be in pristine condition, but look at it. Someone else has already been playing with her. She's already been broken, something I had long dreamed of doing myself and that's been taken from me. I traded in good faith and I didn't get what I paid for. I figure she wants whatever is in that hunk of rock and you are going to take it away from her. Or at the very least, you'll make trouble for her and that suits me just fine."

I nodded. As demons went, Balchain was as close to honest as any of them ever get, even if it was still miles away. He was not so much into the lying and deception as in to the wholesale destruction and pain.

The hairs on the back of my neck stood up and got hot. I looked back and noticed my latest tail only about thirty seconds before Balchain sensed him crossing his borders. I could tell by the subtle turn of the Lord of the Dance's head. This troubled me as the demon wouldn't have been here if he hadn't been following me for some time. I hadn't noticed him and I always check to see if I'm being followed.

A closer look showed me he was a spigh. Yeah, it's pronounced spy, but spelled different. Spighes worked directly for the Devil himself, watching things on Earth and in the Pit in order to report back. They are practically undetectable. The only reason I noticed him when I did was Balchain's power was so strong in his domain, not just from his status as Fallen, not only because of his multitudes of souls but because he is constantly having his damned performing rituals to raise power. All that dancing wasn't just for fun and punishment. He has as much, if not more, power to draw on than any demon lord in the Pit. It won't allow anyone to come hidden or unknown into his domain. The spigh didn't count on that.

The thought that the Devil was having me followed crossed my mind, but I dismissed it. Our dynamic involved me getting called on the carpet, not followed. I have more to lose than most in Hell. Without the manna I get for doing my job, I'd be heading out on a one-way ticket to oblivion. Drawback of being a forgotten god. I'm not going up against Nick without a damn good reason.

Besides spighes are professionals. One in his right mind wouldn't have made the blunder of setting foot near Balchain's infinite dance of the damned. However, one blinded by lust…

"Friend of yours?" asked Balchain. It wasn't above him to do me a favor by allowing one of my cops to go if they had been stupid enough to trespass uninvited. It meant I'd have to let him finish the next ballet he was at or something of that sort. If I admitted the spigh was tailing me, he also might let him go in order to see what happened, just for ha-has.

A spigh that had it out for me was too dangerous to let loose. Once I left Balchain's realm, I'd have no way of knowing where he was. When Red gave the word, I'd never see him coming and I might find out if a forgotten god can die in Hell. However, while not high ranking they, like me, work directly for Nick. He'd frown on me for disposing of one, even if his service was preempted by Bambi.

The Devil was more powerful than any demon lord, but not more than all of them or even a large number working in concert. He liked to keep the lot infighting, but even the Devil has to honor treaties and diplomacy. By being caught, the spigh had made a major diplomatic blunder. That meant Balchain could punish him to his heart's content with no real consequences. The Devil didn't care enough for most demons to risk a squabble with someone of Balchain's power levels to get them back. I just had to convince the Lord of the Dance that he wanted to keep and punish the spigh.

"No friend of mine. Certainly not of yours," I said.

"Oh?" said Balchain. "Why's that?"

Remembering my own suspicions of information given too freely, I played hard to get. "I'm not sure I should say. It falls out of my jurisdiction. It was only words. I'd just as soon stay out of it."

"We're not in the mortal world where I'm weakened and you're not. We are in my place of power. Are you sure you wish to deny me a simple request?" said Balchain, moving into a threatening position. Oddly enough, he went up onto the tips of his toes when he did. Some would say being threatened by someone in a pink tutu could never be intimidating. Those people had never met Balchain.

I made like I was speaking only because of the implied threat, which meant that I had to try to save face. "I suppose since you were so free with the information regarding The Crone..."

"I was."

"This makes us even on that account, right?" I said. I need his help, so I couldn't risk him think he was getting something for nothing. I'm not noted for caving in easily. Not that I haven't done it, just not easily.

"Sure."

"That spigh was talking about your dancers," I said.

"What about them?"

"Mostly that they moved like three-legged, blind hell hounds who had never met a choreographer," I said meekly.

"He did? What else did he say?" demanded Balchain, his fangs showing as he spoke.

"I don't really want..."

"Tell me!" he shouted and the ground shook. The dance even halted for half a beat, before quickly resuming.

"He insulted you personally. Said there was no way you were really one of the Fallen. That you were the weakest of the demon Lords. That you were a... poof," I said.

"A what?" asked Balchain.

"A poof. Light in the loafers. A pansy." He looked confused still. I held my wrist up and let it go limp. Now homosexuality is not the sin some think it is. It falls into the same category as abuses of heterosexual sex do, but Balchain had endured many insults on his masculinity over the years because of how he dressed. It was a sensitive topic for the demon. Balchain's eyes narrowed and the surrounding mountains trembled in a staccato beat. "Said you only wear the dancing clothes because you can't dance anymore. Doubted you ever could. Of course, he was trying to impress a succubus at the time." Might as well lay the groundwork for stuff the spigh will spout under torture. "We've all been there. He probably figured he'd talk trash about the badest demon lord he could think of to look tough. I mean he works for the boss, so he could hardly disrespect Him."

"How would you know this?" he asked, his anger tempered by suspicion. Balchain was no lesser demon, easily tricked.

"Knowing things in the Pit is my business," I said.

"What succubus?" he asked.

I hesitated before answering. "Bambi."

"So why would he be dumb enough to come here?" asked Balchain.

I took a page from the Devil's playbook, interspersing enough truth in the lies to make it seem feasible. "To impress the dame. She has an interest in what The Crone got from you."

"Which is?"

"I'll find out when I find it. She's been sending lovesick fools after me since I started this case," I said.

"Can you prove it?" he asked.

Did I want to? No. But could I? "Yep." Or close enough.

"Stop him from leaving," I said. "I assume you can hear anything in your realm?" Like the omniscient thing, the demon lords like to make others think they knew everything that happened in their realms, but the truth is, outside of certain security measures, they had to be focused on the event to eavesdrop.

"Of course," he lied.

"Then make sure you get an earful," I said. I had been maneuvering myself so Balchain was between me and the spigh. Fire is a popular motif and there was enough for me to ride across far faster than I could run. I ducked out of sight, doubled outside of Balchain's realm and back in behind the spigh, blending in with the flames so I wasn't seen.

"Vacationing?" I said. I had to give the spigh credit. He only startled slightly.

"Why would I come here?" he said.

"Not a fan of dance?" I asked. I got lucky. The spigh made a sarcastic grunt. "So I guess you quit working for Nick. Why? Bambi have better fringe benefits?" I didn't get a rise. Guess I wasn't aiming low enough. "The whore certainly has enough practice. Tell me, do you have to take a number or do you just wait in line until the thousand demons in front of you are done? Not too bad if you don't mind sloppy second thousands. Or are you so ugly you have to wait until she's tired and numb and slip it to her in stealth mode so she doesn't even know you're there?"

That did it.

"You don't know what you're talking about. Bambi and I have something special," the spigh insisted as if convincing me would make it true.

"Yeah, you and half this circle," I said. "She sent you after me?"

"Sure. You're so dense you didn't even know I've been following you," he said.

"Then why'd you stop short the first time I looked back at you?" I bluffed. I look back at regular intervals and glare. Spighes aren't the only things that are hard to spot in Hell. I fell outside the normal range of demon abilities, so most aren't really sure what I can or can't do. From the look I got, he bought the bluff.

"How could you know I was there?"

"Sun god. Light reveals all that is hidden," I lied.

"I didn't know you could do that," he said.

"Why advertise?" I bluffed. "So you going to give up your mistress and get back to your job?"

"Maybe after I kill you," he smiled, the four fingers opposite his right thumb merging together to make a talon blade. "But probably not."

"So you'd do this in Balchain's realm?"

"Why not? You'd see me just as well out there. At least here, I'm ready for you," he said.

"I doubt it," I said, grabbing his bladed hand and kneeing him in the groin. I followed through by gutting him with his own living knife. The spigh wasn't exactly skilled at hand to hand. Didn't have to be normally. It's kind of hard for people to defend themselves from an unseen attack they don't know is coming. I reached along to his back and made the fire dance up from the ground to surround his body blade and grabbed it. To me, fire, even the Hellish variety, can be used as if it was a solid and I didn't want to touch the sharp edges directly. Too easy to get cut and he might poison them. By slicing and moving it around inside of him aiming for delicate organs, I maneuvered him to his feet and marched him toward Balchain.

"You want him for trespass and the rest?" I said.

"You're willing to just give him to me?" he asked.

"Think of it as an advance apology for the next time Nick asks me to escort you home," I said, being careful to emphasize that it was the Devil's insistence that made me keep bringing him back.

"Accepted," said the Lord of the Dance with an evil grin. Balchain grabbed the spigh by both shoulders and pulled him away from me, lifting him up into the air.

He started with the spigh's pinky and called for a change, ordering everyone to switch over to doing the Macarena.

I shivered and got the blazes out of there. I was off to see The Crone.

The Crone was one of the Fallen. Not all fallen became demon lords. In fact, most didn't, but the ambitious Fallen do have an advantage over the hell born demons in that they were allowed to keep their own domains and still have quite a bit of political pull.

The Crone, like Balchain, had been seraphim before the rebellion. While Balchain's job was to keep the dancing going, her job was just to stand there and look pretty. Literally. The Crone's job was to channel some of the creator's own beauty through herself to inspire those who could not always stay by the throne. She was one of the most beautiful things in heaven and therefore all of creation.

In Hell, she's one of the ugliest, and that's saying something. Yes, her skin was scaly and oozing, but that wasn't uncommon. She was lumpy in places that might look good on a tree but not a woman. And as much as she tried, her two eyes could never point in the same direction and they tried constantly. Neither could her nostrils for that matter. She had no hair of her own, but constantly tried using the scalps of the damned as wigs, but they turned to multicolored straw soon after being placed on her scalp. Her hands were talons and she was unable to touch herself even to scratch her misshapen nostrils without leaving a gash on her skin.

It was no secret she pined away for her lost beauty and whether it was a reward for her loyalty in the rebellion or punishment for having fallen, she was given the damned who's sins involved abusing their beauty in life to take advantage of others. The Crone took great pleasure in finding new ways to mutilate her damned and unlike so many other hell spawn, she never seemed to have gotten bored by it.

Because she didn't have the power of a demon lord I could approach her domain, which she called Beauty's Edge, without her knowing about it. The problem is once I set foot inside she'd know I was there and I wanted to catch her with the goods.

The best way to do that is to get in there fast. At least I was fairly confident she wasn't planning on destroying the evidence, not after going to such lengths to get a hold of it. Now technically, I do have officers of both demon and damned that work for me as well as a network of spies and informants throughout Hell. The problem is I don't trust a one of them and I've always felt that going in with large numbers was a sign of weakness and the last thing I can afford to be perceived as is weak.

I do have a means of traveling quickly over a linear distance that's not blocked, but Nick hates it when I do it. As a former sun god, I can travel in a sunbeam. Problem is sunlight and the denizens of Hell don't mix well together. With the sun shining overhead it's easy. Here, much more difficult. Also, it's risky. If someone knows I'm coming, I can be caught in a bottle or vessel that is lightproof. I do it rarely because of that risk. Plus, in the Pit, it uses up my personal supply of power, which is on a limited basis until my next trip topside to Earth to sunbathe. Despite all that, sometimes it's worth doing it to make a grand entrance. I set my sights on The Crone's chambers, stepped one foot into her domain and shot ahead as a sunbeam right through the window. Its magic, not science, so I don't quite travel at the speed of light, but it is pretty swift. It does take me another couple of seconds to shift back into a physical form. It was still enough time for The Crone to start acting like she wasn't doing anything. The Fallen was hunched over a pretty mortal soul, slowly tearing small strips of flesh from her face, but I could tell it was just an act. Maybe a third of the face and almost none of the body had been touched.

"Negral, how dare you invade my domain without my leave!" The Crone was angered and indignant, but she came across a little too much like a kid caught with her hand in the cookie jar. "You need the Devil's permission to come in here."

It was amazing how many demons, even the Fallen, didn't fully realize how Hell worked. No one needed anyone's permission for anything, including the damned. It was just a matter of the strongest imposing their will on the weakest.

"Its okay. I have a warrant."

The Crone's eyes went wide. "You do? I've never heard of such a thing.

Let me see it."

"Always happy to oblige a lady," I said pulling Bambi's contract out of my inside coat pocket. I held the folded document up and The Crone leaned in to look at it. I smashed her in the face with my fist.

"You'll pay for…" I hit her again just to shut her up.

"Okay, where is it?" I demanded.

Her skin can't take physical abuse and each blow made her even uglier. The skin above her upper lip had opened and demon ichor was oozing down her mouth in gooey rivers. The Crone wiped it with the back of her hand and smiled. "I'm sure I don't know what you're talking about."

I slipped the contract back into my pocket and The Crone made a move on me from behind as I looked around her torture chamber. I let my sun fire flare from the back of my head where she was aiming her talons. Her whole arm caught on fire.

It made her back off long enough for me to finish looking around the room.

While I'm not a lava god, lava and fire have several affinities and I was able to feel for the magma. The Crone actually had been rather clever in hiding it —she plunged it into the abdominal cavity of the damned she was torturing. While it was not the last place I would have looked, it would have taken me a while to search there. I pulled aside the stomach flap and pulled out the stony chunk.

"That's mine!" screeched The Crone, still trying to put out her burning limb. The solid magma had shown several signs of damage as if someone had been trying to chisel or claw it apart, but several eons of layer upon layer wasn't exactly the easiest thing to break apart. Otherwise, she wouldn't have needed Balchain's help.

I snapped my fingers and the flames in her arm went out. "Why do you want it?"

"Do you even know what it is?" she asked.

It's not like I was the only one who could have been fooled by a pretty face, but I was pretty sure no one had pulled the bloody wool over my eyes. "Let's not insult either of our intelligences by pretending we don't know what's in here. Tell me why you want it."

"That priss Bambi didn't have a fraction of my beauty in paradise, but down here men and demon alike fall over themselves to fawn on her. It makes me sick. One of my damned was not only good looking but a psychic as well and gave me the information in hope of getting out of torture; it worked. He got all of five minutes to relax. If I had her virginity, I would control her. I could make her do what I want with whom I want. I could make her uglier than me if I wanted to." The Crone was grinning with evil glee. "I'm not going to let you take it from me."

"You can't even get it out of there," I said.

The crone cackled. "And I suppose you can?"

I raised a single eyebrow in answer. "I'm taking this with me."

"You steal from me and you will have made an enemy for eternity."

"Oh, goodie. I hear my enemies have a club now, even have weekly meetings. Maybe you can join and learn the secret handshake." The Crone was not amused and still was waving her flaming arm. "That's not the handshake, but it's surprisingly close. The middle finger needs to be extended more."

"Didn't have the balls to come alone, Chief?" she growled.

"I assure you I did." Outside, there was raking of claws on stone. Something was climbing up the side of the building. Red had decided to send more tails en mass. It was starting to piss me off, but at least she was getting smarter and sent a group. It sounded like this time there were at least five.

"I don't believe you," said The Crone.

"I don't give a damn what you believe, but you make another move and it means you are starting a war with me. If that's what you want, bring it on. I'll burn you and your domain to the ground. Then I'll let you grow back and do it again." I was exaggerating my power a bit. Back when I was at the height of my power, I could have done all that and more. Now, I'd have to be in direct sunlight to do more than the building. "Of course, there are other options." I snapped my fingers and her blazing arm went out. "I offer you a gift." At this, The Crone's eyes widened. "Bambi has many admirers, those who as you say fall over themselves to do her bidding. That is who has invaded your domain, coming after what you have taken. I offer you my assistance in capturing them for your amusement." As Bambi had her choice of suitors and partners, she only chose the handsomest or most powerful. "What could you do to the hellish beauty of several of her devoted? It would not be as good as controlling her, but it would be something of hers that you have that she does not."

"It's not the same," said The Crone.

I shrugged and held my hand like I was about to snap my fingers again. "It's the best offer you're going to get. And this time I won't contain the blaze to a single limb. And she'll keep sending more and more of her admirers here after it. What happens when she convinces one of her trinity of demon lord friends to come for it? Are you prepared to fight one or all of them?"

The Crone looked at me, peering deep into my eyes. "You don't have the look of one of her thralls."

"That's because I'm not."

"You're not going to give it back to her?"

My only answer was a laugh. If Red had honored our deal by not coming after me, sure. She hadn't.

The Crone rubbed her chin. She wasn't buying my threat entirely, but she wasn't convinced it was a bluff either. And she knew there were demons heading her way. I was offering her a way to save face and she decided to take it. "You have something of a reputation. If you will not give it back to her, you must have something else planned. It won't be as good as what I would do to her. It might be adequate with the rest of your offering."

I nodded my head in thanks. "Excellent. If you will allow them to enter through the window, I'll see if I can't gift wrap them for you."

The Crone cackled. "Do you think I will allow trespassers to go unpunished by me directly? There are only seven of them." Looks like I underestimated. "You can have my leftovers."

"A contest then?" I suggested.

The Crone smiled and something gooey and brown oozed down her chin. "Sure."

The septet climbed in the same window I had beamed through, not even suspecting that we were waiting for them.

I stood directly in their view, while The Crone waited to the side.

"Negral, you may have escaped the others, but they weren't as devoted to Bambi as we are. You shall not escape us so you may as well hand the stone over to us," said the largest of the septet. Even in Hell, guys can talk like a B-movie. Sure, I may ape Bogie, but those flicks are strictly the A-game.

Big boy didn't have a chance to take another step before The Crone speared him in the chest, pinning him to the wall. The Crone enjoyed nailing her damned like insects being dissected and had many impaling instruments laying about, just waiting to be used. I helped myself to a pair of spikes and pinned the closest demon to the same wall. I was jumped by three of the remaining, while the remaining pair went after The Crone.

My assailants came in quick and quiet, getting me between them. I tried to burn one, but his fellow attacker jumped in front of my flames. As the guy was a sulfure demon, it didn't do as much as I hoped. Those guys are bred for fire, even sunlight. They're also big as sin. I slugged him in the jaw and didn't accomplish much more than hurting my hand.

The sulfure managed to get me in a full nelson. The other two used the opportunity to start working me over. Big mistake on their part. They should have gone for the kill while they had the chance. One was pounding my breadbox while the other was alternating between my groin and my knee. As I had lifted my feet up to make the sulfure work hard, my knee swung like a pendulum instead of snapping, but it wouldn't take long for them to adjust their attacks. One thing even the dumbest demon is good at is inflicting pain.

These jokers were strong and the breadboxer grabbed hold of the cherry stone and pulled it out of my grip. The three of them were laughing like baritone schoolgirls.

They had what they came for. Either I made my move or they were going to have me at their mercy. This being Hell, I knew they had none. I waited for the groin gouger to try another shot at making me sing soprano and kneed him in the jaw, then head butted the sulfure. The big guy was expecting it, but it loosened his grip enough for me to gouge his eyes out with my thumbs. I dug both his demon blues out like my fingers were melon scoopers. The pain combined with his world going dark made him drop me like a living man would a skunk.

Instead of running or even backing up to regroup, the pair who had been working me over pressed their attack. I grabbed them both. My hand closed around the throat of the demon that had been socking me in the gut, but I returned the groin gouger's attention and grabbed him by his neither regions. I lifted both of them up. Normally, I'd just beat the crap out of both of them, but my balls hurt. Bad. I incinerated the neck of the breadboxer, so his head fell off. I'm sure it hurt, but nowhere near the pain that the other had when I cremated his demonhood. Then I stomped on both his knees until they were bent at improbable angles.

I picked up a trio of spears and impaled the body of the headless breadboxer where he fell through his gut. I did the same to the groin gouger but put the spear a lot lower. If The Crone left him there, his demonhood would have to grow back around the shaft. I had no problem with that. I wanted nothing more than to put an icepack on my godhood and, considering my affinity for fire, that was saying something.

The Crone had disposed of her two attackers without much problem, but ten more lustlorn demons had come in the window. The sulfure was one tough bastard because he was back on his feet and listening. He must have heard me breathing because he charged right at me. Fortunately, eyes take more than a few moments to grow back and he was charging blind. I sidestepped and tripped him as he roared by. The sulfure lost his footing and smashed headfirst into the wall. I raised the spear but caught The Crone out of the corner of my eye. I stepped back and motioned with my arm that the honor of pinning the sulfure was hers. She acknowledged the gesture and pinned the bastard with a spear of her own right into the mouth and out through the spine. The sulfure's legs twitched wildly for a moment, then went still.

The ten newcomers saw the cherry stone and dove for it. One I recognized as Fallen got it first and yelled, "Cover me and I'll bring it back to Bambi." The other nine moved to obey. Even The Crone looked a little nervous. Most of them were Fallen, with power levels close to or exceeding hers. They had sent the others in as crone-fodder.

I pulled out a cigarette and lit up. "What a bunch of suckers." The advance stopped. "Bambi's offering a reward for whoever brings her that stone, am I right?"

"And your head, Chief," said another sulfure, bigger than the first.

"Good luck with that," I said. "And good luck getting your share of the reward."

"We're going to split it," said the sulfure.

"How are you going to divvy up the favors of the queen of the succubi? Take turns?" I said.

The sulfure paused before answering, "Yeah." I laughed. "What's so funny?"

"Well, the bozo by the window is going to be the first one back with the stone right?" There was agreement on that point. "You think the first thing on his mind is going to be telling Bambi that the nine of you helped him? Or do you think he'll get right to partaking of that reward? I bet she'll be real grateful too. Probably take days showing her gratitude."

"Oh yeah," said the sulfure, but some of the others were already figuring out where I was going.

"So she'll finish him up and if he remembers to mention the rest of you, maybe she'll screw the lot of you, but she'll be tired for the second one. Probably ready for sleep by the tenth one. Who figures out the order? I don't know about you boys, but I'd want to get my share of the reward first, while she'd still be fresh, not stinking of him. Or any of you. But if you lot don't mind, far be it for me to screw up such a great plan," I said, blowing out smoke in the shape of Red. My next exhalation had a demon joining her, followed by a long line of bored looking demons. I can control smoke and got pretty good likenesses and some nice animation.

"No way you're getting Bambi, first," said the big sulfure.

"Now wait, I'm the fastest and we agreed…" said the demon holding the cherry stone, backing toward the window. Two Fallen had already cut him off.

"Give it to me," said the big sulfure.

"What makes you think you're going to be the one to take it to her?" said another.

"Cause I'm taking it to Bambi," said a third.

Things went downhill from there, at least for their side. The logical decision to all deliver it together never occurred to them. It's not like Red wouldn't have taken all comers with a smile and a moan.

Instead, it was a blood bath as one of the Fallen beheaded the guy with the cherry stone, but the sulfure was the first to grab it. He was skewered by the spike tail of a Cerotops, who himself was ripped in two by a bulkhiad demon. And so it went until there was only one demon standing, although he had lost one of his right arms in the struggle. He raised the cherry stone over his head and bellowed in triumph, which is when The Crone and I did a double impalement on him from behind. We found a nice empty spot on the wall and parked him there.

The Crone rubbed her hands together. "They are all so very pretty." She was already gathering up the wounded and imprisoning them, calling for her underlings whom she had kept outside because she had wanted her possession of the cherry stone to remain secret. "I think I shall enjoy this bargain, Negral. I shall forgive you this trespass if you go make that bitch's life miserable."

"As long as you're having fun," I said. The Crone was almost giddy as she started peeling back the first sulfure's face. I picked up the now bloody hunk of lava and took my leave of her and Beauty's Edge.

Of course to make Red's life miserable or otherwise, I had to first find her. Bambi was a kept demon with her own little piece of anti-paradise. It was right on the border where three demon lord realms met. They spent centuries fighting over the area until she offered to set up shop there in exchange for services rendered. As rent in Hell goes, it wasn't too steep.

The place was about the size of a shopping mall with a parking lot-too small for any respectable demon lord to claim as a solo territory, but more than respectable for anyone else. She didn't have the same tie with the land as a demon lord would or even a Fallen who had taken the land and made it their own like The Crone had. Still, she was Fallen and had the home field advantage. Part of me debated about making her come to me, but decided against it, mainly because it's what she'd assume I'd do. No doubt the way back to my office was littered with her obedient lovers, some of which might be very competent attackers. As I now had her cherry in my possession, she'd demonstrated she had no reason to tell them to hold back. That is assuming the others hadn't foolishly just been demonstrating initiative and overstepping their bounds.

I had the sunbeam option, but I didn't want to over do it. That ability wasn't common knowledge, but it wasn't impossible for someone to know about it. One of her lovers might be clever enough to be waiting to capture me.

Better to do things the old fashioned way. I hit her ground running so to speak. It was more of a brisk walk. Her various boy toys moved to stop me, but I was faster and none of them were really motivated enough to try and come after me after I disemboweled the first two with a flaming sword. I would have used it on my attackers earlier at Beauty's Edge, but it takes a bit of concentration to form it and ignoring them even for those few seconds they would have had me pinned. It could have been fatal.

I slowed down and strolled into her boudoir. It was decorated like something out of Arabian nights meets the Marquis De Sade. There were chains and various spiked instruments of torture and pleasure, mixed in with satin pillows and silk sheets, some of them even on the walls. Like her clothes and skin, the overall coloring was red. She was right in the middle of a bit of a gangbang with four demons and two damned, although one of the damned was standing in a corner watching, but obviously more than willing to participate, but forbidden to. His hands were removed to limit his other options.

I cleared my throat. "How many tickets to ride this ride?"

Bambi startled and stopped short, although the other five members of her party didn't even slow down.

"Chief, what are you doing here?" said Bambi, although she was having some trouble speaking as two of the demons kept trying to put parts of themselves in her mouth, but she swatted them away.

It was obvious she hadn't expected me to still be moving under my own power, so I just smiled. "I agreed to find something. You didn't think it would take me that long, did you?"

The succubus started to look nervous. "No, not at all. Everybody off and out," she yelled. It took some kicking and squeezing of delicate organs on her part, but eventually, they did listen and leave.

"Not to critique your methods of punishing the damned, but I don't quite understand. The damned in the corner watching makes sense. It must be torture for someone who lived their whole life for sex to observe and not be able to participate, but what about the one in the mix?"

"He's gay."

I had seen the man's face and he seemed to be enjoying himself. Maybe the sight of his other male playmates was enough to get him going, but he seemed to only have eyes for Red. I was guessing he conned her. Good for him. It's rare for the damned to do anything but get walked on. True, he was low man on the orgy totem pole and I'm not sure how much he was really getting out of humping her left foot, but he seemed to have risen above the rest of the damned.

Once the room had been cleared of anyone who might overhear about the unusual and literal condition of her cherry, Bambi could not help but stare at the molten mass under my left arm.

"Is that it?" she asked, the desperation in her voice surprising even her. Red was used to causing the emotion in others, not having it herself.

"Is this the hunk of cooled magma taken from the Western Lava Pit? Yes, it is," I replied.

Bambi lunged for it and I pulled it out of her way like a matador's cape before a bull. Red stumbled but didn't fall. She had done that a long time ago.

"Not so fast. You seem a little surprised to see me. Why would that be?" I asked, full knowing the answer.

"I don't know what you're talking about," she said with a pouty innocence that, if had she been wearing a Catholic schoolgirl uniform, would have reduced some human males to blithering and drooling idiocy.

"And I suppose all those admirers of yours took it upon themselves to come after me?" I said.

She put her finger to her lips and nibbled suggestively on the end as she shrugged. "I can hardly be expected to be responsible for the actions of every demon that's ever taken a liking to me."

"But you can take credit for more than a few."

"What are you accusing me of?" she asked, brewing with indignity. I wasn't going to swallow a cup of that nonsense.

"No accusations, just that you were foolish enough to try and have me knocked off. You're lucky the first few didn't work out because I hadn't found your cherry yet and then you'd be up a creek wouldn't you?" I said. "You asked me to do you a favor and this is how you repay my kindness?"

Bambi morphed into her evil succubus form, this time making sure she went all the way. Red became twice as tall as me and had talons as long as my forearms on her hands and feet. Her breasts grew even larger in proportion. Little mouths with rows of sharp pointy teeth appeared where the nipples had been.

I was supposed to be scared but I have a problem with what I'm supposed to do. It's part of why I ended up in Hell.

"This really isn't a good look for you."

Bambi ignored me taking a swipe at my head. I stepped back out of the way but had to move so quickly that the lava stone fell from my grasp. Everything else forgotten, Bambi dove on it, swiping it with her talons trying to dig in through the protective stone coating, but all her efforts barely made a scratch.

She started laughing and talking to herself. "It's still safe." She turned towards me, an evil grin on her face. "Now its time to take care of you, Chief. I'll dismember you and scatter the body parts throughout all of Hell. I'll even drop your head in the Western Pits. The lava will cover it and nothing will ever cut you out. Imagine eternity trapped in stone."

That was assuming Hell extended to me its courtesy of not allowing death to affect those within its borders. "We had a deal. I find your cherry and you do anything I ask."

"I told you to call it my treasure and since it's still buried, consider our deal broken."

"I don't think so," I said pulling a round red ball from my pocket. I held it tightly between my thumb and fingers and squeezed it ever so gently.

Bambi fell back into her more pleasing form, one hand grabbing her neither regions, the other the right side of her mountain range, all the while moaning in fear and ecstasy. "That's my… how did you get it out? The lava should be almost impenetrable."

That much was true. Balchain had found it by smashing away at the wall and picking up what didn't crumble. Her dipping method mixed with the magic of her cherry had made an incredibly dense coating. Luckily, I don't use brute force as my first course of action. "Well Red, you may or may not know that the key ingredient of lava is fire. That stuff there is just the cool version. Add a little flame and it starts oozing around again. I'm good with fire, so it wasn't much to get it out."

"Give my treasure back to me or I'll…." Her sentence ended in a moan.

I had squeezed the cherry until it was oblong instead of a ball and rolled it between my fingers. Bambi fell to the ground writhing in what looked like pleasure, screaming louder than she had for her quintet of lovers. "You're not in much of a position to be threatening me. You're already on my list for trying to break a deal and going back on your word. I don't like it when someone goes back on their word. Particularly to me."

"I'll do anything…"

I shushed her with the movement of my hand and a shake of my head. "We've been there and done that it didn't work so well the first time."

"I'd be happy to go through with our deal."

"No, you wouldn't. However, I will still stick to our agreement." A look of disbelief and relief flowed across Bambi's face and she held out her palm. "I never said I would give it to you."

"But the contract said you'd find it for me."

I nodded. "You should really read the fine print." Demons are dumb that way. If they figure they can get out of a deal, they don't worry about the fine print so much. That's why so many mortals get their souls back. "I just said I would find it. I never mentioned or wrote anything about returning it. I suspected you would double cross me. If you had followed through with the deal I would have asked for my request before I returned your virginity, but I would have given it back to you. Multiple attempts to wipe me out have ruined any charitable intentions I might once have harbored." I took a pin out of my pocket with my left hand and moved it slowly towards the cherry.

"Noooo!!!!" she screamed loud enough to shake the building. The males outside started banging on the chamber doors in an attempt to save the object of their desires. Sadly for Red, she had the place built too well. Most architecture around here is designed to withstand an attack, which in the Pit is usually wise thinking.

Magic likes to do things symbolically, so I couldn't risk squishing or smashing it. Bambi threw herself through the air at me, transforming in mid-leap to her less attractive form, her claws slicing for my throat. My pin was tiny, but as always when taking away virginity, the size of the prick doesn't matter, just the penetration.

I decided it was best for all involved, or at least me, it I got this over quick, although I doubted it would be painless. I pushed the pin into Red's cherry and you'd think I had stabbed her in the heart by the way she screamed, but even that sound was drowned out by the explosion released by the small red sphere. I guess it had built up power every time Red had sex, but truth be told I think most people would find it easier to figure out pi than the number of times this succubus had gotten carnal.

The resulting shockwave demolished the entire building, vaporizing it with all the intensity of a nuclear blast, throwing anybody nearby miles away with two notable exceptions. Bambi it flattened into the ground and turned sexy again. Me? I was protected by being the one to do the popping, so all that happened to me is my trench coat flapped around a bit, but I could feel my limbs fill up with the released power.

"How could you?" she cried.

"What? It wasn't good for you?" I said, taking out a cigarette and lighting it. "Want one?"

Bambi was suddenly back into her murderous demon form, coming at me.

"Stop," I whispered, waving the coffin nail at her. Red froze in midair. The popping had given me total control over the succubus, far more than another demon would have if she had been deflowered right after the Fall. Whether she liked it or not, my every word was law. My favor had gotten a bit more complicated now. "Bambi, from this moment on, you work for me. You will never do anything that in any way would or even conceivably could cause me harm, either by word, deed, or inaction. You will do everything I say and always look out for my best interests. In exchange, I will allow you an illusion of freedom, to carry on as you always have. But there will be times I will want you to find information or do something for me, and you will do it without question or hesitation."

"And I suppose I'll have to service your every twisted need," she said.

It was tempting. I had moved my coat to cover that fact that the male parts of me were at attention and almost screaming to do just that. My brain was overruling it. If I gave the order, she'd make sure I had the most incredible sex of my very long life and lots of it. But I'm a guy and sometimes in the heat of passion we say things we might mean at that moment, but not when the moment has passed. For instance, if she asked if I wanted the best for her and I said yes without qualifiers, that word would let her try to kill me as being out of my power would suit her best. With this kind of mystic control, the latest command will always overrule any previous ones. Any misspeaking on my part could literally come back to bite me in the ass or worse.

"Like I told you, I'm not interested." Bambi's entire sense of twisted self-worth was tied up in her being the ultimate object of desire. Taking control of Red to make her my sex slave would still be acceptable to her in a sad, twisted way. My rejection hit her someplace my mystic dominance couldn't even reach. There was hatred burning bright in her eyes as I smiled. "And you're not allowed to tell anybody about our arrangement." Bogie always had the best lines so I ripped off one of his best. "This is the start of a beautiful relationship. For me at least. Don't worry, I'll show myself out. Come by my office tomorrow." I looked at the succubus, as always covered head to toe in some form of red or another and smiled. "And wear something green."

I left walking tall, glaring at every demon I passed. Vaporizing her so-called realm would only help my rep. I didn't linger. I had a lot of extra manna at the moment. I wanted to get back to my office and figure out how to store it for a rainy day. And in Hell, it rains pain every day and those who don't plan ahead get drenched in it. At least now I'd have another umbrella.

PATRICK THOMAS is the author of almost 40 books including the beloved fantasy humor Murphy's Lore series, which includes *Tales From Bulfinche's Pub, Fools' Day, Through The Drinking Glass, Shadow Of The Wolf, Redemption Road, Bartender Of The Gods, Nightcaps, Empty Graves, The Mug Life* — as well as the future space adventures *Startenders* and *Constellation Prize*.

The Murphy's Lore After Hours spin-offs star the half pixie/ogre Terrorbelle (*Fairy With A Gun, Fairy Rides The Lightning*); the former demon-possessed serial killer Agent Karver of the Department of Mystic Affairs (*Dead To Rites, Rites of Passage*); the cursed magí Hex (*By Darkness Cursed and BY Invocation Only*); Vince Argus, the Soul For Hire (*Greatest Hits*); and Negral, a forgotten Sumerian god who works as Hell's Detective (*Lore & Dysorder* and *Bullets & Brimstone*).

Co-Written with John French and Diane Raetz, his Mystic Investigators paranormal mystery series includes *Bullets & Brimstone, From The Shadows* and *Once More Upon A Time. Assassin's Ball*, his first mystery, is also co-written with John French.

He also wrote the steampunk *As The Gears Turn* and the space epic *Exile & Entrance*. He co-edited *New Blood* and *Hear Them Roar* and was an editor for the magazines *Fantastic Stories of the Imagination* and *Pirate Writings*.

Patrick's darkly humorous advice column Dear Cthulhu has been running since 2005 and includes the collections *Have A Dark Day, Good Advice For Bad People, Cthulhu Knows Best, Cthulhu Happens, Cthulhu Explains It All* and *What Would Cthulhu Do?*

His short stories have been featured in over sixty anthologies and more than forty-five print magazines.

A number of his books were part of the props department of the CSI television show and have been spotted on the program. Nightcaps was even thrown at a suspect's head. His urban fantasy Fairy With A Gun had been optioned for film and TV by Laurence Fishburne's Cinema Gypsy Productions. Top Men Productions has turned his Soul For Hire Story, *Act of Contrition*, into a short film.

He is also writing books for kids as **Patrick T. Fibbs** including the *Undead Kid Diaries: Over My Dead Body*, the *Babe B. Bear Mysteries: Bad Hair Day* and the picture book *5 Silly Monsters Jumping On The Zed: A Ughabooz book* (all with artist Shawn Evans).

Please drop by www.patthomas.net or follow him at I_PatrickThomas at Twitter or www.facebook.com/PatrickThomasAuthor to learn more.

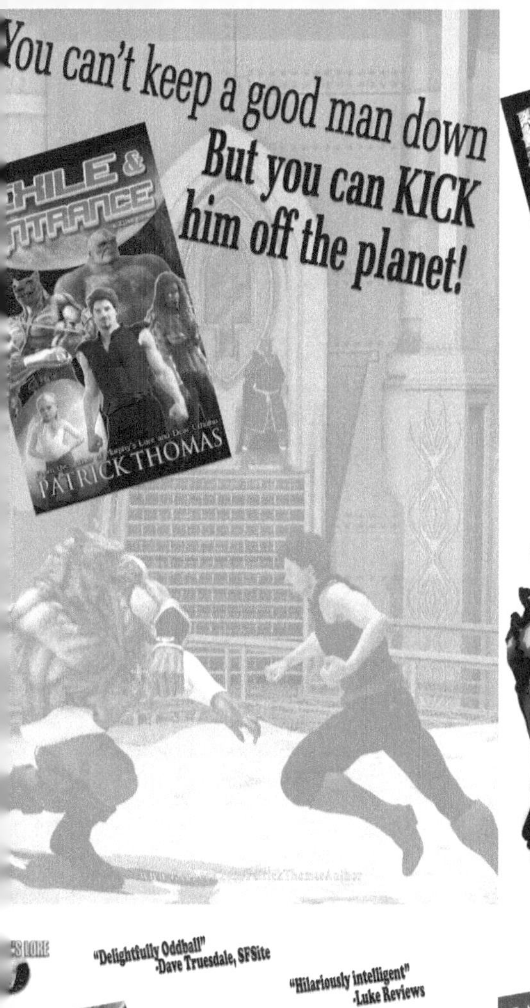

More GREAT Science Fiction!

THE STARSCAPE PROJECT

As his quest begins, an artificial intelligence life form enters the galaxy and launches a series of covert attacks against the Empire. The Teconeans assume that the Federation is responsible, and galactic peace is about to unravel. As Stryker chases his nemesis into Teconean space, he finds himself thrown into the middle of the battle. Knowing that Earth will be the aliens' next target, Stryker must decide whether to let them destroy the Empire, or to join forces with his Teconean enemies against the invaders. The key to the mysterious aliens lies buried on the moon of Kennedy Prime, and it's up to Stryker to solve the puzzle before war begins. The fate of the galaxy is at stake.

...NE OF THE TENTH DGREE

...1912, an alien ship crash lands in the Atlantic ...ean, setting up a secret colony that remains ...detected for centuries, allowing them to ...nipulate some of the most important events in ...man history -- from the sinking of the Titanic to ...Bermuda triangle to global warming. Now, ...technology of the 26th century has ...covered the aliens' distress beacon, and it's a ...e against time as the Navy tries to stop a ...rorist armed with a nuclear weapon from ...stroying the colony and triggering an all-out ...r as the mother-ship approaches

Now available from

PADWOLF PUBLISHING

Shape up...
You only get
ONE Warning

Hell's Detective

No One Is Above The L
Even In

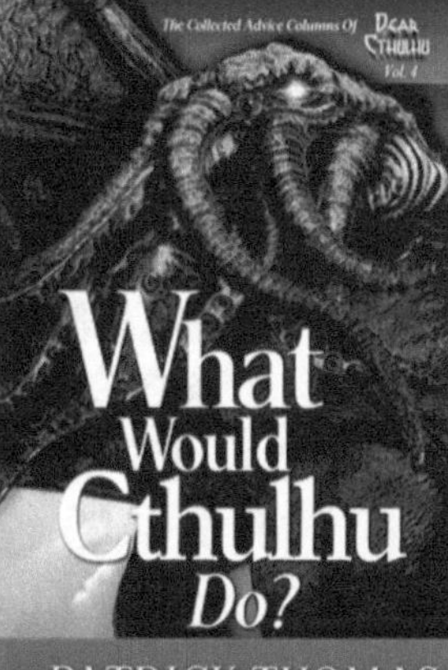

DEAR CTHULHU

The advice column to **END** all advice columns

WWW.DEARCTHULHU.COM
WWW.PADWOLF.COM

A detective's work is never don
And don't call him Baby Bear . .

NO TEACHERS.
NO PARENTS
SCHOOL IS OUT....
OF THIS WORLD

15th Aniversary
Omnibus of
Books 1-6

The zombie
apocalypse
is over...

Now even undead kids have
to go to school

5 SILLY
MONSTERS
JUMPING ON
THE ZED

a picture book
for kids

www.talehaven.com

DOWN THESE MEANS STREETS
of Magic & Monsters walk the

MYSTIC INVESTIGATORS